Il
Comandante

By
James Solomon

[signature: James Solomon]
[signature: Lt. Col. Inf. USA Ret.]

JAMES SOLOMON MARKETING
2822 Allen St.
Allentown, PA 18104

1072 Egret's Walk Circle, #203
Naples, FL 34108

ISBN: 0-615-11244-7

Manufactured in the United States of America

Library of Congress Cataloging-in-Publication Data:
Solomon, James
IL COMANDANTE

To order copies of this book
(via e-mail)
JSOL123@aol.com

PROLOGUE
May 30

"SIR! SIR! Lieutenant! Lieutenant!" Discordant and demanding, that call struck at the core of James Mitchell's heart.

Above the din of the sounds of war, Jim heard those desperate and strident cries coming from men to his rear.

It was May 30, 1944. Memorial Day.

The U.S Fifth Army was breaking out of the Anzio beachhead in Italy. Lt. Mitchell and his men were in Co. H, 2nd Battalion, 135th Infantry Regiment, 34th (Red Bull) Division.

The sun was beating upon them unmercifully, their throats were parched but they dared not halt to drink from their canteens. Leaden shoes seemed to encompass their feet. The gear being carried weighed heavily on their chafed shoulders. This battalion was in regimental reserve and following the tanks that were just ahead.

Suddenly the platoon encountered heavy machine gun, rifle, and small arms fire coming from their right flank. They had been crossing an open wheat field and were observed by the enemy. Naturally, all hit the dirt. It was exactly what the Germans knew they would do because their artillery and tanks immediately opened fire on the American group. The G.I. infantrymen clung to the earth, fingers embedded in the foreign soil and laid low while the shells exploded around them.

The shelling ceased and as the lieutenant arose to get the men going towards their objective, he heard the dreaded sounds calling him to come to the rear.

All the soldiers were still in a prone position. The medic and Jim arrived at the tragic scene at the same time. Mitchell immediately saw that two of his men, Rowe and Ozzie, were wounded. The shell had struck between them. As he crouched beside Rowe, the medic, Bandy, looked at his leader pleadingly, his bright blue eyes tearful, "What shall we do? He has a sucking wound."

Rowe's breathing was hard and a sucking sound could be heard coming from the gaping wound in his lower chest. The ground about him was poppy red where his blood had

I

immersed itself in the hot earth. Rowe was dying.

"There's nothing you can do!" Mitchell shouted to the medic so that he could be heard above the noise of the American artillery that was now returning fire to the German tanks on their right.

"Nothing!" The medic cried. They moved to the next victim, Ozzie.

Ozzie was gone. They could see his brains scattered about. Jim needed to see no more. He turned quickly to meet the Bandy's glance with a shake of his head. "Let them be, and let's get the hell out of here. We must keep moving or we'll all die."

The assessment of the injuries only took a few seconds. The platoon commander had to immediately move the remaining men to a safe position.

Up until then, many members of the unit were unaware of the casualties. As Lt. Mitchell ran back to his original position, he called to the men. "On your feet! Let's go, let's go. Follow me!"

They moved out quickly and at a trot.

Two hundred yards later, after placing his men in a slight defilade, Jim took a head count and found that half of his men were missing.

"Sir," Sergeant Waldrop said, "Somebody didn't pass the word to move out. They're still lying where we were pinned down. Shall I go for them?"

"No," The lieutenant replied. "I'll go. You stay here until I get back with them."

He was not going to let the sergeant correct something that was his fault. The men were his responsibility and he went back for them.

It was a grueling couple hundred yards and Mitchell was still carrying all his equipment that included a pack, walkie talkie (hand held radio), field glasses, two rounds of bazooka ammo, and a carbine. Halfway, he dropped the walkie talkie, field glasses, and the bazooka ammo, with the idea that he would pick them up on his return with the men.

Panting from his run he found the men still in their prone positions in the wheat field. They were in the column behind the casualties, Rowe and Ozzie. Carefully, he led the men around in a manner in which they would not see their fallen comrades. In doing so, he got off the path that he had followed to find his troops.

As a result, Jim could not pick up his equipment at the halfway mark. Instead, he led the men to safety immediately. He was determined to regain his gear later.

Needless to say, Lt. Mitchell was exhausted and decided to wait until things quieted before returning to reclaim his belongings from where he had dropped them. The items were vital and in short supply, he could not even think about abandoning them.

An hour before sunset, steeling himself Jim set out in a run towards the spot where his equipment lay. Upon arriving there, he could not find them because of the many new shell holes that pock marked the area. Fresh dirt was thrown everywhere and the articles he sought to recover could not be readily seen.

Brrr-rrrp, brr-rrp! He heard machine gun bullets whiz by and automatically dove into a bomb crater that was a short distance away. The well-positioned enemy troops were active once more. The 5th Army artillery units had not silenced those guns after all.

Several rounds from a not too distant tank landed nearby, showering the grimy officer with dirt. He lay huddled at the edge of the crater that faced the enemy and praying with great feeling as the shells landed closer and closer.

A fleeting thought passed through his mind; what a great story this would be to tell his brother, Sam. Digging his fingers into the soil, he ventured to try another tack. He had used it many times before and it seemed to work. While lying there, he tried to project his thoughts into the future and by doing so he was somehow shielding himself from the perils of the present.

When an 88mm shell struck the edge of the crater opposite Lt. Mitchell's position, he fearfully cringed waiting for the deadly explosion but only received some soil that was thrown his way by the impact. It was a dud! There was nothing more. It was the last round fired in his direction.

The officer waited several minutes before leaving his sanctuary, and then picked up his equipment, which was almost totally covered with Italian soil. Losing no time in returning to where his men had been positioned, he did not mention the ordeal he had been subjected to just a few minutes earlier. One never spoke of those things because they occurred all the time to one soldier, or another. It was a commonplace experience and not worth mentioning.

Sitting down to rest for the first time in hours was some comfort to Jim, except that he experienced a jolt to his backside and realized that there was an extra wallet in his back pocket. It was not his. Then he remembered stooping to pick it up while crossing the wheat field just moments before that fatal barrage. Taking out the wallet, he opened it and looked for the owner's identification. It contained no money, only a V-mail from his mother with his name and APO address. His mother's return address was in the city of Bethlehem which adjoined Jim's hometown.

Lt. Mitchell decided to send the wallet to the G.I.'s mother when he had the chance. He had a great deal of other things to think about. There was still a war to be fought.

Prologue Continued
May 31

One day later, while following in the wake of the tanks that preceded Lt. Mitchell's platoon, they found five of them burning, their dead crewman strewn about. The smell of burning flesh intermixed with gasoline filled the air. The sight of their dead comrades and the odor was nauseating. The heavily laden soldiers turned their heads away from the picture that would remain with them for all their days. All focused on getting to safety. One soldier vomited violently.

The deadly Panzers (Tiger tanks) were very superior to the American tanks and had exacted their toll. The German armor was almost invulnerable. The unit hastened to seek cover in what was later termed "Bloody Gulch." It was nothing but a dried streambed and drainage ditch, five to seven feet deep and about six feet wide. It was considered good cover under the circumstances. The shelling was continuous and very heavy. The enemy was making a last ditch effort to keep the Fifth Army from liberating the city of Rome.

It was standard operating procedure to make a position more tenable by digging foxholes. This time they dug into the sides of the banks to obtain more shelter from the constant rain of artillery and mortar shells. The narrow but long ravine was crowded to its maximum. Hundreds of soldiers were contained within the crooked walls of the ditch. It was the only cover in that area of the beachhead. Campoleone, a railhead, was nearby and the Germans were defending it with all their might.

The size of the Allied position did not lend itself to the dispersal of troops, but it was the best that could be found under the horrific shellfire that they were encountering. Despite great precautions, the holes they laid in did not offer too much protection from the onslaught and as a result the Allied troops experienced very heavy casualties up and down the line.

At one point, a Sergeant Wolf who had posted some fifty feet down from the lieutenant's position came running up to him shouting, "F--- me! F--- me! Damn it, damn it!" plus some other choice cuss words.

Mitchell was surprised at the language. He had never heard Wolf swear before. The sergeant came from Mormon country and was of good Christian stock. Wolf was a farmer.

Then he continued with, "A dead man just fell down from the bank and landed right on top of me!"

Wolf rambled on and on, very shaken by the incident. His body was trembling vigorously and his mustache was visibly bristling. Recognizing that he was in a state of shock, Lt. Jim gave him a drink of water from his canteen and told him to lie down and cover himself with a blanket. Sgt. Wolf returned to his position with his teeth chattering and hopefully to heed his lieutenant's advice.

A major was crouching nearby and obviously scared to death at what he was witnessing. He was not from the 34th division, probably from some rear headquarters, and sent up to the front to observe and later make a report. At that moment he was only interested in nature's call because he called out to someone, "Where's the latrine?" His voice was trembling with emotion.

"This is it, sir!" Someone responded.

And the major peed. Mostly in and on his pants.

Realizing that his canteen was now almost empty, Jim walked in a slouched position towards a five-gallon can of water, which was about fifteen feet to his right. As he reached the can, an artillery shell hit in the exact position where he had been only a few seconds before. Mitchell was knocked to the ground, but was otherwise unhurt.

Loud and insistent, once more he heard the cries, "Lieutenant, lieutenant!"

Pushing himself to a standing position he rushed to where he was needed. Private Snow, a Native American Indian, was completely buried in the hole he had dug. Using no tool because time was of the essence, Jim desperately clawed at the soft sandy earth with his bare hands, hoping to reach Snow before he suffocated. Mitchell swiftly uncovered Snow's head. Snow was still wearing his helmet. There were no wounds on his body. He was killed by the concussion instantly.

Sergeant Reagan who was closest to the can of water lost three toes on his left foot. Privates Woodward and Beal were also wounded, but not seriously. Private Arno, who was in a hole next to Snow, was standing in a daze and his nose

VI

was bleeding. He was shaking from shock. Mitchell put his blanket around Arno and told him to stay put. The medics were totally occupied dressing wounds. It was a hectic period.

Private Arno was about twenty years of age, slight of build, and with blond hair. He grabbed Jim's hand as the lieutenant was about to leave to tend to others, and said, "I'm fine, Lieutenant, just give me a drink."

Mitchell knew Arno was not "fine" and handed him the canteen that he was about to fill before the shell landed and changed their immediate world. Arno drank the tepid water with relish and wiped his mouth with the back of his hand.

"I'm fine." He repeated. "Thanks." Arno was courteous under the most trying conditions.

During the first lull in the shelling, Jim sent Arno with a medic to the nearest aid station. They were accompanied by Sergeant Reagan who limped along with a temporary bandage on his foot.

The following day Lieutenant Mitchell received word that Arno had died from internal injuries caused by the concussion.

Jim realized then that going for the water in a crouched position saved his life. He mentally acknowledged that there were no heroics on his part. He only happened to be there.

The visions that were evoked of the occurrences and tragedies of the Anzio Beachhead, and other battles, came upon him again and again in the years after World War II had ended. Soon he felt that it was time to share his experiences by showing his family the sites where they happened. To accomplish this, he would have to take them to Italy. Thus the idea of a pilgrimage was born. It took twenty-five years to get to that point where he felt it would be wise to tell them the stories in graphic detail. The urge to go to Italy welled up like a strong tide and in 1970 he responded to that feeling. Renewing friendships with his Italian friends was high on his agenda. He was not prepared for the ensuing events.

Mrs. Olive Denti, Il Comandante, and Tilde (sec'y) at Lago de Garda – August 26, 1945.

VIII

ACKNOWLEDGMENTS

Many friends supported me in the project "IL COMANDANTE" and without their encouragement I probably would not have published the book. Since it was written in my twilight years, it would have remained on disks and in the notebooks which held the printed pages.

Ruth Howard Marcon put me on the right path with her meticulous corrections in punctuation. It was Leila Elias, a writer in her own right, who imbued me with her enthusiasm. Then Labiby Joseph's praise strengthened my resolve. Katherine Charles Seideck, a prolific novelist, who managed to squeeze time for me between novels, gave suggestions that had great impact. While in Florida a steadfast friend, Mary DiMarinis proofread the printed pages during a period when her time was limited. It was a writer of travel books, Robert Johnston, whose guidance in publishing was invaluable. My Creative Writing Class in Naples, Florida critiqued my writing favorably and verbally applauded my attempt at publishing. Tracy Kiernan who designed the cover took special pains to please me.

For bearing with me, my gratitude goes to: My son James Jr.; wife Elaine Gannon; their sons and my grandsons: James P. (Jimmy) and John (Jack) J. Solomon. And of course my daughter aand her husband, Judith A. and John W. Cacciola; and their daughter and my Granddaughter, Gina Marie.

I love you all.

JAMES SOLOMON

Jim Solomon in Florence, Italy on March 12, 1945

BIOGRAPHY

Born in 1916, I was brought up during the eras of the "Roaring Twenties" and "The Great Depression". At the age of twenty five, I found myself embroiled in a war of far reaching dimensions. For five years I served my country in the capacity of an infantry soldier. First, as an enlisted man rising to the rank of corporal, and then after an intensive ninety days at Fort Benning, I was commissioned as a second lieutenant.

I was wounded in combat in Italy, received the Purple Heart, the Bronze Star, and other awards and decorations. When the war in Italy ended, I was assigned to The Allied Military Government (AMG) and ordered to command and operate a refugee camp in Modena, Italy. I was only 29 years of age at the time and with awesome responsibilities in processing thousands of European Jews, Polish, Austrian, and other Continental refugees, plus feeding and housing them.

It was that part of my life that influenced me in writing this book.

Completing five years on active duty during World War II, I continued serving in the Army Reserve for an additional thirty years until I retired from the service in 1976.

From 1957 until 1978, my wife, Dorothy, and I owned and operated a Lincoln-Mercury Dealership in Allentown, Pennsylvania. We retired in 1978 to spend our winters in Naples, Florida.

While Dorothy was recuperating after having a heart attack in July 1998, I wrote "IL COMANDANTE" after she had retired for the night. The first draft in the first person was completed in a few weeks.

However, Dorothy Loscalzo Solomon never recovered because she was suddenly overtaken by cancer. She died April 8, 1999. We were married for forty seven wonderful years.

This book is dedicated to her with all my love. She was the first to read it and the first to give me, and the book, her blessings.

JAMES SOLOMON

CHAPTER ONE
The Coming

Modena, Italy. July 15, 1970.

It was hot in Andrea Cavelli's office. The air conditioning system was not working too well. The fan on his desk was oscillating with a gentle hum. The correspondence spread nearby would rustle each time the fan reached a certain position as it turned. Cavelli was slouched in his well-padded leather chair.

"So he's coming?" Directing his question at Cavelli, Mandelli casually glanced at his well-groomed fingernails.

Giacamo (Jacob) Mandelli was standing and assuming a position of power and authority by being on his feet and looking down on Andrea Cavelli. It was a tactic used throughout the ages by authorities in questioning prisoners. He knew how to do it well.

"Who's coming?" Countered Cavelli his face darkening.

"I saw the letter on your desk."

Andrea Cavelli was infuriated but quelled his temper. He did not respond for several moments. Since he had been afflicted for years with perpetual hoarseness, his voice rasped, "That was private!"

"Not as far as I am concerned! Nothing, and I mean nothing is private in our relationship! And, I might add, in our organization! You should have alerted me!" Mandelli scolded. He was seething inwardly.

"Why is he returning after all these years? I was under the impression that Il Comandante was under your control!" Mandelli added.

"I don't know," Andrea responded. His voice was now steady and firm. "I suppose that I thought he would pose no threat to anyone."

"No threat?" Mandelli screamed. "He must be taken care of now, sooner than later! I'll see to that!"

"No, No!" Cavelli choked. "That's not necessary. He wants nothing more. I'm sure of that."

With eyes blazing and looking directly at his partner, Mandelli adjusted his dark horn rimmed glasses then firmly asked, "Why do you say that? Why are you so sure? He's just like us - no better, no different."

1

"He's a man of character. He will ask nothing of us. Besides," Andrea continued, "He's a decent human being."

"Human being? Less than human, I'd say. Just like us."

"Don't fool yourself. Morally, he's better than we are. You, Mandelli," Cavelli continued with his finger pointing at his partner, "You keep away from him. Don't see him. Don't let him see you. Everything will turn out just fine."

"Yes, I'll keep out of his way, And no, I'll handle him my own way. That's final!"

Mandelli's voice was curt and with a quick gesture he held his right palm out in front of him indicating that the conversation was over. He turned and stalked out of the office.

Cavelli was muttering under his breath. "Mitchell.....Why him?.....Why now?"

His face was ashen as he slumped backward in his leather chair. He had used all his options. Knowing what was on Mandelli's agenda caused his mind to crumple as well as his body. Andrea's mind and body were completely exhausted. Slowly and carefully he reached for a bottle and a glass in his desk drawer. He needed a long drink.

Desperately Andrea Cavelli tried to collect his senses. He did not feel threatened. as did Mandelli by the man who was to intrude into his life after twenty-five years. He had other things to worry about of which IL Comandante had not an inkling.

Andrea tried to formulate a plan which would not need drastic actions and which would yield results in his favor. He still had some time. The drink had bolstered his confidence in what he would do. Soon he felt that he could convince his partner to accede to his convictions.

"I need another drink." Cavelli told himself. He was losing the confidence that the first long drink had instilled in him.

Mulling things over, his thinking changed when the thought entered his mind that he really did have something to worry about! Maybe he had better not interfere with Mandelli's plans and let the cards fall where they may.

*   *   *

In his private office, the worried Mandelli reached for his phone and hastily dialed a number from memory. He often made calls from this special phone to that person and to other special people he was involved with. Cavelli did not have access to this phone line under any circumstances. He spoke quietly in Italian interspersed with some guttural sounds that were foreign.

"What do you think I should do?" Mandelli asked in a muffled voice.

"That serious?" He put forth another question. The response was evidently not to Mandelli's liking.

"But Cavelli says that he could handle it ....well, I don't know. We may be able to work things out without being too drastic." Mandelli was perspiring. He seemed to be under severe pressure from the person on the other end of the line.

"Yes, sir, I'll do as you say." He hung up with shaking hands. Mandelli was now in turmoil and in the same condition in which he had placed Cavelli.

He sat in his chair and wiped his brow. Thinking about the awful fix he was in made him reach for his bottle and glass.

"I must do it," He said to himself. "I must do it, or they will do it to me. I hoped that this day would never come. Now it is here. They have put me in the position where it is either Comandante Mitchell or I. And it's not going to be me."

A sound that was like a sob disgorged itself from his stout body as Mandelli slouched deeper in his chair.

CHAPTER TWO

The Arrival

With passports in hand, carry-on luggage strap tearing into his right shoulder, James Mitchell approached the custom booth and shoved all four passports through the glass opening to the officer. He eyed Jim intently after glancing at his passport then turned his eyes downward at what was apparently a sheet of paper. His eyes seemed to narrow as he read something written there. He quickly brought his head up and with a half smile asked, "Why are you coming to Italy?" Mitchell was taken aback by the question. He wasn't asked that in the other countries he had visited. They were always ready to welcome American tourists. American dollars were needed everywhere.

Nervously, Jim responded by saying that he and his family were coming to tour Italy and see the sights. The customs officer glanced at the Mitchell family of four and saw that a long line of people was forming behind them. The officer glanced at the paper again, shrugged his shoulder, stamped the passports and shoved them back to Jim. Not another word was said. He just waved them on, but his face had a puzzled look as he reached for the phone. His eyes followed the Americans as they made their way to the exit.

Everyone is always in a hurry to get away from the customs area and the Mitchells were no different. However, Jim did momentarily wonder what was in the officer's mind while he held them there. He reasoned that the officer probably had some English words written on that piece of paper and was going to put them to practice. Mitchell forgot about it immediately after he remembered that he had to pick up a rental car at that Roman airport. His worries about the car were soon realized when he saw the autos that were available were not Mercedes Benz, or any large car, for that matter. He had to settle for a small station wagon and the luggage had to go on the roof. Not in the style that he had imagined!

This was their second trip to Italy. This was the year 1973 and they had been there in 1970.

The first trip included England, France, Italy and Spain. It was a memorable one, especially for Jim, because he was in Europe during World War II but mostly in Italy as an Infantry officer. He wanted to see Europe in peacetime. As a foot soldier, he had walked the length of Italy, from Naples to the Italian Alps and Ventimiglia at the French border.

In 1970, while preparing for their first trip, Mitchell had written to friends that he had made in Italy while he was the Commandant of an Allied Military Government Displaced Persons Camp in Modena. It was twenty-five years since he had left there and he didn't have much hope of receiving any replies. Unlike Americans, the Italians are not a "moving population". They stay in their family homesteads for generations.

England and France were great and Jim had high expectations for Italy. Some of his enthusiasm rubbed off on his children, Judy and Jimmy, but his wife, Dorothy, was noncommittal since she was of Italian heritage.

They rode the train from Paris through the rest of France, into Austria, then Switzerland and down to the next reserved hotel in Milan. Venice was their next stop. Getting there was not going to be a problem, or so they thought.

It was August and it was hot. Italians don't work in August if they can help it. They take the whole month off. Factories close for that month. Everything stops. The trains still run...if ....and there are many ifs. The Mitchells entrained for Venice. The train moved swiftly and was making good time...until Padua. It was a regular stop according to the schedule. Suddenly, some shouting and yelling was heard and the passengers were told to get off and to take their luggage. Why? "SCIOPERO!" "STRIKE!" In Italy strikes can erupt at any moment and without any notice.

CHAPTER THREE
Sciopero! Strike!

Hundreds detrained. There were Austrians who invited the Mitchell family to join them and get on a train, which was going to Yugoslavia. Others sought hotel accommodations. Hotels were booked solid. Jim asked a cab driver if he could drive to Venice. Certainly, he said. The American fares wound up on the Autostrada ramp and found that the highway was closed in sympathy with the train strikers. The driver claimed he knew the back road to Venice. That was a mistake. For a while they traveled on a fairly decent highway, which was highly trafficked and then he cut off another cab. That cabby was furious and followed closely bumping the tourist's vehicle repeatedly, then coming alongside and sideswiping the cab with a horrendous crunch. Needless to say, Jim's family was frightened and implored the driver to get off the road. He complied, and lost their adversary, and found themselves on rural roads for the rest of the journey to Venice. The cabby really didn't know any short cuts or the route, for that matter. He drove east and relied on luck to get there.

No Italian will ever admit that he doesn't know the way. He'll lose face. If you ever stop to ask directions in Italy, a small crowd soon gathers and each person will give you a direction in sincerity. As you walk away in bewilderment, the group of advice givers remains and discuss among themselves the merits of their directions. Their arms keep waving and their voices get louder as the arguments heat up. Never a dull moment in Italy!

CHAPTER FOUR
The Stranger

Jim had studied Italian the hard way. Before landing on the Anzio Beachhead the troops were given pocket size booklets. They contained information on the customs of Italians and a dictionary of sorts with words and phrases we could use in communicating with the natives. It was in a foxhole along the Mussolini Canal that Mitchell studied and memorized all the words and phrases it contained. He would recite the words out loud over and over again until he thought that he had the right pronunciation. The soldiers remained in their foxholes all day; they dared not stick out their heads until the sun went down. After dark the beachhead would erupt like the Vesuvius they had left behind in Naples. Of course, during the day the shelling was continuous from the German side because they had the advantage of the heights that surrounded the beachhead. The Allies were in the flats and could easily be observed by the enemy. No one moved until night clothed them with its invisibility. At night the Jerry bombers would fly over and drop their bombs indiscriminately. Large bombs on the port area and anti-personnel bombs everywhere else. The skies would light up with the Allied anti-aircraft umbrella; the colors of the tracers were beautiful but deadly. Every now and then a shooting star would plummet to earth spewing blinding light. That comet would turn out to be enemy aircraft succumbing to the onslaught of thousands of rounds of ammunition emanating from the beachhead's anti-aircraft weapons.

So, naturally, Jim made good use of the daylight hours to study Italian. After a couple of months on Anzio he considered himself fairly proficient in the language. It was an accomplishment despite the trials and dangers he endured while there. The benefit he received was learning the language. He tried to forget everything else.

Incidentally, at the Hotel Excelsior Galia in Milan Jim's wife, Dorothy, ordered her dinner by using her best Italian. The snooty waiter floored her by asking where she learned the language and at the same time telling her that she spoke the way the Italians spoke a hundred years ago. Oddly enough it turned out to be true because her grandparents came to

America not long after the Civil War and her father was born in New York City in the 1880's, hence she picked up the language from her grandparents who spoke 19th century Italian. But, of course, Senor Mitchell spoke perfect Italian - in choppy phrases.

During the war, the Italians Jim met were pleased at his attempt to speak to them in their own language, and he was thrilled by their response. Strangely, the American G.I. was not interested in speaking a foreign tongue. They thought everyone in the world should speak English. The G.I.s knew the words: 'vino, signorina, casa and ciao.' They suited all their needs, but were not enough for Lt. Mitchell.

Jim had been to Venice during the war and got slightly seasick riding in a gondola on the choppy waters of the bay. This time he took his family through the canals on a gondola and to all the tourist traps the gondolier takes you. That included the famous glass factory.

Mitchell's plan was to pick up a car and travel to Modena after a few days of basking on the beach of the Lido, chasing pigeons on St. Mark's square, and having breakfast on the verandah of the Danielle Royal Excelsior where they resided.

While walking around Marco Square with his children, Jim noted that they were being observed by a man who was toting an attaché case. Most Italian men carried some sort of leather bag or briefcase so that was not unusual. Mitchell attributed the man's curiosity to being interested in Americans. As the man persisted in following them, it gave the American family some discomfiture, but was dismissed in their attempt to make the best of it and have a good time.

Later, they noticed the same man on the beach at the Lido, which was a good distance by speedboat from the Hotel Danielli.

It was with great anticipation that they left Venice to a place where Jim had been before under different circumstances. They had reservations at the finest albergo in Modena. It was the Hotel Fini.

CHAPTER FIVE
The Warning

During the drive to Modena, Mitchell noticed that a car seemed to be following them. In order not to alarm his family, he said nothing.

Prior to their departure from the United States Jim had written to several of his friends in Modena, advising them of the date of arrival and informing them that he had reservations at the Fini. His wife was unaware of this but the children did know because Jim told them that he was going to try to contact some of his friends by mail. Since he wasn't sure that he would get any kind of response, and to avoid being embarrassed in front of his wife, he purposely neglected to tell her of his attempt at a reunion with his Italian friends.

The Mitchells pulled up the front of the hotel and parked. Glancing around, Jim saw no crowd waiting. Sheepishly, he walked into the lobby to register and have a bellboy unload the luggage, etc. The room clerk eyed him with a half smile and asked, "Comandante Mitchell?"

"Yes," Jim responded, smiling broadly and relishing with great pleasure the sound of the title, 'comandante.'

Upon hearing his reply, the clerk reached behind him, grasped a sheaf of messages and handed them to the startled American. Needless to say, he was overwhelmed as was his family that had followed him. All of the notes, except one, were greetings of enthusiasm and asked the comandante to call one telephone number and they would all come to meet him and his family. Jim was puzzled with the odd note. It merely said: "GO AWAY, DON'T STIR THE POT". He hastily folded it and shoved it into his pocket. What did it mean? He mentally shrugged off the uncomfortable feeling it had upon him and handed the telephone number to the room clerk who dialed and informed the person on the other end of the line that the comandante had arrived.

The Mitchell family was agog with expectancy and just stood around speculating as to what was going to happen next. As for Jim, being practical, he began unloading the station wagon intent on getting his family settled and comfortable in a nice air-conditioned hotel. He wasn't sure what to expect and had no idea as to the type of reception they were going to receive. It was twenty-five years since he had seen any of these people or heard from them.

When he left Modena in 1945 he made a clean break. He was young and had been away from home for two years and anxious to leave Italy and everything else behind. He was homesick and cared little about making bonds with anyone there. He had been trained as an Army officer not to become too attached to anyone while in combat. Officers were taught to remain distant because they would lose their efficiency when combat losses consisted of personnel who were close to them. Jim managed very well in that department and kept his sanity. Being detached was part of his personality during combat, however he did melt somewhat when he came in contact with the thousands of refugees that he took charge of at the Duke of Modena's Palace (Ducal Palace). And of course, he maintained his distance to some extent with the personnel and staff who worked for him. He had a good relationship with almost everyone. But he did have some people among the refugees and his staff with whom he had problems.

CHAPTER SIX
Reunion

The 'Campo' was under Allied Military Government (AMG) control. The Brigadier in Rome was British and Lt. Mitchell's commander. Jim gradually saw the logic in replacing the British Captain with an American Officer because the American Supply Bases were easily accessible so he could easily requisition American rations and supplies for the refugee camp's use.

How naive this twenty-nine year old officer was! He felt like a scapegoat at times, however he was under military orders and had a job to do. It was a huge jump from being an infantry officer just out of combat, going into a refugee camp and commanding a garrison of 200 Italian officers and men plus another 190 or so civilians required to run things. His nucleus of Americans included a second lieutenant, two sergeants and a corporal. They were there whether they liked it or not. The Americans were assigned to First Lieutenant Mitchell. He had never met or seen any of his American staff before. They were thrown together and none of them had an inkling of the job that was in store for them.

Therefore, in 1970 Jim did not have any high hopes as to what was in store for him in the prospective meeting with his Italian friends at the Hotel Fini.

Mitchell had just retrieved the third piece of luggage from the roof of the station wagon when a caravan of autos rolled up in front of the hotel. Such excitement! What a thrill! His family was agape at what was transpiring. Twenty five or thirty people emerged from their cars and enveloped them. Jim was being kissed by men and women alike. And his family stood in awe. Dorothy wept.

Cavelli, who had been Jim's right hand man and administrator in charge of the civilian employees, whisked Dorothy and Jim into his Ferrari and started out to an unknown destination unknown. Judy and Jimmy were taken into custody by others. Mitchell's car was left at the curb, the luggage still on the sidewalk - all left in charge of the concierge who was still bewildered by the invasion of people and cars. Dorothy sat in the back with Cavelli's wife, Lina, who was fanning herself vigorously and mumbling about the oppressive heat. She complained constantly about how they had to leave the seashore for the heat of the city. Her husband was only intent on demonstrating how fast his car could go and how loud the radio played. There was no air conditioner, so all the windows were open to their fullest and the air whipped at the passengers furiously. The conversation in the front seat was muted by the sounds of the rushing air, the loud radio, and the roar of the high-powered motor. Dorothy would never forget that ride and neither would Jim.

The other cars trailed behind, trying desperately to catch up. The Italian racing car sped on up some hills and then into the mountains. This speed demon, what was he trying to do? Impress them or kill them? Jim did not know the answer to that question. Some years later he would find out.

The road was narrowing, but the speed was not abating. No guardrails were visible on that narrow road and a person could look straight down for hundreds of feet. No time for sightseeing; just hanging on for dear life. Jim's wife, Dorothy, was petrified. Lina was still fanning herself and asking Dottie over and over again, "Why did you have to come in August."

The gears of the car really took a beating that day; Cavelli was downshifting, then stepping hard on the gas to gain momentum enough to shift to a higher gear. He was in his glory, or so Jim thought. Mitchell didn't realize until years later that Andrea Cavelli was angry and almost to the point of self-destruction. And all the while Jim thought he was showing off.

CHAPTER SEVEN
Salute!

Rounding a curve they had a near miss with an oncoming car. Cavelli dismissed that occurrence with a "niente" (nothing) and a wave of his large arm. They were high up in the mountains and since the road was ever winding, Jim could not make out where they were going. Although he did ask several times, he was dismissed with "wait and see".

Suddenly, they were there. The high-powered car zoomed into the parking lot and from there they saw a large modern restaurant and hotel with a wrap around verandah. It was outdoor dining at its best. They were at the peak of the mountain and diners and guests could look down on all sides and see magnificent views. Besides that, it was cool. Lina perked up as the air touched her face. Her mood changed. The fanning stopped and so did the complaining . Soon the whole entourage was seated at a long table overlooking the valley's most scenic view. The table was already set and reserved for the party. The Mitchell family was surprised and elated at the beautiful setting and at the reception they were receiving. Jim was deeply gratified and moved. He hastened to express his appreciation to all his friends.

The three Valente brothers were there with their families, so was their sister, Camille, and her husband and son. Marta Giaroli was there with her husband, Ermano. Marchese Casate's daughter, Sonia, was there. Her mother, she informed Jim, had died fifteen years before. She didn't have her mother's title and she had to work for a living now as a nurse. Then there was Franco, the comandante's driver. His arm was broken when he tried to crank the British lorry when the battery was run down. He showed Jim how it had healed. His forearm was a bit out of alignment.

None of the greeters spoke English, so Mitchell had to manage with the fractured Italian that he remembered. His wife managed very well with her nineteenth century Italian. She learned new words as she listened intently to what was said to her. Jimmy and Judy talked to their counterparts with their hands and use of the English-Italian dictionary that Jim had provided.

13

Mitchell caught Cavelli staring at him in a strange way and noticed that he eyed Franco and shared some sort of hidden communication with him. They were probably noting that Jim was not the 29 year old they knew but a mature family man anxious to renew friendships and that things were now different. Jim was no longer the Comandante who was their boss, but just another friend. Or so Mitchell thought.

Camille called everyone to attention by tapping her wine glass with a knife and her brothers chimed in by doing the same. All became quiet except for a slight hissing sound by the disgruntled Lina which Camille politely dismissed by tossing her head to one side, and smiling at all of them at that angle. It was uplifting to us in particular because she began her speech with, "......Mitchell who saved our lives twenty-five years ago!" She raised her glass, her brothers followed suit, and then all the others. Camille took a sip and then continued, "We were still lying on the floor in our farmhouse where the Germans had left us, when Mitchell entered and saved us. It was the turning point in our lives and we owe our lives to him. I wish our Papa were still living so that he could tell you the story of that day! Salute!" And all clinked their glasses and took a drink.

Then Efrem took the initiative and went on to say, "I was so happy to be rescued that day that I gave Mitchell my bed to sleep in that night. None of us will ever forget that day!" His brothers echoed some of the words that would ring in Jim's ears for many years to come.

Mitchell was deeply touched, and a spate of tears washed down Dorothy's cheeks.

CHAPTER EIGHT
Reggio-Emilia

James Mitchell sat at the head of the table and could see everyone from his vantage point. All his Modenese friends were talking at the same time and with gestures and body language that was truly magnificent. It was the real Italy accompanied by fine cuisine and the best of wines. And COCA COLA! Large bottles of coke were place at strategic intervals. All for the Americans. Their taste for Coca Cola had preceded them. The wine was for the natives. A large bottle of red wine and a large bottle of white wine were placed in front of every male adult present. They drank it with gusto, saluting their visitors with every refill. Their children drank wine also but it was watered down with either sparkling water or plain aqua. All the water was bottled. The table was laden with food, for this was the main meal of the day.

The expansive table had everything, soup, pasta, chicken, rabbit, but very little beef. The rolls were odd shaped. They looked like a man's hand, fingers protruded from the main part of the roll, if you could call it a roll. That type of bread can only be found in the Reggio-Emilia region of Italy.

The wine was of local origin. It sparkled and was sudsy when poured, especially the red. Their Italian friends drank wine with all their meals, except breakfast. Breakfast was just a small 'espresso' and a biscuit or piece of bread. That's all, no orange juice, cereal, bacon and eggs, pancakes, waffles, sausages, or ham.

After several attempts, Jim was finally able to sample the wine. He insisted and they relented, and they were very pleased that he was going to drink with them. Evidently, they had been brainwashed into thinking that Americans only drank Coca Cola. It was obvious by all the coke bottles that were placed on the table. The Italian children relished the Coca Cola and made great inroads to the supply. For that the Mitchells were grateful. The vino was sweet and easy to drink. Jim added sparkling water in his glass to cut down the intake of alcohol. The wine was newly made, fresh and had a low alcohol content. That's why they could drink a bottle of vino

15

at a sitting and not get drunk. Of course, they were used to it. The average American could not survive drinking in that manner. Jim was a Coca Cola guy.

The party was toasting everybody and everything. Hurray for the waiter! Hurray for the cook! Viva Americani! Viva bella Italia (beautiful Italy)! And on and on.

The conversations mainly dealt with the changes in the region. The Valentes told how they were no longer share-croppers. The three boys,now grown men, were truckers and had their own business. Camille still lived in the country with her husband and son. Efrem, Mario and Renzo lived in Modena in their own apartments. They insisted that the Mitchells cancel their reservations and stay with them.

" No, no," Lina whispered to Dorothy, "You're not used to living like they do. You better stay at the hotel because you are used to air conditioning."

Dorothy got her husband's attention and spoke in the clear telling him not accept the invitation until the matter was discussed by the family. Jim thanked the Valentes and told them that he would talk about it later. Their mother, Mama Valente, was not with the gathering. She was at home and would see Mitchell and his family later. She was anxious to see Jim.

Mama Valente was now up in years and was homebound. Her children told Jim and Dorothy that their father had died several years before. He and their mother always spoke about "Mitchell" as the person who saved their lives during World War II. At the time of their 'liberation' in April 1945, the ages of the children ranged from eighteen down to twelve years. The girl, Camille, was the eldest. However, at the first meeting she told the young officer that she was fifteen. That was so that the soldiers, German or American would not bother her. Twenty five years later Jim learned that she was eighteen at that time. Needless to say, it would not have mattered. His men never pursued girls while in combat. It was their mission, first and foremost, to stay alive.

16

CHAPTER NINE
S.S! Out Of The Past

Cavelli's voice was always hoarse but it was now more pronounced and Jim Mitchell had some difficulty understanding what he was saying. It became tiresome asking him to repeat his sentences and it probably bothered him too. So Jim allowed him to ramble on and went with the flow of words, grasping a word here and one there and managing to get the gist of what he was talking about. He reminisced about the days of the Refugee Camp and how they had to struggle to feed and house all those many thousands of Jews, Poles, Austrians.

"Remember the Jews", he said, "remember all those thousands who claimed to be Palestinians? They were German Nationals, Polish Nationals, and Slavs but they would never admit it. They have their own country now!"

Mitchell responded by saying, "I knew that. I spoke Arabic and by interviewing the Jewish refugees I only found six true Palestinians. They spoke Arabic and were happy to find someone who could speak their language."

As they sat around the table at the restaurant in the mountains, faces flashed through Jim's mind.

The faces he remembered were like a conglomeration of many visages, some smiling, others serious, some whose bodies were wracked by disease and malnutrition. Suddenly, one face emerged, very clear, and in living color.

"Why," He thought, "Did this guy's mug intrude on my memories?"

And just as quickly Jim had the answer. Stifling a smile, he got Andrea Cavelli's attention and with that all conversation ceased at their end of the table.

"Do you remember a refugee who was a ringleader of sorts and who was caught selling our blankets and other paraphernalia on the black market? He was the fellow I threw into the brig to put a scare into him. I recall that a week or ten days later the Italian Captain came to me and asked about the disposition of the prisoner. I clapped my hand to my head because I realized that I had completely forgotten about Yacob... Yacob...that was his name. Yacob Klinger.....Kleiner.....Klimmer.....Kimmel?"

17

At the mention of those names, Andrea turned ashen and his lips trembled. Likewise, Franco bit his lip and watched Cavelli intently. Both puffed on their cigarettes, to hide their true feelings. Mitchell was aware of this peculiar change in their demeanor. He went on to say that in retrospect it was very funny and that if the Captain hadn't taken it upon himself to ask about the prisoner, Yacob would still be in jail. Jim laughed heartily at the thought and all around him laughed too, Andrea and Franco joined in with the rest but seemingly with some hesitancy.

Why were they so affected by this reminder of a funny incident? Then Jim remembered another incident involving Yacob. Why he reached far back into the past to pick out that memory was beyond him. Perhaps he saw the somewhat odd reactions and wanted to see what other consternation he could cause. At least he was enlivening the conversation and had piqued everyone's interest. Then Jim went on to recall a very scary incident in which Yacob...(last name unknown at this point)..was involved. As a matter of fact, the whole riot was centered around him. Yes, they had a riot in the courtyard of the Academy. Mitchell could see it all as plain as day. Then he went on with recounting what he recalled on that eventful afternoon.

"Listen," Jim ventured, "Remember the mob of people in the courtyard on that hot August afternoon, when they were all screaming 'S S' - 'S S' over and over again? There was a man in the center of that melee who was being pummeled and kicked and who would have been killed if we hadn't intervened. And then that idiot Italian soldier fired his machine gun."

At that point, Franco contributed something to the conversation. "Yes," he answered, "If it hadn't been for you there would have been casualties. You grabbed the weapon and raised the barrel as the soldier was beginning to fire and bullets went high, hitting some of the statuary and the ceiling."

That was true. Jim deflected the machine gun upward and wrested the weapon from the soldier's hands. He did it without thinking and was glad he did. With his nerves shaken, he scolded the soldier unmercifully and then continued with the business at hand. It was a crucial moment, the mob was hysterical and at a high pitch incited by the sounds of gunfire.

18

Jim stood by the fallen figure of a man who was sobbing and possibly in great pain by the beating he had taken.

The crowd fell back slightly, enough to enable the soldiers to pick up the injured person. This refugee's face was quite swollen and unrecognizable. He was taken to the camp hospital which was on the second floor. Meanwhile, the soldiers dispersed the crowd. It was no longer a mob. The people were now sobered and much quieter. Several men approached the Comandante respectfully and asked if they could speak to him about the incident. They were invited over to a corner of the courtyard while he was still clutching the machine gun.

"This man," They said, "Worked for the SS and had been recognized by someone who was in the concentration camp where he was a high official. He's not a Jew," They insisted, "He doesn't belong here."

The Comandante told them that he would look into the matter and dismissed them. He had lots of other things to do besides listen to complaints. The had constant gripes from the refugees. Some of them were about food, some about money, some about the crowded conditions, about privacy. The staff dealt with their complaints as best they could under the circumstances. Jim remembers telling Cavelli to see to the man's injuries and to keep him advised about his progress.

As Mitchell concluded narrating the mob story, Cavelli was wiping his brow and nervously lighting another cigarette while the one glowing in his ashtray still had a way to go. He suddenly arose, excused himself while muttering something about calling his place of business.

CHAPTER TEN
Valentes Vs. Cavellis

While Andrea was gone, the Valentes talked about what they had done after war's end. There were no jobs so the boys worked on the farm. Camille was given a job by Lady Raus, a Red Cross Volunteer from England. Camille was hired after Jim left the Academy (Displaced Persons and Repatriation Sub-Commission Refugee Repatriation Camp). Since he was under the impression that Camille was only fifteen he did not employ her. Before leaving for the United States, Lt. Mitchell had introduced the family to Lady Raus. She took a liking to Camille and offered her a job as an assistant, after Jim was gone. When the Valente sons grew older they labored at odd jobs, pooled their resources and bought a truck. Soon they purchased another, then a third. Three men, three trucks and the world was theirs.

The Valentes were content. All were happily married and with children. They said that all three families lived in one building. Mitchell couldn't imagine that and neither could Dorothy. It was hard to picture all of them and their mother under one roof. What would the Mitchells get into if they accepted their invitation? Was Lina right? How were they to get out of that predicament?

"Oh, heck, let's live for the moment and enjoy ourselves in this beautiful setting." Jim communicated that thought to Dorothy. He overheard the Valentes calling Dorothy by her baptismal name-Donata.

Noon is dinnertime in Italy. The dining was great. The cameras were clicking and many pictures were taken amid laughter and some exaggerated poses. The teenagers were showing off. The smaller children were calling for attention. For that period of time it was a joyous occasion, just like a family reunion. On that day the Americans and the Italians really bonded, especially the Mitchell family and the Valentes. All Jim needed to see was Mama Elena Valente to make it complete.

After dinner, the Italians take a two or three hour siesta. The shops and all businesses close for the afternoon. Everything stops. Most people take naps. Business commences about five in the afternoon and remains open until eight. Unlike the Americans who work from morning until night. And vacations! At least four weeks per year. Factories cease operations for the entire month of August. It's a good month for travel in Italy because the whole country takes a holiday.

The party began to break up and all arose to stretch a bit before departing for the city. Lina implored Dorothy not to accept the Valentes' invitation. But Lina never extended an invitation to the Mitchells and it was hard to understand her motive. By that time Andrea had returned to the table. He appeared to be more composed and affable. Jim assumed that Cavelli had some problems in his business and that he had solved them with his phone call. It was at that time that he asked what type of business he was in and expressed the desire to see his place. Andrea put Mitchell off by saying that Jim wouldn't be interested in seeing it and that it was nothing to brag about. Mitchell couldn't understand why Cavelli took that position. Reasoning that he was anxious to resume his vacation, Jim put it out of his mind for the nonce.

Before leaving, Dorothy and Jim thanked their friends for the wonderful reception and hoped that someday they could reciprocate when they would come to the United States.

While walking to the parking lot, the Valentes insisted that the Mitchells return with them to see their mother and, of course, to see their home. The Cavellis did not object and they said their good byes and also stated that they would try to see Jim and his family again before they left for the seashore. Lina began fanning herself once again as they drove away.

CHAPTER ELEVEN
Cavelli Vs. Valente

Franco eyed his former comandante curiously and appeared as though he wanted to talk to him about something. At least Jim got that impression. But he didn't have the chance with the Valentes all around him. Franco shook Jim's hand and wished him well and said "arrivederci."

Again Franco lingered for a moment or two after that, hesitated, and then waved while striding off to his car. His Fiat sputtered as it left the lot. No Ferrari for Franco, he was still a workingman with his whole future tied to Andrea Cavelli. Jim could still picture Franco at the age of twenty driving a British lorry for the Comandante at the Accademia Militare.

As he digressed, small pockets of memories were loaded into the lines of communication to his brain. Like a computer it created images, which it extracted from the deep recesses of his mind, delving into things and occurrences that he thought had been erased completely. A word, a picture, a voice, almost anything triggered some mechanism in his head -- a flash would rise to the fore. It put itself at the forefront and Jim would recognize the incident immediately and then the details spilled forth. This had been happening to him throughout lunch (dinner).

There was so much to remember; yet by merely sitting at home and racking his brain he could not conjure up many memories. Here, his memory was jogged often and the flashbacks were many. But how can a person recount those memories before several more are resurrected? So you just sit there and enjoy the moment and hope that at a later date you could communicate those flashes to anyone who would be interested. That's how Jim gathered a wealth of memories in that period. He thought it was amazing!

As they traveled down the mountain the temperature rose and upon arriving at the bottom it was again quite warm. Jim thought of Mrs. Cavelli and wondered how Andrea was able to cope with her constant moaning about things. It was not a bit flattering in how they dismissed his desire to learn more about what they were doing, their business, especially in the light of what the Comandante had done for Cavelli during his darkest days while in employed at the camp. However, Jim was grateful that Andrea did, at least, participate in the event of the day and to come from the seashore to meet them. That, too, puzzled Jim. Why would he go to all that trouble, help arrange the party, and spend the afternoon with the Mitchell family?

Efrem Valente drove sensibly, not wildly like Cavelli. All the windows of the car were wide open. The rushing air made it difficult to speak, so Jim had time to think of the afternoon's events. He reached down into his pocket and pulled out some of the notes that he had received at the hotel. Cavelli's card stood out. It was folded twice and when opened measured about four by eight inches. It was certainly a large business card. In red letters beside a black coat of arms it read "ditta A. Cavelli" and underneath his name and in black letters: MODENA. The coat of arms had a crown on the top and the letters in descending order: A, a larger C, and then an M. Diagonal stripes separated the letters and the C had an ebony background. "A" for Andrea, "C" for Cavelli, and "M" for Modena, Jim reasoned. The address of the warehouse and store was listed. The rest was advertising the products they handled. Liquor of all nations, it said, and a vast assortment of sweets. In large red letters on the bottom of the card it asked you not to throw the card away but to save it for future use. Good advertising, Jim thought. At least, now he knew what Andrea did for a living.

The Valentes had not maintained any friendship with Cavelli during the last twenty-five years. They knew of each other only because of Jim's mutual friendship with both families. They never visited each other but the Valentes did patronize Cavelli's shop now and then for liquor and other sundries. That was the extent of their relationship.

CHAPTER TWELVE
The Liberation Party

Recalling the great favor that Jim had accorded Andrea was easy; it was firmly etched in his memory. Lt. Mitchell had taken command in June, 1945 and it was about a month later that a serious problem occurred involving his administrator. A delegation of three men came to see him in his private office. They demanded that the Comandante fire Cavelli immediately and handed Jim a letter signed by the 'Sindaco' (mayor) of Modena. The letter was from the Liberation Party of which the mayor was the head.

The mayor listed the reasons why they requested his ouster. It seemed that Andrea Cavelli had served a couple years in prison for selling in the black market, had committed several misdemeanor crimes during the war. All in all, they didn't like the idea that this man had such a prestigious position and one that paid well. They could easily replace him with one of their own. He didn't belong to their party and they wanted him out. Just like that! Comandante Mitchell didn't care for their attitude, but hid his feelings for the moment. Then he thanked the group for their interest and told them that he would look into the matter and give them an answer in a few days. Jim marveled at how he handled the situation being such a greenhorn in the art of diplomacy. He was only twenty-nine years of age and recently off the front lines where diplomacy had no place.

Jim read the letter as best he could, called in his chief interpreter, Olive Denti, and asked her to give him the fine points to add meaning to the words that he may have had misread.

CHAPTER THIRTEEN
The Meeting

It was a hot, dry day and the stuffed furniture in the sindaco's (mayor's) office emitted an odd smell. The room was airless and the men sitting were very uncomfortable. Not only did they feel that way because of the stifling heat, but they were in surroundings in which they were unaccustomed. They tried to feel important because they represented a constituency of laborers and farmers. THE COMITATO PROVINCIALE DI LIBERAZIONE NAZIONALE was formed immediately after the fall of Italy little more than three months earlier. They were the so-called 'partigiani' (partisans) who stepped into the void of the fallen fascist government. Communism was their goal.

It was August 1945. The city was Modena, Italy.

Their ill fitting and unpressed clothing reflected the tough times that the committee members had endured for several years and also projected their abject poverty to all those who viewed them. These were poor and desperate people. Hats were being twisted in their rough hands as they listened intently to their leader whom they had elected as their mayor.

"........Since we have finished with the business of this meeting, I would like to bring up a subject, which was pointed out to me by one of the members of this committee.

As you know, it is our goal to help each other with positions of honor whenever we can. One such opportunity has presented itself and I wish to advise you that this certain position will become available to one of you. I will give you that facts and I would like you to come to a decision as to how we should proceed. I will abide by your wishes."

The mayor looked at each individual in turn with a smile seemingly to indicate that each member was eligible. The pause was a long one and none interrupted with a single word. All waited in anticipation.

"There are some jobs available at the Academy but those are menial jobs. Now there is one in particular that should be filled by our own comrades. It is the top civilian position there and it is held by Andrea Cavelli."

A low murmur filled the room and several men nodded their heads vigorously indicating that they knew Cavelli and

25

would approve of his ouster. The others stared blankly at their hands. They did not seem to agree.

The mayor sized up the committee's reaction and decided to continue, "I have some evidence here that could secure his dismissal immediately. I gather that some of you know Cavelli and the problems in his life."

He held up some documents, then adjusted his glasses and began to read out loud from a paper that had the seal of the surete.

".........black market.......convicted........time spent in jail............." and on and on.

Putting down the sheaf of legal papers, the mayor centered his attention on the group in front of him. He had already made his decision. All that had to be done now was to let the committee think that it was theirs.

Seeing that the response by his fellow committeemen was almost non-committal, one of the men got to his feet and pointing his finger at his cohorts angrily said, "We must do something about this! With his bad record that man Cavelli has no right to such a position! It should go to one of us! I think we should show his honor that we are behind him and that he should do everything possible to get that job for our cause!"

The mayor hurriedly seized the opportunity that was presented to him.

"He's right, comrades. Shall I do what is necessary?"

Again there was a loud agreement from several and a clapping of their hands.

The reluctant ones were intimidated into agreeing with the majority.

All were in favor of actions to be taken and to get the job for a supporter of the liberation committee.

Slowly the committee members rose to leave still clutching their hats and anxious to get out into the open air where they would feel more at ease.

Lining up each man in turn shook hands with the 'sindaco' and muttered his goodbye.

CHAPTER FOURTEEN
The Letter

With the room clear, the mayor called to his secretary who just happened to be his sister-in-law and asked her to take a letter.

"It is to "Al Comandante il 24 Evacuation Camp ex Accademia Militare.""

The secretary scrambled to write the address and then poised to take the mayor's dictation.

"Mark the letter 'personal' and to Lieutenant James Mitchell. He's just a boy and we'll have some fun with him." The sindaco winked and with a broad smile continued, "He doesn't realize that he is up against a powerful organization. Those Americans, they don't know anything about politics. He'll do anything we ask him to. You know soldiers; they'll take the easy way out. Americans are big showoffs with their money, their food and cigarettes. I've been told that Cavelli is on a good footing with his comandante but I am going to change that with this letter!"

"Si, Peppino," The middle aged secretary agreed.

"Don't call me by that name here! Address me as Your Honor, or Signore. We must respect the dignity of this office! Now let's continue."

"Al Tenente....," He began dictating a letter that would be dated August 4, 1945.

The mayor put his hand on his wet forehead and pursed his lips. He smiled at the thought that his brother could fit into Cavelli's job at the refugee camp in the Academy. His responsibility for his brother's welfare would cease and all concerned would be happy. His action could easily be explained to the committee. After all, his brother was a member of the political organization too.

The secretary waited patiently for her boss to dictate the letter. When he began she laboriously wrote down his words. It was to be her only letter for the day.

On August 4, 1945 Mitchell received the following letter:

COMITATO DI LIBERAZIONE NAZIONALE
MODENA

Modena, 4/8/45
AL TENENTE JAMES MITCHELL
COMANDANTE IL 24' EVACUATION CAMP
M O D E N A

Oggetto: CAVELLI ANDREA fu Alberto

Si trasmette per conoscenza alla S.V. copia della lettera inviata dalla R. questur di Modena relativa ad informazioni sul conto del nominato in oggetto:

foglio n' 0220/U.P./N.I. div. I in data 26 luglio 1945.
" CAVELLI ANDREA fu Alberto nato a Castelfranco il 4/1/1912 domiciliato a
Modena Via Bosco n. 942 rappresentante, ha i seguenti precedenti penali:
Sentenza Corte d"Assise di Firenze-10/7/37 detenzione e spendita di monete false-anni 4 di reclusione- L 400 di multa e sottoposto alla liberta vigilata.
Sentenza Pretore Modena-28/2/1938 Truffa - non doversi procedere per amnistia."

IL PRESIDENTE
[seal]   [signature]

28

MITCHELL'S TRANSLATION:
NATIONAL LIBERATION COMMITTEE
MODENA

THE LIEUTENANT JAMES MITCHELL
COMMANDER OF NO. 24 EVACUATION CAMP
MODENA

Subject: CAVELLI ANDREA son of Albert

For your information we are transmitting copies of letters and ask you to take in account the following subject:
File #0220 dated 26 July 1945
"CAVELLI ANDREA born in Castelfranco on Jan. 4, 1912, residing in Modena on Bosco St. has received the following penalties in the past:

Sentenced in the court of assizes in Florence on July 10, 1937 for passing counterfeit money -4 years imprisonment, paid a fine of 400 lire. (and probably after release subject to surveillance)

On 28 Feb. 1938 the Judge of Modena ruled out parole."

SEAL

PRESIDENT
sig.

CHAPTER FIFTEEN
The Black Shirts

The interpreter, Mrs. Olive Denti, had come from Palestine with her family before the war. She and her husband, Salvatore, spoke Arabic fluently and incidentally with the same dialect or accent that Jim had acquired from his mother and grandparents. Salvatore was Italian by birth; Olive was born in Italy of an Italian father and English mother. Olive's father had been in the diplomatic service. Mrs. Denti was highly educated and was fluent in English, Arabic, French, and Italian. She had some fluency in other languages, too.

It was with some hesitancy that Lt. Mitchell asked her to look at the letter because it dealt with a very sensitive situation. A man's livelihood was at stake and in addition to that Cavelli was his right hand man, a very efficient person, and one who had the respect of all who worked at the Academy, including the American and English staff. Andrea immediately acceded to all Jim's wishes (or commands), never giving him an argument, and kept the Comandante up to date with all that was going on. Cavelli was on the job long before Mitchell arose in the morning and he only left in the evening when all the work was completed. One could not ask for anything more. He was very respectful and did not mind taking orders from someone many years his junior.

At times Cavelli could be brittle with some of his workers, but not without justification. They respected him for that. Jim got to know his family, his wife, Lina and daughter, Carla, who was a teenager. Mitchell and his American staff were often invited to the same parties and affairs that were held by local gentry.

Marchese Casate often had them over to her villa some evenings for drinks and dancing, some snacks but not much. The Americans contributed some things from their rations that were very much appreciated. Sometimes, a relative of the Marchese would show up. She was introduced as a princess. Both the princess and the Marchese did volunteer work at the refugee camp. The princess only came now and then, but Marchese Casate worked every day. She wore a Red Cross uniform and applied herself diligently in the hospital that had been set up in one wing of the Academy.

From the point of view of social life, Andrea seemed to be respected by all. His family life was beyond reproach. He was very attentive to his wife and child. He never got drunk, and only drank the usual wines but not to excess. He was a heavy smoker, which contributed to his perpetual hoarseness. There was no violation of law or of ethics that Mitchell could see.

The Comandante ran a tight ship as far as expenditures were concerned. Jim's accounting experience was used in good stead in the finance department. His American team was as diligent as he was and it was reflected in their work. Lady Raus handled the Red Cross finances; the Americans were not involved in that except that they paid the doctors and nurses that Jim had hired for the hospital.

Olive Denti enlarged on the points that Lt. Mitchell had missed; he did not recollect any major difference between his own interpretation and hers. She was shaken by the allegations stressed in the letter and said that she knew nothing about his record. In her responses to Jim's questions, she admitted that she sensed that there was some political motivation. That rather frightened her.

"It's not like America," she said. "Here this sort of thing is very serious coming from the Liberation Party. They are known to have done terrible things to people who got in their way. In their minds they are still at war with the Fascists and anyone who stands in their way is in danger."

Mitchell couldn't understand her thinking but did give her the benefit of the doubt and decided to play his cards carefully. He would talk to Andrea and try to get some of the facts of his life during the war years and even prior to that in the late 1930's when Fascism was predominant and necessities of life were scarce.

During that period Italy was girding for war and the black market started then. The Black Shirts (Fascists) got everything they needed, the rest had to take the crumbs. Meanwhile, Mussolini strutted on the world stage beside Hitler.

The Fascists were ruthless. They commandeered everything they needed despite the complaints of the poor sharecroppers and laborers. The elite lived grandly, while oth-

31

ers starved. The black market flourished, Fascists participated heavily because they had the goods and got rich. They were not prosecuted, but the poor person who was caught was jailed and his family suffered as well.

CHAPTER SIXTEEN
The Jewish Refugees

The entire staff at the displaced persons and repatriation camp treated the refugees well and with respect. They understood the problems themselves. The civilian workers included many different nationalities. A number of them had been refugees as well, so they understood the problems of the guests.

At any given day, the camp had a count of five thousand or so guests. About ninety per cent of them were Jews from Europe. They came from Poland, Germany, Austria and other countries. However, when they were registered they all claimed that they were Palestinians. It seems that people from various Jewish agencies from England and the United States gathered the Jews at different points in Europe and put them on trains to Italy. Destination: Bari. That was to be their port of embarkation.

The agents of JDC (Joint Distribution Committee) instructed the Jewish refugees to claim that they were native Palestinians. At registration time they said that all their papers were lost and would not admit that they were Polish Nationals even though they spoke Polish when answering questions. It was a huge conspiracy, well thought out and well planned. All other nationals responded in the same manner, speaking in their native tongue and declaring their nationality to be Palestinian.

The rabbis also told the same untruths. Mitchell questioned many of them personally in Arabic. They understood not a word and insisted that they were from Palestine. The rabbis tended their flock like shepherds and ministered to their people in a way that was admirable. These same rabbis came to Jim and demanded kosher food.

"Impossible," He had replied, "You must eat whatever we can provide. You can't make that kind of choice in these times."

His answer did not deter them; they came to see him again with a larger delegation.

"Now," They said, "We will cook ourselves. Just give us beans and some vegetables, and some oil. We'll do the rest."

Lt. Mitchell remembered seeing a "Jerry" (German) kitchen at one of the American Army vehicle depots. He sent two of the non-coms to the depot with a requisition for that unit. The rabbis were delighted when it arrived and was parked in an alcove adjacent to the courtyard. It was an outdoor kitchen, but it was the best Jim could do. The rabbi and some members of his flock proceeded to clean it post haste.

Late that afternoon the Comandante was invited to the kosher dinner in the mess hall. The meal had been cooked outdoors and the people were fed inside. He accepted the invitation and had a great kosher meal. It was meatless and consisted of beans and vegetables cooked in olive oil.

The Orthodox Jews watched him as he ate and when Jim nodded with approval and cleaned his plate they applauded. Cavelli was also a part of this; he saw to it that they were given what had been requested. He never complained about how we deviated and made available special food for a comparatively small contingent. At that time, most of the Jewish refugees did not care whether the food was kosher or not, as long as they were fed.

Yacob was kosher, conveniently perhaps, and that was before the mob scene, which was held in his honor.

And Yacob seemed to be everywhere, ingratiating himself with the Italian soldiers, the cooks and even Cavelli. One day the Lieutenant walked into the kitchen to make a surprise inspection, and there sitting at a table was Yacob eating some specialty of the house. This was something that could not and would not be tolerated. Jim flew into a rage and ordered Yacob out of the kitchen. He then proceeded to raise hell with the head cook and told him that no preference was to be shown to anyone. That order was obeyed as long as Mitchell was in command. Yacob kept out of his way for a short while.

Next time Yacob came into the Comandante's presence he was leading a delegation of men who wanted reparations, pay and the same food the Americans were eating. They claimed that UNRA (United Nations Relief Assn.) was supposed to give them reparations and pay at so many dollars a day. They saw the rations that the American soldiers picked up from the Army Depot and they wanted the same food and claimed that it was their right. Mitchell really exploded that time and told them that he earned those rations by fighting their war and that they were no different than any of the other refugees. He also told them to take their demands to the Joint Distribution Committee. The lady who represented the JDC and who visited the camp often also turned them down, much to Jim's amusement.

CHAPTER SEVENTEEN
The Ducal Palace

Every day the count of inhabitants of the refugee camp remained close to five thousand and that was despite the fact that they had new arrivals almost daily in numbers of four or five hundred. It appeared that several hundred Jewish refugees would "escape" every day. Guards were posted at all the exits not to keep the people in, but to keep order and not allow anyone to leave bearing luggage. The refugees found a way, however. Whole families would leave ostensibly to walk around the town and their compatriots would throw their belongings out the windows to the square below. It was impossible to control. The staff looked the other way and did not pursue them.

Earlier, it was said that it was a "grand conspiracy" and Mitchell stuck to that notion. He observed that almost daily British lorries, large vehicles that could easily hold up to forty persons, would park several hundred meters away. Not out of sight, mind you, but at a distance where they could say that they were not interfering with the operation of the refugee camp. It may have been overlooked in explaining this before, but this was a very unusual 'camp.'

At one time it was the Duke of Modena's palace and had over two hundred rooms, including large halls and a huge dining and entertainment room. One hall had a stage and had been used as a ballroom. Marble floors were throughout the building, the ceilings were high and the frescoes were ornate and covered with gold leaf. Bathrooms were adequate. The kitchen was all-electric; the soup vats were very large and controlled by electricity. By all standards very modern. Despite all of these conveniences, people were leaving.

As stated earlier, the trucks were parked legally and at one point the Comandante confronted some of the drivers and learned that they were not British soldiers, but Palestinian Jews who volunteered to man this truck brigade. It was called the Palestinian Brigade. They did no fighting, only transporting for the British Armies. Now, here they were in an unofficial capacity picking up the 'escapees' and taking them to the port of Bari where ships were awaiting them for transport to Palestine. The British Government overlooked these

36

actions and unofficially sanctioned them. The drivers were using British lorries, British gas, and Palestinian troops who were paid by the British, to transport thousands of Jewish refugees to their 'Promised Land.' It was clearly political.

CHAPTER EIGHTEEN
"When In Rome"

Jim's musing about the past was interrupted when Efrem honked his horn as they drove up to a large apartment building. Someone opened up the gate to the courtyard and Efrem's car entered followed by four other cars. So this was their home! It was nothing like the picture that Lina had formulated in the Mitchell's minds. This was a magnificent apartment building, built of marble and stone, with verandahs encircling the building on all the upper floors.

Mama Elena was there to greet them, with tears and kisses and hugging. She was overjoyed that Mitchell had come to visit them. She greeted Jim's family in the same manner. The American father was greatly pleased and especially so, because his family was impressed. They had no idea that their trip to Italy was going to be like this. They were overwhelmed with their hospitality.

The Valentes proudly showed the Mitchells their apartments. Mama had her apartment on the first floor and the three apartments above were occupied by Efrem, Renzo, and Mario and their families. The rooms were large with marble floors, high ceilings, with built in closets and furniture. The bathrooms were ultra modern and with that extra facility used exclusively by women. Jim's family filed from one apartment to another, congratulating them on their tastes in furniture and decor. Efrem handed Jim the keys to his apartment and said it was theirs to use for as long as they liked. His wife and son were going to go to Lago di Garda, a lake resort, with his in-laws. He would stay with one of his brothers because he had work to do.

Despite protests Efrem insisted, "You slept in my bed in our farmhouse the night you saved us from the Germans and I'd like you to sleep in my bed again. Besides that you saved my life when I had meningitis and you took me to your hospital and treated me and I got better. I will never forget that."

With that, who could refuse such an invitation? All were deeply moved and accepted. The Mitchell family remained at the apartment while Efrem drove Jim to the Hotel Fini to retrieve the luggage and passports. As was customary, they had relinquished their passports at the reception desk upon registering.

Canceling the reservation posed no problem. The hotel

staff was very cooperative.

As they were leaving the concierge confidentially whispered to Jim, "The police were here early today to check your passports."

That bit of information caught Mitchell by surprise. It is not usual for the police to make a special visit to check passports. That inspection is done routinely on a daily basis. He wondered why they were singled out. He thanked the concierge for his concern.

Needless to say, Jim felt troubled on the way back to Efrem's apartment.

All the meals were furnished by the families in residence at the apartment building. Breakfast with one family, then dinner at mid-day, when everybody would attend at one of the apartments. Cena (supper) was held in any apartment. At the dinners, Mama Elena's cooking was evident. It was the finest cuisine in northern Italy. Dorothy said her sauces were light, but supreme in her book. The dinners were classic, with lots of wine, loud talk and banter. Very enjoyable. When the Americans desired "quiet' time, they excused themselves and retired to their apartment. Their Italian friends respected their privacy and the Mitchells appreciated that. Besides, after dinner the Italian friends took naps. So did the Americans. When in Rome.........

CHAPTER NINETEEN
Out of The Past

The third morning in Modena, armed with a map of the town, Jim decided to drive around to see some of the sights and to acquaint his family with the city. The Valentes had told the Mitchells that they already had made arrangements with the Commandant of the Academy for a tour scheduled for the fifth day of their visit. Therefore, it was Jim's intent to stay away from that part of town. He had the address of Cavelli's shop in his pocket and after looking at the map, he was determined to find via S. Giovanni Bosco.

The large business card that he had said "nuova sede magazzino," meaning "new, main store." He probably had several branches and the one Jim was going to drive by was the principal address. From over a hundred meters away he could see a theater-like illuminated sign with hundreds of light bulbs attached to a very new, and modern building.

The lighted bulbs shone brightly with many colors and flashing one name "STOCK." It was the name of a very popular liquor that was imported from another European country probably Germany. Jim did not intend to stop there at that time. Traffic was heavy on that street. But there it was, a parking space big enough for a big Lincoln. So on impulse, Mitchell pulled over and parked.

His family got out and started walking towards some shops that had attracted their attention. Jim let them go and crossed the street and slowly walked past the entrance of Andrea's store. The building was half a block long and thirty five paces wide (about a hundred feet).

From the signs and the displays that were shown in the storefront, Jim gathered that Cavelli's sold to wholesale and retail customers. Liquors from all over the world were available there. He recognized the names of the best American and British whiskies, plus beer of all nations.

They had everything. They sold the finest chocolates from Switzerland; American Hershey bars, and British Cadbury. Gift boxes of all of these products were displayed so beautifully that he was tempted to go in and purchase an item or two to give the Valentes as tokens of his appreciation.

The doors at the main entrance were wide open and as

Jim walked towards where he had last seen his family, he heard someone call, "Comandante! Comandante! Come in! Come in!"

It was Franco. When Mitchell turned to face him he could see past him and into the store. There was some sort of confusion going on inside and he knew that the ruckus started when his name was called by Franco. He did notice that a man was running to the rear of the store. He also heard a familiar voice shouting something to Franco, but he could not make out the words.

Franco paled, then stuttered a few words of greeting and ended by saying that he had something important to do and had to go. As he turned to enter the store, Andrea appeared. Wiping his brow, the red-faced Cavelli tried to cover his annoyance with a half smile, and then shook Jim's hand. His palms were very wet. The American had never seen him so agitated and nervous. It was as though he had been caught red-handed in some illegal act. He did his best to welcome Jim to his establishment after they had some small talk for a couple of minutes. Franco had disappeared after the man who had taken to his heels. Both were now hidden in the deep dark recesses of the store.

Andrea only showed Mitchell the front part of the store and tried to minimize the importance of his business. Jim congratulated him on his success and his ability to get all the franchises of all the name brand products that he traded. He was fascinated by Cavelli's accomplishments.

Andrea had many clerks waiting on customers and at the side door some men were loading a truck with cases of liquor and other merchandise. Jim was told that the load was going to Milan.

The truck had large letters on its side "STOCK" and in smaller letters "ditta A. Cavelli." The coat of arms with a crown on top and the letters "A,C,M" in descending order was painted on the rear doors of the truck. It was big as life, in black and gray. A person could easily distinguish that logo a half mile away. Jim was truly impressed.

CHAPTER TWENTY
Mysterious "Silent Partner"

Several minutes passed by and Cavelli and Mitchell lapsed into a strained silence. Jim lamely excused himself, saying that he had to go and find his family. Andrea very politely invited him to come another time but to please call him beforehand to make sure that he would be in. He added that he and Lina were supposed to go back to the seashore that day but he had to attend to some urgent business and probably couldn't leave for another few days. They shook hands and Mitchell exited by the main entrance.

While leaving to seek his family, Jim looked around to see if he could see Franco and the mysterious person who was fleeing to the rear of the store. It was of no account, he reasoned; that incident didn't happen because of his intrusion. Was it something that was caused by Franco? Jim hoped he didn't get in trouble for coming out to greet him. No, that wasn't it either.

The Mitchells did a little shopping that day and had a nice lunch in a small restaurant. Modena was not a tourist town and was not geared to handle travelers. True, some buses came by from Germany and France but only to stop over at a hotel to spend the night. Today, Modena is industrial, being the center of the ceramics industry. The Ferrari, Lamborghini, and DiTomaso automobiles are made there.

There are quite a few points of interest in Modena, some churches dating from the twelfth century, and "IL PALAZZO DUCALE di MODENA". The latter is now the West Point of Italy - a military academy, and that is where Jim was the comandante in 1945.

While relaxing in Efrem's apartment and while the rest of his family was napping, as is the Italian custom, Mitchell had the sudden urge to find out what was going on at Cavelli's store.

He would have to talk to Franco about that. In addition, while emptying his pockets of some of the junk one accumulates while traveling, he came across a crumpled piece of paper, which he was preparing to toss into a wastebasket.

Bells rang in script but in English words: "GO AWAY, DON'T STIR THE POT". It's one way the Italians tell you to mind your own business. Jim was puzzled. What business? He did not mention the note to Dorothy.

He looked at the note again; the writing was in German script, not Italian. That made it more puzzling. He knew no Germans in Italy. That type of script was familiar to him. He had studied German for two years in high school. At that point he knew that the warning did not come from any of his Italian friends. But who could it be? Besides, into what kind of business was he going to poke his nose? He was on vacation and only looking for a good time for himself and family. Now he was intrigued and therefore decided to investigate the mystery of the German's note.

At the evening meal at one of the Valente's apartments, (it didn't matter whose apartment, because all the families in the building came), Jim decided to see what information he could garner by asking seemingly innocuous questions about various things. They talked about the Valente's trucking business, where they obtained their large demijohns of wine, etc. Asking about the wine gave Mitchell an opportunity to ask about Cavelli's wine and liquor business. He mentioned that he had seen the store and talked to Andrea, then asked how long Andrea was in business.

Right after the war, they said, Cavelli opened up a good sized store at that location and it has been growing in leaps and bounds ever since. Even in years of depression, his business grew. The latter information was given to Jim with a suppressed smile while the Valentes exchanged knowing looks with each other. They had whetted the American's appetite for information. He pressed them for more.

With an innocent look, Jim told them that he was curious about the coat of arms that was on the business card and on the back of the truck, and what was the meaning of the third letter, "M?" They almost roared at the last question. Between smirks and guffaws and nudging each other, they informed Mitchell that was the "silent" partner's initial, a man by the name of Mandelli.

The man came from the Tyrols, they thought, because he had a funny accent that bordered on Austrian. They said he was not a true Italian but became one with the name Mandelli. They snickered at that. But they did say that he was very wealthy and endowed the various charities and

43

churches in the area with large contributions. And politically, he had a lot of clout by supporting the leading party of the period. He seemed like a great person to Jim, so he couldn't understand their picture of Mandelli.

CHAPTER TWENTY ONE
Surete Chief On A Bike?

The morning of the fourth day in Modena, after a leisurely continental breakfast consisting of a local biscuit and coffee, Mitchell went to the balcony overlooking the courtyard. He stood there a short while before his family joined him. They were admiring the scenery and the difference in architecture between the very old homes and the new apartment buildings and villas, when a man on a bicycle rode into the courtyard ostensibly to look at the racing pigeons that Efrem was raising as a hobby.

The pigeons were housed in a cote on the top of one of the outbuildings. Efrem was on top of the stairway leading to the cote with feed in a receptacle. The bicyclist called up to Efrem who then turned to acknowledge the greeting. Their conversation continued for a while as the pigeons were fed. Naturally, Jim thought that this other person was a friend of Efrem's and possibly another pigeon fancier.

Efrem noticed Mitchell on the verandah and motioned for him to come down. Jim eagerly went down, hoping to learn more about their hobby of raising and racing pigeons. Approaching them he put out his hand to greet the newcomer as he would a friend of his host. He was introduced as Signore Gabrielli who lived nearby. Gabrielli was very friendly and politely asked Jim where he was from, and how long was he going to stay in Italy. He particularly wanted to know the Mitchell's departure date. Interspersed with conversation, he would interject other questions that Jim thought were a little off base.

He was a little too nosy perhaps. But Jim answered his questions without hesitation and honestly. Gabrelli was not really abrasive; he was congenial and acted as though he was a long time friend of the Valentes. Therefore, Mitchell excused his sometimes-pointed questions. He called Jim "comandante" at one time and the American thought that was a little odd, since he was not there in that capacity.

Conversation turned to the pigeons and Efrem was then included. Later they talked in generalities; it was not about Jim or his family. Gabrielli took leave by shaking hands, getting astride his bike and riding off with a wave.

45

Jim remarked to Efrem that it was nice of his friend to come to his home to meet his guests. Efrem looked at him peculiarly and said, "He's not my friend, this is the first time he has ever come here. I know him because he lives not too far from here, and he is the Chief of the Surete in Modena. He is a well-known person and I only know him that way. No, Gabrielli is not really a friend of ours."

Mitchell hastened to explain that he saw him ride in and thought that the Chief was another pigeon enthusiast.

Efrem shook his head, "This is the first time he has ever come here."

Both were puzzled.

"Efrem," Jim asked, "But he asked me so many questions as though he was a good friend of yours and wanted to know more about me. That would be natural. But why?" Efrem shrugged, then climbed back up the ladder to tend to his pigeons.

Now Mitchell had more food for thought. The plot was thickening and he was at the center of it all. It probably was nothing. But it did amuse him and not without some misgivings.

Jim mentioned the conversations that he had with Gabrielli to Dorothy. She had observed the meeting from the balcony and thought it was only good Italian stuff going back and forth between them.

Dorothy thought that the Chief looked like a nice personable person and that he rode the bicycle with dignity. That's a woman's observation for you.

CHAPTER TWENTY TWO
Motive For Investiation

Later that day, over the evening meal, Mario and Renzo were told about the encounter with the visitor. They thought that it was nice of the Chief to stop in and acknowledged that it was his first time. They also thought that it was only coincidental that he dropped in while the Americans were there. Now, they said, we will have better security with him around (joke).

Mitchell slept fitfully that night; something was nagging him and he couldn't put his finger on it.

Morning finally arrived and he arose and prepared himself for the day, while the rest of his family slept on.

He couldn't understand why, but he was determined to get some answers before the day was over.

Jim could hardly contain himself while waiting for Efrem to show up at pigeon feeding time. The Italian found the American nervously pacing around the courtyard. Mitchell explained that he was taking a little exercise before breakfast.

After some small talk, Jim posed the question of the day, "When did you tell Gabrielli that I was a comandante?"

"Never," He responded, "I didn't even mention your name before you came down to meet him. He was only told that you were an American friend who was visiting. I told him nothing about your history."

"Did I hear him call me "Comandante" or was I just imagining it?"

"Daverro," He answered, "That's right. I wondered at the time why he called you that! He's a wise one, that Chief, I am now certain that he got that information before he came here. Why is he investigating you? You have nothing to hide. I wonder what his motive is?"

Mentally, a phrase came to the fore in Jim's mind. It was something he used to hear the kids say when they were questioned. It was "For me to know, and you to find out." As if that made any sense. Now he knew it had to be the other way around. It was, "FOR ME TO FIND OUT!"

Fortunately for Jim, Noris (Camille's son) drove in shortly after breakfast with the intention of taking his wife, 'Donata,' and Jimmy and Judy for some leisurely sightseeing. That was great. Now he could do some sleuthing on his own. He would have to hurry though, because they were going to go to the Ducal Palace (Academy) for the tour scheduled for that afternoon.

Jim drove directly to via Bosco and the grand "magazzino" (store) of Cavelli's. Franco was right there at his designated place near the entrance. He greeted Mitchell cordially and with great respect. Rightfully so. Jim had taken good care of him at the Camp. He had treated Franco well and his former driver still appreciated it.

Franco was about forty-five years of age now, married, and with one child, a boy whom he had named "Giacamo." He sheepishly said that it was the closest he could come to "James." Jim was flattered; he had named his son after him. He never thought for one minute that he had made that kind of impression on him, or any one else that he had left behind in Italy.

Things were calm and peaceful in the store. Cavelli and his wife had gone to the seashore to join their daughter, Carla, for a few days.

Mitchell understood, from Franco, that he was sort of a general manager in the business. He had no investment in the enterprise, but was making a good living. Franco said that he probably would work there for the rest of his life. He was happy with the arrangement with Cavelli. Franco did not mention Cavelli's partner, Mr. "M."

Not having much time, Jim did not mince words with Franco and asked him pointedly what the "M" stood for on the coat of arms. The response was slow and deliberate, as though he had rehearsed it. He knew that Signore Mandelli was a partner, he explained, but he very seldom saw Mandelli. Franco went on to say that he never had to deal with Mandelli in any way.

Cavelli and Mandelli met in private from time to time and Franco was never invited to attend the meetings. Since that was the case, he never had any information as to what went on and did not care to know. He was treated well and received bonuses each year for doing a good job. The business was doing fairly well, according to Franco, and he was generously paid.

"Confidentially," whispered Franco, "I think I am over-paid, but who am I to argue about that. That's why I am very loyal to Andrea. What he does with Mandelli does not concern me. I am content."

The two talked about the past, the fun they had, and the problems of the times during the post war period. He told Mitchell that Cavelli took good care of him after the refugee camp was closed. Cavelli gave him a job in his store and kept him there all these years. Andrea was best man at Franco's wedding and later was the godfather to Franco's son. His son was now nineteen and a student at the University of Bologna.

CHAPTER TWENTY THREE
Accademia Militare

As the conversation lagged, Franco lit a cigarette, inhaled deeply and forcefully expelled a large cloud of smoke. He was relaxed and at ease.

On a hunch, Jim slowly reached into his pocket, pulled out the note that was written in English and dropped it on the floor. A few moments later he let Franco see him stoop to pick up the crumpled piece of paper. Mitchell smoothed it out, glanced at the writing, and handed it to Franco.

Franco let it lie on the palm of his left hand and without thinking Franco said, "That's Mandelli's handwriting."

He recovered quickly and added, "I pick up the mail and take it to Andrea's office. Sometimes I see envelopes with that type of handwriting. We get letters from all over Europe, and even America."

Franco seemed a bit flustered because of what he had blurted out and did not seem to mind when Jim took the note out of his hand and put it back in his pocket. As if in agreement, they changed the subject. Mitchell had learned that Franco could not read English and therefore did not know what the note said.

Having heard what he wanted to know Jim excused himself and prepared to leave. As an afterthought, he told Franco that they were going to go to the Ducal Palace later in the day and invited him to meet the group there.

"Great," He said, accepting graciously, "I'll take the rest of the day off."

It was at that moment that Cavelli drove up in his Ferrari and they walked over to meet him.

"I changed my mind and am not going to the seashore today," Andrea said as they approached him, "A friend of ours took Lina there and so now I am free." He ended his sentence with a broad smile and shook Jim's hand.

Not to be outdone, Mitchell invited him to go to the Ducal Palace with Franco and meet the party.

"If we are all there together, I would enjoy it more," Jim said. They both nodded in agreement and shook hands with their comandante in parting. They would meet at 3 P.M.

Three o'clock came soon enough and there were many gathered in the square at the entrance to Accademia Militare. Camille was there with her husband and son, as were the Valente brothers. Maurizio, the son of Efrem, came with his father.

Cavelli and Franco stood apart smoking.

The Mitchell family was busy taking pictures of everyone and using the Ducal Palace as the backdrop.

As the group approached the main gate where the comandante, Colonel Giannangeli, was to meet them, a green Fiat sped towards a parking space and screeched to a halt. It was the interpreter of many years ago, Olive Denti, and her husband, Salvatore.

That was indeed a surprise and the seeing them was very heart warming. Olive shed tears and Jim swallowed hard.

The Colonel greeted his visitors as they entered the large courtyard, thanked the contingent for coming, and told them that Colonel Mitchell's family and the group were welcome to go anywhere with his appointed guide except the restricted areas. All understood that and thanked him for his kindness. The Italian comandante then turned the party over to his aide, a young captain, who proceeded guide them to points of interest. He spoke English fairly well and in turn used both Italian and English in describing the various items. He handled the questions very well and all moved right along without any problems.

CHAPTER TWENTY FOUR
The Riot

Mitchell's family was in awe of the art and the history that the Ducal Palace represented.

The Palace was built in 1634 to give the Este family a palace in keeping with their place among the royalty of Italy. It became the "ACCADEMIA MILITARE DI MODENA" in 1859.

The "Steps of Honor" leading to the balcony that surrounds the courtyard was magnificent. Made of marble the wide staircase curved softly upward. The balcony was a museum in itself. The many niches along the wall contained statues and busts of historical figures. They were priceless treasures.

While approaching a familiar bust, several of the viewers moved hastily forward leaving the rest of the group slightly behind. All, including Jim, exclaimed in unison, "There it is, there's the mark left by a machine gun bullet!"

It was put there the day a mob of Jews almost killed one of the refugees.

As the group edged forward to take a look at the chip on the face of the marble bust, Cavelli explained to the Italian captain about their interest in that particular piece of art. Mitchell took the opportunity to ask Olive in English if she knew what happened to the victim, Yacob...Yacob something or other. She finished his sentence with "Klein."

Yes, she remembered him well because he was always doing something that got him in trouble with others, and forever irking the refugees with whom he came in contact. She said that when he left the camp things went back to normal.

"Refresh my memory, Olive," Her former comandante asked, "didn't that riot occur in August?"

"No," she responded, "It happened in the last half of July. I remember it well because I had just come back from Rome after visiting my mother. A week or so before the first A-bomb struck Japan, Yacob Klein got out of our hospital and asked Cavelli to take him to the railroad station so that he could leave Modena and the camp. He must have been afraid to stay."

So that's what happened to Yacob. Andrea had never reported it. It was understandable. Lt. Mitchell had forgotten all about him anyway and probably the director, Cavelli, didn't want to bother his boss with such triviality.

Olive hastened to add, "I remember that period of time like it was yesterday, and of course you recall some of us went to Lake Garda; Cavelli and Franco took a couple of days off to go to Lake Como or the mountains. It was a few days after Japan surrendered and we all celebrated one way or another."

Mitchell remembered Lago di Garda, but nothing about Andrea and Franco leaving together. Cavelli was supposed to take his wife and daughter somewhere for an outing.

Andrea finished telling the mob story to the captain and the other listeners and the tour continued.

As though she had read Jim's mind, Olive Denti moved over towards Andrea and asked in a voice loud enough for all to hear, "Whatever happened to that refugee, Yacob Klein, after you took him out of the hospital?"

Cavelli stopped in his tracks, obviously stunned by the question. He did not immediately turn towards her to respond, but seemed to hesitate to gather his wits, and then answered, "I don't know, I only took him to the train station."

Franco, standing close by, seemed to be taken aback by Andrea's short explanation. Jim was interested in seeing how this question and answer period was affecting the people in the party. At that point, he thought he had heard and seen enough.

The rest of the tour was quite interesting. Valuable pieces of art were on display everywhere. Paintings hung on the walls of the large salons, in the grand ballroom, even in the Princess' apartment that the comandante had occupied while he was there. Mitchell showed his family the apartment, where he slept, the anterooms, and the large dining room that still had the table on which his staff had dined. The dining room table was very long and could easily accommodate forty people. It was more ornate than he remembered. At the time he was in occupancy he was not interested in art or furnishings, for that matter.

The gold leaf and murals on the ceilings fascinated everyone, especially Donata.

The tour ended on a fine note, the captain being a great

guide and a good companion. The colonel had made a good choice in choosing him.

As they were thanking the Captain and shaking his hand, Colonel Giannangeli came to the exit and shook hands with all as they thanked him too. Courteously, he saluted Colonel Mitchell when they met. Jim saluted him in return and was moved by the honor that had been accorded by that gesture.

CHAPTER TWENTY FIVE
Castle de Zena

That evening the Valente men and their sister, Camille, entertained the Mitchells at a local restaurant. They had reserved the entire facility for the evening. All four Valente families attended including the family members who had returned from the resorts late in the afternoon. In-laws and some of their relatives were in attendance. Salvatore and Olive Denti came too.

The main salon was filled to capacity. The children of the Valente clan were having a great time. It wasn't very often that they were taken anywhere at that hour of the day. Again, the American family was overwhelmed by the kindness and respect they showed.

Noticeably absent was Cavelli. Franco appeared at the last minute with his wife. After introductions he said that Andrea had some urgent business and couldn't attend. Jim understood because he had noticed that for some reason or other Andrea was not at ease with the younger Valente men.

Course, after course, appetizers and entrees were served in family style. The tables were loaded with food, wines, and two kinds of bottled water - with gas and without gas (that's how they distinguished plain water and club soda). The kids chose their water and their parents added the wine. No mixed drinks served there. No martinis or manhattans. Just plain good Italian red and white sparkling wines. As usual there were toasts and more toasts. Jim responded in kind. So did Dorothy and Jimmy and Judy.

Franco sat near the American family with his wife, Anita, by his side. She was shy but after Dorothy spoke to her for a while, Anita opened up a bit and talked about her son and his accomplishments. She told us about her house in Villanova, a suburb of Modena, and invited the Mitchells to pay her a visit. She had never met any Americans and wanted to get to know them. It was very complimentary and spoken with sincerity. One could see that Franco was very proud and pleased that Anita was comfortable with her new friends. Jim congratulated him for choosing such a beautiful and charming wife. Anita blushed and hid her face laughingly.

Mitchell had noticed that while the women were in earnest conversation Franco seemed to be on the verge of telling him something. At one time while Jim was pouring some wine in his glass, Franco asserted, "It's not as bad as you think, working for Cavelli and Mandelli. As you can see, my wife is very happy living the life we are leading. And I am thankful for that."

That was it, nothing more, nothing less. Why he thought he had to reassure Jim about his position in the Cavelli Store, and his position in life, was a mystery. What did he think was known about his arrangement with his employers? Mitchell really only knew what Franco himself told him, or what had been observed in his visits to their place of business.

The party broke up about eleven, long past the children's bedtime although most of the kids were as lively as ever. The waiters were tired and wishing the party would leave. The Mitchells bade good-bye to Franco and Anita, for they would not see them again.

Dorothy and Jim rode home with Efrem, his wife, and son. Judy and Jimmy went along with Noris.

On the return to the apartment, Dorothy remarked about how charming Anita was, and how well they were able to communicate. Anita gave her some recipes and tips on Reggio-Emilia cooking. Of course, Anita was very proud of her home and how it was furnished. "----and it was all possible through the kindness of a Signore Mandelli ---," thusly Dorothy ended her summarization of her talk with Anita. That last sentence meant nothing to Jim's wife, but it meant a lot to him. Parts of his puzzle were falling into place.

Knowing that he could not continue his search for more information because they were leaving the following day for Florence as a continuation of their Italian holiday, the former comandante decided to shelve his curiosity.

Before retiring for the night, Jim informed his family that on the way to Florence he wanted to stop at a couple of places where he had been during the war. He wanted to show them some of the battlefields, places he would never forget, like the Castle de Zena which stood at the bottom of Monterumici (a mountain that was stained with the blood of American G.I.s). And then there was Livergnano (soldiers called that town 'Liver and Onions') which was nothing but rubble when last seen by him. He had a lot of close calls during World War II, but the one he had experienced there was one of the most memorable.

CHAPTER TWENTY SIX
War Criminals and The Chief

The following morning, as the Mitchells were loading their car with luggage, Gabrielli rode into the courtyard on his bicycle. Efrem was helping load and he kept on stacking the bags, completely ignoring the visitor. Jim politely acknowledged the Chief's presence with a nod. This time he was dressed in a business suit and he wore no hat. HAT? With a hat he could be the man who was following them in Venice. Jim dismissed that thought as impossible.

Gabrielli parked his bike and walked over to shake hands. After the usual 'nice day' and 'not too hot today' - weather talk, he looked at Mitchell squarely and mentally took off his gloves.

Jim did not know what to expect and he could sense that this man wanted something. He could not venture a guess as to what the Chief was up to, or the reason for his second visit. All the American could do was stand his ground and look the officer in the eye. Jim was a little nettled at this point. He was in a hurry to leave on their journey, and wasn't at all pleased at the prospect of being held back.

"Where are you going in such a hurry," Chief Gabrielli demanded.

Efrem stopped what he was doing and came over to Jim's side.

"Why do you have to know?" questioned Efrem, "I don't like the idea of you coming here to my home and asking questions in this manner!"

"I'm sorry," Gabrielli said in response, "I am very sorry to 'incomodare' you and your guests, but I do have a couple of official questions of a personal nature that I must ask of the Comandante before he leaves."

At that, Efrem calmed down a bit and accepted the Chief's apology. He then moved away to give the two others privacy.

Gabrielli reached into his shirt pocket and pulled out folded letters that looked faded and old. He passed them to Jim and upon opening them he recognized them as letters and supporting documents from the Liberation Party and Surete. The letter from the 'COMITATO DI LIBERAZIONE

NAZIONALE - MODENA' was dated August 22, 1945 was directed to the 'Prefetto,' (chief of police).

In essence, the letter complained that the governorship of the Camp had not responded to their request for the ouster of Cavelli. It also said that they were prepared to 'occupy' the position of Cavelli and wanted to know what the police department could do to further their cause. At least, that is what Mitchell understood.

Attached to the letter was a paper outlining the allegations against Andrea Cavelli going back to 1937 and 1938. Another paper was the copy of a letter of transmission to Tenento James Mitchell from the Surete also dated August 22, 1945. That letter was for his information saying that their had been complaints about Cavelli's behavior towards the refugees and the service personnel at the Academy. In the last sentence of the letter from 'Il Prefetto,' he invited the Comandante to act on that notice.

As Jim held the documents in his hand, he went back twenty-five years and recalled that incident vividly. He remembered the first complaint that had been received on August 4, 1945. Both of those letters and attachments were in his personal file, and as a matter of fact, he had most of the file in his luggage including the two in question.

The first communication was interpreted in full by Olive Denti. It was done in the strictest confidence and Jim was sure Olive never revealed the contents to anyone. When he received the second communication and its attachments, he kept the matter to himself. He also decided to handle it personally.

Handing the documents back to Chief Gabriella, Mitchell asked, "Why are you bringing this up at this time? I settled the matter to my satisfaction with the Surete and the Sindaco who was the head of the Party at that time."

"Well," Gabrielli said as he lit a cigarette, he offered one to Jim who refused, then he continued, "We've been having some communications from Israel through diplomatic channels regarding some war criminals that had infiltrated Italy during and after the war. I thought it would be a good chance to talk to you, since you were the head of the Refugee Camp and may have some insight into this matter. Through various sources, we heard that you were in Modena. Now I have taken the opportunity to speak to you about it. It is a very sensitive issue for our government and I appeal to you not to reveal this conversation to anyone, not even your wife. I will appreciate that."

The Chief became more and more friendly and he was really sincere in what he was saying and, in addition, was taking this matter very seriously because of the high priority the Italian Government had placed on this case.

"I appreciate your candor in telling me all this, but what have these documents do with war criminals?" Jim posed the question to Gabrielli.

"Maybe nothing at all, maybe everything. These letters were written to you because the Surete and the Mayor of Modena suspected something. The black market was very strong at that time and some of your personnel and some refugees were suspected of being involved in the trafficking of goods illegally. I have a feeling that Cavelli and his man, Franco, may have been involved. They could not prove it at the time but the police were very suspicious of their actions during the period when the letters were sent to you. I could find no record of how you resolved the problem that they threw your way. I would really like to know how you proceeded to deal with the question of Cavelli's criminal record."

Gabrielli took out his handkerchief and wiped his brow, then reached into another pocket and pulled out a small notebook. He slowly leafed through it until he found a certain page.

Glancing up at Jim, he continued, "In the old files I found some notes on the surveillance that was kept on the two men they thought were involved in illegal activities. They evidently learned nothing, although they once followed them to Milan where they dropped off an ailing refugee at a hospital there. It also seems that after you left Modena to depart for the United States, the same two men made at least three trips to Milan, but it was not for contraband. The case must have been dropped after that, because there is no record."

CHAPTER TWENTY SEVEN
Letter of 1945 Surfaces

Mitchell rapidly digested all the Chief said and came to an almost immediate conclusion that the fleeing refugee was Yacob Klein. It could be none other. The case of the missing holiday was complete in his mind.

He prepared to answer the question that was directed at him regarding the disposition of Cavelli and his prison record. He hoped that Gabrielli would understand the American mentality regarding fairness, equal opportunity and paying one's debt to society.

It was Jim's turn to mop his brow. He faced the Chief and began to recount what happened on the day he received the second letter with its demands.

He told Gabrielli that upon reading the letter of August 22, 1945, he became furious because it was unAmerican to cast out someone working for you because he once violated the law and was imprisoned.

"As far as I was concerned, Cavelli had paid his debt to society. Secondly, he was doing such a great job as the director, I could not, in conscience, fire him for no reason. The Liberation Party only wanted the position for one of their own. To me, the matter was political; therefore I would not accede to their wishes As a matter of fact, I was so incensed that I had my driver, Franco, take me to City Hall where I walked in on the mayor (Sindaco) and told him off in no uncertain terms. I told him that I was in command at the Camp and would brook no interference from him or the Committee. I actually raised my voice to make it clear and I stalked out of his office in high dudgeon."

In relating his actions of a quarter century earlier, Jim gazed steadily into the Chief's eyes. Ending his explanation on a rather high-pitched note, he waited in anticipation for a response. Mitchell's eyes were still fixed to the Chief's.

Gabrielli listened to him intently but seemed puzzled about the reference to the "American Way." He did accept the explanation with a half smile.

Then he said. "Bravo! You did well by attacking that bunch; they were a bunch of disgruntled politicians. They did not last long in their positions after that period. The

Sindaco almost went to jail for corruption. However, he is still high in government and is a man to be feared. I learned from others that he hated you with a passion. Be careful; don't step on his toes. Keep out of his way. Even I can't help you."

(Don't worry, Jim thought, I have no desire to come in contact with him.)

"Thank you," Mitchell said, "I thought I did the right thing at the time. I never spoke to Cavelli about the letter because I did not want to upset him or his family in any way. He was a good man as far as I was concerned."

"Well," Gabrielli mused, "We will see about that."

The opportunity presented itself and Jim took advantage of the situation to ask, "Did you follow us in Venice?"

The Chief momentarily blanched and recovered quickly.

"Yes," He admitted. "I was under orders. I make no excuses."

That ended their talk for that day. They shook hands and the Chief left on his bicycle.

Meanwhile, their vehicle being loaded the Mitchells left the Valentes with some regrets and many "arrivedercis."

On August 22, 1945 the Police delivered the following letter:

R. PREFETTURA DI MODENA
Divisione 5   N.   di   prot.   86735
Modena, 22 August 1945
Risposta a nota_____
Allegati_____
OGGETTO:____Sig.   Andrea
Cavelli_____

Al   Sig.COMANDANTE   DEL   CAMPO
SMISTAMENTO N.46
Tenente James Mitchell MODENA
e per conoscenze
AL SIG. ANDREA CAVELLI
ccademia Militare
MODENA

AL C.P.L.N.
MODENA

Dato,I precedenti penali accertati cul conto del Sig. Andrea
Cavelli e I reclalmi pervenuti circa il suo comprtamento verso I profughi e il personale in servizio, wu richiesta del C.P.L.N., dispongo
i'allontaneamento immediato da codesto Campo del predetto.
Invito il Camandate a prendere provvedimenti del caso dandomene notizia.

IL PREFETTO
(Signature)

62

MITCHELL'S TRANSLATION:

The preceding penalty verified on the account of Mr. Andrea
Cavelli, we are sending you this complaint about his behavior towards the refugees and the service personnel. We request you make available his removal immediately to better the aforesaid conditions. We invite the Comandante to act on this notice.

Mitchell's translation of the letter from the NATIONAL LIBERATION COMMITTEE of MODENA to the Prefect of Modena:

Modena, 22 August 1945.
To the Prefect of Modena
This committee has already renewed to occupy the position of Cavelli Andrea,
Director of the Evacuation Camp No. 24.

We recently sent a letter of the Governorship to the Camp Commander and a summary of the information asking for the results of the Cavelli case which we deem very grave.

Since we have not received an answer to our communication, we would like you to take an interest with urgency. We are including copies of the information from thePolice Department.

With great respect,

/S/ Secretary   /S/ President

SEAL
    COMITATO   PROV.   di   LIBERAZIONE
NAZIONALE

CHAPTER TWENTY EIGHT
Bloody Feet and Shock

The last conversation that Mitchell had with Chief Gabrielli gave him a lot to think about. Who were his friends and who were his enemies? Is the former sindaco out for revenge? Unbelievable! After twenty-five years? Where does he fit in?

Jim was determined not to dwell on that matter and to concentrate on the road ahead.

As he was driving away from the Valente's apartments he saw the sign, "Marzaglia 3 km," which pointed the way to the old Valente farmhouse. A larger sign in the form of an arrow blazed the name: "BOLOGNA." His division, the 34th Infantry, had liberated that city on April 22, 1945. It was exactly four years to the day that he was inducted into the Army. He also remembered the day before when they were in Zula and attacking the last German line of defense before Bologna.

The Americans were on the receiving end of heavy artillery and mortar fire. Machine gun fire was intense and kept the leading companies pinned down. Lt. Mitchell's position was in a slight defilade and in the middle of a vineyard.

Since there was no cover Jim faced his men and ordered, "Dig in, dig in."

To set an example, he tried to dig with his shovel. The ground was hard as a rock It was useless.

He saw that the troops had given up, too. They had to do something, so the lieutenant had the men set up the 81mm mortars and fire in the direction of the enemy. The noise was deafening, yet above it all he heard crying like mewing coming from nearby. All were in crouched positions except a replacement that had come to the platoon only the night before on the ration jeep. Jim did not remember his name. The green soldier was on his knees and scratching the ground with his fingernails and sobbing.

"What's the matter?" The lieutenant shouted in order to be heard above the noise.

"Everybody's hollering at me to dig a foxhole........ and all the noise..... and the firing..... I don't know what to do! I'm scared......I must dig......I must do something............"

He was out of it. He was helpless, no good for himself or his fellow soldiers. He was a detriment to himself and to the Army. It was best to get rid of him fast before the other men caught the same sickness. It is contagious.

The poor kid was barely eighteen. He was blond and had never shaved. It was his first day in combat and a bad day to be christened in the art of war.

Jim looked around to see if his actions had affected any of the other men who were nearby. If they noticed, they didn't show it. All were busy at their mortar and machine gun positions. Their outgoing mortar shells seemed to be doing the job of silencing some of the enemy, because the incoming mortar rounds were decreasing.

Mitchell took a moment to write a note to the medics: "This man is of no use to me, help him any way you can. Lt. Mitchell."

Looking around for a medic he saw none. They were all too busy. All of the action that has been related took less than a minute.

It was necessary to find someone to take the shell-shocked boy back to the aid station somewhere to the rear. As the troops had moved forward earlier in the day, Jim had noticed that Pvt. Morgan, the youngest soldier in the company, was limping. He ran back to where the private was laboriously carrying mortar ammo forward.

Taking the rounds from him, Jim ordered, "Take off one of your shoes!"

"I'm O.K., honest, Lieutenant." Morgan said pleadingly.

"Take off your shoes, both of them." Mitchell commanded.

"Yes, sir!" Pvt. Morgan responded.

"I'll be right back!"

Jim carried the ammo to the nearest mortar position and then ran over to gather up the replacement that was still on his hands and knees.

With the replacement in tow, he returned to where Pvt. Morgan was dejectedly sitting. The sight that he came upon shook him inwardly and outwardly. He had seen men get wounded and killed, but this hit him to the core of his being.

Morgan's shoes were filled with blood. His socks were sopping with blood. The soldier's feet were raw with wide cracks caused by "athlete's feet." This young hero never complained and would have continued on until he dropped. The lieutenant was touched, but was also angry and had to restrain myself from letting the young private know how he felt.

Quickly with a stub of a pencil Jim wrote another note, "Pvt. Morgan is of no use to this org. Send him home. Lt. J. Mitchell"

Jim hoped that it would get the young hero back to the states. It would take months for his feet to heal. He was only eighteen and had already had two years of combat experience. Morgan signed up at the age of fifteen, a mere boy. He was a man now. The company records showed his age as twenty-one. By the grapevine that entwined my men, the lieutenant knew that Private Morgan was three years younger.

His last order to Morgan was, "Take this man to the aid station and give the medical doctor these notes."

First Lieutenant Mitchell never saw or heard of either of them again.

CHAPTER TWENTY NINE
The Fatal Decision

That same day, Mandelli and Cavelli confronted each other once more on the subject of 'Comandante' as they referred to Mitchell.

"What are you up to?" Cavelli demanded angrily.

"Just what you should have done long ago. He has bled us long enough and he has the nerve to return to face you. And you...you...greet him and entertain him!"

"It's not what you think. It's not that way at all! He won't hurt us. I guarantee that. He has only come to tour Italy with his family and see his friends." Cavelli was wringing his hands.

"I can't believe that. He must still have his hand out. There is only one way to cut him out and we have made that commitment." Mandelli let the latter slip out and he regretted it instantly.

Cavelli jumped into the breach. "What commitment? I've made no promises of any sort. I wanted things to remain the same. What horrible thing are 'we' going to commit this time?" Andrea was tearful and dreading to hear what Mandelli's organization had ordered to be done.

"I'll get Mitchell to discontinue his demands.....starting immediately....I'll do it....I know I can handle it personally. Just don't do anything now." Cavelli pleaded to deaf ears.

Mandelli seemed to be enjoying the scene that they were enacting. It filled him with power. He regretted sending the warning note to Mitchell. It would be the only thing that could tie him to the Comandante.

"I'll go see him now." Andrea continued with his plea. "I'm certain he'll listen and will cease making his demands. He is reasonable. I'm sure he has enough. Please cancel whatever plans you and your friends have for him. I will make it right....please..."

Cavelli's promises had the wrong affect on his partner. Mandelli was hardening his stance. His inherited hard line was not softened and his stubbornness remained intact.

Seeing that his partner was unmoved, Andrea groaned and moved towards the sanctuary of his private office. He would find comfort in his bottom drawer.

Mandelli picked up his private phone and dialed.

In hushed tones he said, "We'll do it today. Our friends are going to Florence on Route 65 this morning. You will have to hurry to catch up and to finish the job."

He slowly replaced the phone.

Having said and done what he was ordered to do, Mandelli began to have some misgivings of his own. He did not relish his position in the matter and sought to ease his inner agony by reaching for his bottle and glass.

CHAPTER THIRTY
Valente Family and The First American Soldier

It was after ten o'clock in the morning when the Mitchell vehicle reached Via Emilia Est, which Jim intended to take until they arrived at Route 9. From there he would proceed to Bologna and going through that city would look for Route 65 which went right through the heart of the battlefields that they were going to visit on the way to Florence....

......and share some of the memories of a quarter century earlier.

They could have gone from Modena directly to Florence on the Autostrada and would have been there in a couple of hours. However, Jim opted for the scenic route hoping that his family would learn something about the war, and share with some of the memories that he could not describe to them at home.

Traffic was rather heavy initially because they had to pass through the industrial area. Trucks were bumper-to-bumper, many of them carrying ceramics and tile for which Modena was noted. Traffic eased in the eastern part of the city and soon they began to make better time.

At one point, Jim's vehicle overtook one of Cavelli's trucks and he beeped his horn, but the driver did not seem to take notice. Looking through the rear view mirror, Mitchell could see a passenger, or helper, sitting next to the driver. That person did look familiar because during one of his visits he had some small talk with some of the personnel that was in the store.

Jim sat back and enjoyed the scenery; he had thirty or more kilometers to go before Bologna and Route 65.

They passed by Castelfranco where they had had that great dinner in the mountains the first day of their visit to Modena. It was then that Judy asked her father if they were anywhere near Marzaglia.

"No," Her Dad responded, "It is back a few kilometers from where we had come."

She said that she had really enjoyed seeing the old farmhouse where the Valentes had once lived. Efrem had taken them there the day that Jim had driven to Cavelli's place of

69

business by himself. It was hard for the Mitchell children to believe that anyone could live under the circumstances that were described by Efrem and Camille who accompanied them.

Camille lived in one of the converted farmhouses in the same area, but her house had running water, electricity, and bath. Jimmy said that Efrem told them of how his family was frightened when Lt. Mitchell entered their house with his carbine at the ready. They had been scared enough when the Germans were there, but when the German soldiers fled they did not know what to expect. That's why they were cowering on the floor of the kitchen when 'Mitchell' entered.

Camille told her American visitors that 'Mitchell' was the first American soldier that they had ever seen and that Jim saved their lives by chasing the Germans away from their home.

It seems that the whole morning was spent showing them where Lt. Mitchell's platoon was spread out in the drainage ditches surrounding their farm. Efrem proudly told them that he offered Mitchell his bed that night and that his offer was accepted. He and his sister also described how Jim gave his parents food that was in cans, coffee, and other types of food that came in cardboard boxes. The Valente children were young and very impressionable.

Feeding the hungry was characteristic of the American G. I. He always shared his food with his buddies and starving natives. Packages from home were always shared with the next guy no matter who he was.

Personally, James Mitchell did not think that it was re-markable that they 'saved their lives' by causing the enemy to retreat, or by giving them food. That was standard operating procedure and was accomplished every day by some soldier somewhere. It was no different at that time. However, it made the Valentes happy to think so and Jim let it go at that. It was an occasion to remember for them, but it really and truly was not that memorable to the retired soldier. Mitchell did recall the incident vividly, but it was just another day in a long war.

There were many, many events during those years that stand out in a long stream of memories. Some were horrible, and some were pleasant. And often combat soldiers would experience both on the same day.

It wasn't long before Jim drove into the center of Bologna and was careful to take the south circle to get to Route 65. He watched the signs because one can get lost in a minute by taking a wrong turn. The streets in Italian cities are usually winding and narrow like a maze, so it is wise to stay on a main boulevard until you are sure where you are. There it was, a small rusty sign saying 65 to the right, and Mitchell got on it with a quick right turn.

Route 65 was the main Army route when Bologna was attacked in April 1945. It seemed like a great highway then and it carried tons and tons of supplies for the advancing troops. It was a lifeline then, but now it was the scenic route to Florence.

CHAPTER THIRTY ONE
Saved By Castle of Zena

Once again the conversation with Gabrielli intruded Jim's mind. The sindaco....... was it too far fetched to draw him into the circle of my enemies? Mitchell doubted if he, or his cohorts, had any reason to bear a grudge for twenty-five years unless he was tied in with the people who were being sought by the Chief. It was too confusing, too mixed up. He was near his wit's end, however he drove on intent on showing his family the sights.

The proud Mitchell wanted particularly to show his family Castello di Zena, which was just off Route 65 near Zula. The map of the area that he had used during the hostilities was still in his possession and with the markings of the target area and objectives still on it. Enemy positions were marked in red and included the names and regiments of the German Army. It was in great detail, so Jim looked for the reference points that he had memorized and low grade roads he had to traverse in order to get to the Castle.

There was not much traffic on the two-lane highway that was Route 65. Most of the traffic was local, small cars and small trucks. In the rear view mirror Mitchell noticed a large van coming at a very high rate of speed for a narrow highway. At the same time he was watching the right side of the road for a dirt trail that would take them to the base of Monterumici. His car was abreast of the mountain and Jim was preparing himself for the sharp right that he would have to make. The van was bearing down on the Mitchell vehicle and did not appear to make an attempt to pass on the left.

As Providence would have it, the narrow gravel road suddenly manifested itself and Jim swung hard to the right in a U turn. The passengers complained, but Mitchell was grateful for the sudden appearance of the road to Castle of Zena.

While the family was griping about his driving, Jim heard the grinding and crashing of metal above their voices. The sound had come from the rear and where the large truck had vanished.

No excuses were made to his wife as to why he had turned so sharply, because it seemed to Jim that the truck was purposely trying to run them off the highway and into the deep ravine that was on the right. No guard rails were on that road. Italy's highway department preferred to use them on the Autostradas which were toll roads.

Jim's heart was still racing and he was perspiring profusely. To put it mildly, he was still in the throes of the terror he had experienced only moments before. Shaking, he pulled over at a turn where the path was wider and parked with the pretense of looking at the scenery below. He gathered his wits by seemingly poring over a map. He did not see the map at all----. The rear view visions that he had seen of a huge truck bearing down on them came upon him over and over again.

Dorothy was distracted by the children who got out a water bottle and began pouring drinks. The water was gratefully accepted by Mitchell and a few minutes later he was calm enough to continue their journey.

The small road that the Mitchells were on was a donkey trail twenty five years before. It was passable by jeep only in those days, no trucks. At this time it was improved somewhat, it was graveled and widened to accommodate one small car at a time. At the sharp horseshoe turns it was widened to hold two small cars. One auto would wait while the other car passed. No speeding on that path. There were no guard rails and one could look down hundreds of feet. Judy and her mother closed their eyes at the sharp turns. Between turns, Dorothy was looking for the Castle.

Once she spied a building and said, "There it is, that's the Castle!"

The trees and underbrush growing around the building disguised its form.

"No," Jim hastened to say, "That's not the castle. It's not anything like I remember!"

He was so positive!

Slowly and surely they reached the bottom safely. The narrow path widened as they approached a farmhouse at the base of Monerumici. A man was standing in front of his home and close to the dirt road and a girl who must have been his daughter was hanging clothes to dry. Casually, Jim got out of the car, only too glad to stretch his legs, and walked up to the farmer to ask the direction to Castello di Zena. He had been sure that it was to the right, but now with the passage of all the years, he was uncertain. Besides, Zena was not the building that Dorothy had seen, Jim was sure of that.

"Si, si," The farmer said, "It's right there."

He pointed to where Dorothy had said it was. She was right and Jim was wrong!

Jim told the gentleman that he was an American, that he had occupied the Castle of Zena during the war, and that there had been quite a battle before the Germans on Monterumici were overcome.

The Italian shook Mitchell's hand and said he was happy to meet him. Still holding Jim's hand, the farmer called to his daughter to bring some wine for the American. Just before she entered the house, the farmer changed his mind calling to the daughter to bring beer because the Americans liked beer more than wine and to make sure it was cold.

By that time, all of the Mitchell family was out of the car and standing in the little shade that was available. Jim thanked the gentleman and told him it wasn't necessary to serve drinks, but the farmer insisted. So now it was up to Mitchell to drink the beer while he and his host talked about the brutal battles the ex-platoon commander had experienced. The Italian remembered those days well and how they had suffered. It was many years before they were able to rebuild and restore their home. It was nothing but a heap of brick and stone when they were able to reclaim their property.

"Bruta guerra," The farmer repeated over and over, while shaking his head.

CHAPTER THIRTY TWO
Bad News

Mandelli felt warm despite the air conditioning units that were operating in full force on that hot day. A fan had been brought in to circulate the air to his satisfaction. He had removed his tie and his coat was draped over a chair. The crooked Italian stogie that he held between his clenched teeth still held the cold ashes after the fire had gone out. Uncomfortable as he was slouched in one of his wide leather chairs, he could not shift his weight because he was drained of all energy. With a sigh, he took the cigar and flicked the ashes on to the floor. He was not a sloppy person but this day was different.

It was a day of ups and downs in his outlook and demeanor. That morning he had felt powerful and invincible. As the day wore on, Mandelli was losing confidence in himself and his superiors. He half regretted his show of bravado in his argument with Cavelli. It was afternoon and he had no desire for food or drink. All he wanted to do was wait....wait.

Cavelli, in his own office, was drowning himself with drink and gorging himself with food that was brought in from a neighboring restaurant. There was a vast difference between the partners' attitudes and their ways of handling problems.

However, both were playing the waiting game. And each was laboring, toiling with their consciences. None had a friend with whom to confide. The two had to carry their burdens alone. It was a waiting game that was almost unendurable.

The minutes dragged on and became hours that seemed long and heavy.

Whenever a phone would ring Cavelli would flinch and Mandelli would hold his breath. As the afternoon waned, neither received a personal call.

Mandelli was sweating heavily as the time slowly passed.

Cavelli was out of food and had opened his second bottle of whiskey.

At last, a clerk knocked on Cavelli's door. "Telephone for you, Signor Andrea. It's the carabinieri from Bologna!"

Snatching up the phone from its cradle, Cavelli hoarsely said, "Pronto, this is Cavelli speaking."

He listened as the policeman gave him the news. "This is Tenente Gregorio of the carabinieri and I'm sorry to be calling you with bad news about your employees........"

Cavelli froze. He barely heard the voice on the other end of the wire go on with the particulars.

"One of your 'camions' had a terrible accident on Route 65. Both the driver and the passenger are dead. We are sorry for your loss. Please come as soon as you can to identify the bodies. We are investigating the cause and will have a report by morning. Are you there, sir? Did you hear me?"

Cavelli was nodding, not saying a word until the carabinieri jogged his brain with the questions. Andrea came to life saying, "Yes, yes.....we'll take care of everything. Give me the name of the hospital. Oh, they're where?" The tenente repeated his answer.

"Yes, yes.....I hear you. Thank you. Where will you have the bodies?"

"I told you that they are at the city morgue, Signor Cavelli. Come as soon as you can, please." The officer was patient with Andrea's nervous responses.

"Oh, sir, was anyone else involved in the accident? I will need the information for my insurance company." Cavelli waited for the answer expectantly and with trepidation.

"No, Signor, it was a one vehicle accident. The truck ran off the road and down the side of the mountain. That's all, sir."

Andrea wearily put the phone down; fell into his chair with a huge sigh. It was a sigh of relief on one hand and a sigh of sorrow on the other. Two of his employees were gone, but the Mitchells were safe.

It was time to break the news to his partner. He struggled to his feet, poured a shot into his glass and downed it quickly. It was his last drink of the day.

CHAPTER THIRTY THREE
"Bruta Guerra"

"Bruta guerra," Jim repeated what the farmer had said. "That means 'brutal war'," he explained to his children.

While driving through the overgrown grounds of the Castle, they passed an old crone dressed in black who was working in a small garden. The Americans tried to talk to her, but she paid no attention to them whatsoever, so they continued on the path to what was left of the building. It was in a shambles, and it seemed there had been little or no attempt to restore it. People occupied the first floor of the wreckage, because a woman had been outside as they approached and she fled inside.

Mitchell knocked on the door and when she cracked open the door he asked for permission to look around the premises. She was not a bit interested when he told her that he had been there during the war. She merely nodded her head indicating that they had her permission. She was rather young, in her twenties, and with a couple of children whose voices could be heard in the background. Her disinterest was apparent, she didn't give a hoot about the history of her home, nor did she care about hearing any more about it from an American stranger. She slammed the door shut.

They walked to the rear of the Castle where there had once been a beautiful courtyard with columns of marble on all sides. The floor still had beautiful mosaic designs. Vegetation had taken over and covered everything. Some of the beautiful artwork could barely be seen. It could never be reclaimed. Jim remember sunning himself there one afternoon and eating C-rations when a barrage of enemy cannon fire was dropping on and around the Castle. He lay prone on the ground, waiting for the firing to cease.

When it did stop, he looked at the field to the right where many shells had struck causing the dirt to fly and making rather deep holes. Still hidden from the enemy in back of the building and in the courtyard, Lt. Mitchell saw many small balls that the explosives had uprooted. They were potatoes from the previous year's crop. It was mid-winter, but since they were deep in the ground they were not frozen.

Jim waited until dark, went outside and felt around where he had seen the tubers and brought an armload in to his men. They had fried potatoes that night on their portable gasoline stove. How delicious!

Dorothy could recognize the magnificence of the castle and could conjure up a picture of how it had looked in its heyday.

There was a small creek nearby and Mitchell tried to get to it but the underbrush was too thick. He wanted to show his family their source of water to drink and to wash with. The troops got their drinking water right from the creek during those days. Of course, chemical tablets were put into the water to purify it.

Disappointed at the condition of the Castello di Zena, the Mitchell family got into the car to go back up the mountain to Route 65. The farmer was still outside his home and he told Jim that there was a more improved road to get to the highway and directed him to it. It was a lot better, wider, and less hazardous. They got up to the highway in jig time but it took them back a kilometer or so from where they had exited earlier.

In doing so they were going to pass the original path they had taken to the castle. As they approached the spot where Jim had taken the sudden turn, which caused much discomfort to his family, he noticed orange cones and red flags in the center of the road. It was an indication of a work area or an accident.

Jim Mitchell slowed down to a crawl as we approached the carabinieri, (state police, who were directing traffic. A tow truck was on the right side of the road with its winch directed over the side, the cables hanging and probably reaching to haul some unfortunate driver and his vehicle up the steep slope.

As the Mitchell car came abreast of the very large towing vehicle, Jim could see the winch grinding and at the same time saw the rear of a crushed van with the logo still partly visible. It was a Cavelli van and obviously the one that had almost crushed them an hour or more earlier.

Upon seeing the wreckage, Jim began to pull over on the side of the highway, but a local policeman stopped him from parking and ordered him to get back on the road. As Jim slowly pulled out he asked the policeman if there were any casualties.

The officer nodded his head and said, "Due morte." Two dead.

Mitchell was quite shaken driving away from that scene. "That could have been us." He thought, "And they were trying to kill me and my family! This is serious business."

His mouth was dry from nervousness. Fortunately, his family did not notice the Cavelli coat of arms. They only commented that it was a horrible accident.

At the moment Jim was content living with the fact that his family hadn't the slightest inkling of what had been intended for them earlier. It was no time to alarm them. It would be best to keep it to himself for the time being, but he was not going to let anything happen to his family.

Why would Cavelli and his crew want to do away with them?

"It must have been me that they were after. But why? Why? WHY? Maybe I know something. I still have the warning written in German script. Did that tie me in with somebody who was German? Could it have been a Jew? Most of the refugees were from Germany who had been interned in the many concentration camps across Germany. It had to be a German, or a German Jew, who sent me that note. Not only that, but it must be someone who knew one of my friends personally, and probably a close friend at that." Jim's mind was racing to determine the reason for the attempt on their lives.

He was rapidly losing his appetite for the scenery or for seeking out places where he had been in Italy. All he cared about was the welfare of his family. That was of the utmost importance. However, Mitchell was not prepared to share his thoughts with his family as yet. They seemed to be enjoying the trip and Jim did not wish to spoil it for them.

Getting to Livergnano was no problem. They stopped on the main street of the town - - - right on Route 65 - - just as a procession was passing by. It was a holy day of some sort and it was rather festive. A priest led and was followed by several men carrying a statue of a saint. Men, women, and children all dressed in their finery. Some men had red sashes, some blue sashes, and the women were dressed in bright colors. The little girls were dressed in white as they do for confirmation. The boys wore school uniforms, white shirts and black shorts. A small band brought up the rear playing the music of the day. It caused some excitement in the town and people lined the sidewalks to watch.

A lady walked by carrying her shopping bag that was filled with bread and other foodstuffs. Dorothy politely asked directions to a restaurant where they could go for a bite to eat. She directed them to one that she recommended and said, " Hurry it will close in an hour. Where are you from?"

Jim told her that they were Americans and that he had been a soldier at Livergnano during the war.

"Oh, yes," She said with a shake of her head, "You left us a great present, our town was destroyed."

With that, she went on her way. They hadn't forgotten. The Americans had saved them from Hitler, but they sometimes resented the Allies because homes and buildings were destroyed in the drive to wipe out the Germans. It was a no-win situation.

When the Germans took over the cities and towns, the inhabitants displayed the swastika. When the Americans drove the Germans out, the citizens brought out the American Flag. And so it went either way. Sometimes, a village would be overrun repeatedly by either side and always the populace would react in favor of the new occupier.

The Americans understood the situation and would laugh over it. Certainly the Germans were aware of it, too.

Finding the restaurant was easy and they chose a table in the garden. Sitting in the shade and drinking bottled water, Jim tried to collect his thoughts. The food looked good and may have tasted great as his children claimed, but it didn't do anything for the worried father. His mouth was dry from anxiety and his taste buds had shriveled and didn't seem to work. He lost his appetite although he loved Italian food. Dorothy could attest to that. She came from a long line of gourmet Italian cooks.

For dessert, Dorothy and the children ordered figs with prosciutto. From their vantage point they watched the waiter peel the fresh figs and throw the parings into the street. He placed the figs on plates, put the Italian ham on top of the figs and brought them to the table. Mitchell's family got a big kick out of that performance, and they really enjoyed their dessert.

CHAPTER THIRTY FOUR
Real Danger

It was now Jim's intent to get to the Hotel Montebello in Florence as quickly as possible. After that he was going to try to find a way to lose the people who might be following. He felt certain that he was going to see or hear from someone again in some manner or form. But he had to protect his family. That was his highest priority. It was still too early to apprise his wife, Dorothy, about what he knew was happening. He had to speak to someone of his suspicions. That had to be worked out also.

The words, "GO AWAY, DON'T STIR THE POT," were burned into his brain. He could no longer ignore the threat that they proclaimed. It ceased to be a casual threat and it meant whoever 'they' were could carry it out whenever they pleased. But why? Perhaps it had something to do with the events of a quarter century earlier and tied in with Chief Gabrielli's investigation on 'war criminals.'

Mitchell was deeply troubled. He toyed with the idea of buying a firearm, but discarded the thought almost immediately. He had his share of using weapons during World War II and had sworn off guns the day he was discharged from active duty in the army in 1946.

CHAPTER THIRTY FIVE
"The Escarpment – Dec. 24, 1944"

Something jarred Jim's memory. He had been sipping water and staring south past the hedges and fencing that surrounded the garden. There was nothing beyond the fence, no buildings, no trees, just nothing. Leaping to his feet, he walked over to the fence - and there before him was "The Escarpment."

It had a sheer drop of a couple hundred feet. Not straight down at all sections, but about an 80 degree angle in one area. That was the point Jim recognized and was drowned in memories of the day before Christmas 1944.

His family came over to where Jim Mitchell was standing and looked down at the valley and beyond. They remarked about the steepness of the cliff and of the beautiful terrain below.

Then having almost forgotten about the urgencies of the moment, Jim reminded them of the street on Route 65 where they had seen the procession and where they had spoken to a woman. It was an opportune time to relate to them the tale of Christmas on the front lines.

The 3rd Battalion of the 135th Regiment, 34th Division (Red Bull), had received orders to relieve the First Battalion on the night of the 24th of December 1944. The message was received that morning and First Lieutenant Mitchell was elected to go on reconnaissance and find the best routes of approach to the positions now occupied by Companies A,B,C, and D. This move was to be made under cover of darkness on Christmas Eve and Route 65 was to be used because it was the only possible approach to where the forward troops were dug in.

It was bitter cold, up to a foot of snow on the ground in the valley and probably two feet of snow on the heights above at Livergnano. All supplies to the soldiers on the front were delivered by jeeps at night. The highway was very treacherous not only from ice and snow but by the many bomb and shell craters on the road, and of course, no guardrails.

Driving by night was very risky under blackout conditions. Going up there to scout the area in broad daylight, under bright sunshine, and with snow as a background was madness. But it had to be done.

Two officers from other companies of the 3rd battalion were assigned to go with Lt. Mitchell. His jeep and driver were ready to go by eight o'clock. The reserve troops were in a so-called rest area where they were being shelled several times daily. Since they were situated behind the escarpment, the cannon fire for the most part overshot the bivouac area. All were well rested, sleeping in down filled sleeping bags in pup tents. A field kitchen kept them fed with food that was not too appetizing, but it was HOT.

Since the escarpment was impossible to climb, Jim's reconnaissance group had no choice but to go north on Highway 65 to contact the people they were going to relieve. Even if they had known about the orders a day or two earlier, a night reconnaissance would have been ruled out. That was final. Purposely, they had to leave quickly, and reconnoiter the area to determine the best routes to take the troops forward to the positions they were to occupy on the eve of Christmas.

The three officers only carried pistols, field glasses and maps. They were warmly dressed, wearing heavy field coats, and with knitted caps on their heads under the steel helmets. The jeep slowly grappled its way up the steep sloping rutted trail that would take them to the highway. They were still riding under cover of the hills and were not under observation by the enemy.

Upon arriving on Route 65 they would be seen from miles around, both by the enemy and friendly troops. Their plan was to go up the highway as swiftly as possible to a certain point, then turn to the right when they reached Livergnano and find some cover for the jeep and the driver. The three officers would then reconnoiter on foot and decide which were the best routes to the various positions. Each one was allocated a sector.

It did not turn out to be easy, because the shelling of the highway started almost immediately upon entering it. The jeep driver sped on the slick road hoping to dodge the shells; there was no alternative but to continue.

Jim continued with his narrative to his family reminding them that at the point on the road where they had asked directions, the bombardment was too close for comfort, so all jumped out of the jeep and laid down behind a low stone wall for cover. The jeep was in the open and on the road and didn't get a scratch, but the men were showered with stones and dirt as the shells exploded nearby.

They remained in that position until the shelling ceased and at that moment ran towards some bombed out buildings and sought shelter there until they could get their bearings. Jim ordered the driver to remain in the relatively safe position that was found for him and ordered him to await the officers' return.

Moving towards the east and away from the highway, the recon group found some peace and quiet with only a few scattered rounds of enemy shellfire still seeking the road and targets of opportunity. They hurriedly ran down a street and came to a small wooded area where they encountered, of all people, Second Lieutenant Clapp, the graves registration officer. He was there with his jeep and trailer with bodies wrapped and tied in blankets.

The bodies of American soldiers were stacked four high and four across. The sight was quite disturbing. The three officers were quiet as they approached Clapp. That officer was standing beside a body that was wrapped but still lying on the snow. That was the spot where that soldier lost his life that morning. His blood was bright red on the snowy ground. Clapp was tearful when he looked at the approaching men.

He pointed to the body at his feet and said touchingly, "That's Lieutenant Fleming, I was drinking gin with him last night. God, I hate this job! But one good thing, officers ride on top."

He looked at each of them individually as he spoke the last sentence as if assuring them that they would "ride on top" when their time came. It was a somber moment, and the three paid quiet respects to their fallen comrades who had given up their lives in a country far from their homes.

Clapp directed them to the Battalion Headquarters. Arriving at the cellar that comprised the Lieutenant Colonel's message center and domicile, they found him in a meeting with the company commanders. The colonel expected the reconnaissance officers and was prepared for them. So were the company commanders.

Lt. Mitchell started the conversation by telling the First

Battalion company commanders that the Third Battalion was preparing to come up to relieve them that night and wanted to work out the details.

To a man, their response was, "We have decided to stay in this position."

And then the battalion commander continued with, Our men do not like the idea of moving from the lines on Christmas Eve or any other night. It is too dangerous. We will lose too many men just for a cooked Christmas dinner, and you will too. No dice! We are staying here with our C and K rations. And we will stay until we can push our way out of here and on to Bologna. The Regimental Commander has agreed to this and so does your battalion commander. We spoke to them by telephone about a half hour ago. Too bad for you gentlemen coming up here under such dangerous conditions. You can go back now. Thanks for the offer anyway."

The three recon officers saluted and left to find their way back to their units. Outside Mitchell noticed many telephone wires, both heavy and sound activated lines, going towards the rear echelons. Possibly a dozen or so wires. Jim looked to see where they would drop off the escarpment. The lines were laid on top of the ground and grouped together. Near the edge of the drop off point some of the heavier wires were wrapped around a tree stump and noticing that, Lt. Mitchell had a brilliant idea.

He asked one of the lieutenants to seek out the jeep driver and tell him to leave whenever he thought it was safe. The officers would leave by another route and Jim pointed to the phone wires that descended down the cliff. The wires would be a shortcut to their encampment.

In a few minutes the lieutenant returned saying that the driver was O.K. with the idea of driving back alone. At that moment the shelling commenced once more and they had no alternative but to grab the wires and slide down with their legs entwined around them. The drop was two hundred feet or more. They slid down to the bottom safely in a couple of minutes while the shells were still bouncing all over the place on top of the escarpment. The officers suffered a few bruises and scrapes and their coats were smeared with mud and snow. It was but a small price to pay to get back to their units safely.

The jeep driver left at the same time (his movement may have incited the barrage), but he arrived at least twenty minutes later. That was really a shortcut!

Jim and Lt.Stratmoen at Zula

CHAPTER THIRTY SIX
On To Florence

As Jim recounted the story, his family looked at the scenery with a different perspective. They imagined the winter with its heavy snows and the cold that they suffered, plus the privations and dangers encountered every day.

After listening to some of the comments of his family, and answering their questions, Mitchell decided to hurry to Florence. There were some objections, but he prevailed, and they continued on to their destination.

Jim asked the waiter if there was a way to could get to the Autostrada instead of continuing on Route 65. He told the Americans that about four kilometers south at the village of Guarda there was a new road that went west and connected to the superhighway. Mitchell thanked him with a generous tip for that information. The waiter's directions were right and the improved road was located easily. It had two lanes, looked new and the bright new green signs announced that it was that way to the Autostrada.

CHAPTER THIRTY SEVEN
Suspicions

Upon arriving at the Hotel Montebello, Jim Mitchell decided that he had to get rid of the automobile. It had Venice plates on it, and if people were looking for him they would look for the car. Whoever they were, they must have seen it many times in and around Modena. Handing the concierge an American twenty-dollar bill (a lot of money in 1970), Jim asked him to return the car to the branch office of the rental agency. He gave the hotel employee strict instructions to procure another vehicle, preferably a Mercedes with automatic shift and air conditioning.

Jim carefully looked around the lobby to see.......see what? He had no idea who to look for or what to look for. Being suspicious of everyone and getting paranoid had become the order of the day. THEY were not going to hurt him or his family if he could help it. Nor did he have the slightest idea where to could go for assistance. In Rome he could go to the American Embassy. His story would sound too far-fetched and he had no proof to back his suspicions. Nor did he know who was responsible.

Could it be Cavelli? He didn't think so and was sure that it was not Franco. It had to be someone connected to Andrea Cavelli's business. He was inclined to discount that, too. Hopefully, the incident near Castello di Zena was only an accident and had nothing to do with him at all. Just a coincidence, he tried to reassure himself. Calling the Valentes the next morning would be the wisest course of action. They could check the morning newspaper to see if there was any news about the crash on Route 65.

As the Mitchell family was going to the dining room that evening, the concierge approached Jim with the news that his mission had been accomplished. A Mercedes was already parked in the hotel's garage for his use. All Mitchell had to do was to sign the papers at the desk when convenient.

Dorothy turned to Jim with a natural question. "Why did you choose to change cars here in Florence when we are only going to spend three more days in Italy?"

Jim hedged by saying, "We will have more room inside the car, and with automatic shift and air conditioning, the

88

ride will be much more comfortable especially since we are going south."

That appeared to satisfy his wife's curiosity.

Judy liked the idea of the change to automatic transmission because she would be able to drive too. Jimmy could care less; he didn't have a driver's license as yet.

In their suite that night, after the children and Dorothy had retired, Jim reached into his luggage and pulled out a pouch that contained memorabilia of the time he served his country as a soldier in Italy. He had three notebooks, one of which was used when he was Comandante. Curiously he turned its pages hoping to find something that he had missed before or never noticed.

On one page he had written the pay scale of the service personnel - 22 lire per hour. On the same page, he had added some figures totaling 4852. That was the number of refugees on one particular day.

On another page Mitchell had written that an Italian soldier was seen in the women's quarters. He was sure that he put an end to that.

One note said: "Order 100,000 rations. Cavelli's pay? Nurses' pay?" Jim was to call a Major Stuart to find out how much. And then on the following page: "Maj. Stuart - raise salary of Cavelli". He knew that he took care of Cavelli by getting him an increase in pay!

Then there was a list of names under the heading of 'BAKERS':

> Gelbart, Josef
> Friedmann, Leo
> Schaumann, Bernard
> Goldberg, Berisch
> Nussbaum, Wilhelm

They were the men who were catering to that refugee, Yacob Klein, when Lt. Mitchell ordered him out of the kitchen. They probably knew Klein from somewhere else. The bakers were refugees too. Qualified people were hired from the ranks of displaced persons. They were not paid as much as the Italian service personnel because they were also housed and fed with their families.

Jim distinctly remembered Josef Gelbart from Poland

who was the head baker. He later became the chef for the American and British personnel who were quartered near the comandante's apartment. Mitchell saw to that.

As he paged through other notes:

"Greeks to be sent to Bari on or about 12th"

"Teatro Comunale--August 22--dancing from 2100-0100--Ge Mason & his band--tickets 100 L per couple"

"2 TB cases very ill"

"600 for train to Adriatic this week"

And there was a signature across the length on one page: "Weksler Adam - I 3045825". The number shown was tattooed on his arm at a concentration camp. Adam was one of the interpreters who spoke five or six European languages. He was a Slav or Czech. Jim remembered him well.

The pouch contained a postcard that Jim hadn't looked at in years. It was dated August 15, 1945 and mailed from Lake Garda. The message was, "Visiting Lake Garda on our day off. We beg to remember you and to send you our hearty and sincere greetings. Respectfully yours, Jeolic Anthony, Weksler Adam, Schaumann B., Yacob xMx K."

The last signature had the letter M x'd as though to cross it out. It was written in ink and the letter M that had evidently been written in error was just crossed out. The men must have been having a good time at the Lake, probably drinking, and decided to send the comandante a card. Anthony was a nice man, still single. He came from Austria. It would be just like him to make all the others sign his card and none dare renege.

It struck Jim as odd that Yacob Klein would be with them because it was about ten days or so after he left the camp for a safer environment. It couldn't possibly be the same Yacob. That was a common name among the Jewish refugees. Since Cavelli was not available to clear up the matter of Yacob Klein, Mitchell had to pass and file it in his head for future reference (as though you could do such a thing). Anyway, it was something he would remember because he had some tangible evidence in his possession........but wait!

Hurriedly Jim searched through his pockets for the note with the veiled threat. He carefully unfolded the note and compared the writing with the last signature on the postcard. The letter Y was a close match, so was the A, and lastly the O was a perfect match.

Jim was tired and did not believe what he saw. Since he was not a handwriting expert, he convinced himself that he was mistaken and all Germans had the same handwriting. He went to bed, unsure of what he had uncovered.

Lying in bed, Mitchell reasoned that he was reaching for straws and at this point had reached too far. Yacob was probably in Israel running some kind of business. Most of the fleeing Jews from Europe got to Israel eventually, so why not Klein? He put that thought to rest, secure in the knowledge that no Jew in his right mind in those days would go back to the country from whence he had fled. No future back there, Yacob was an opportunist and a leader of sorts in his own way. He'd certainly go to the Promise Land that his elders had always dreamed about.

Jim had a restless night; filled with wild dreams, and many faces of people he had met and spoken to during the past several days. In addition, the faces of the people whose names appeared in the notebook and postcard appeared before him looking as they did a quarter of a century earlier. Yacob's face was most prominent among them. Jim awoke several times during the first three hours in bed, and upon falling asleep again the same dreams returned to harass him.

It was near daybreak when Mitchell finally fell into a deep and dreamless sleep. He had probably worked all the demons out of his system. It was a hard fight but he won. Maybe those visions were intended to give him a message of some kind. Maybe........

CHAPTER THIRTY EIGHT
Search For Nazi War Criminal?

When Mitchell awakened the next morning, the room was flooded with sunshine. Dorothy was already dressed and ready to go to breakfast. The children had gone down to the lobby. Jim wrestled with himself in trying to get out of bed. Most people get that feeling at times, one part of them wants to get up and the other part desires to get that extra few minutes of rest.

Wide-awake and refreshed after a shower, Jim put on his touristy clothes of shorts and short sleeved shirt. Dorothy selected the socks to match. They took the wide-open stairs to the lobby, since they were on the second floor. As they were going down the stairs, Jim looked down into the lobby for his children. Not too many people were in his line of vision and they all seemed like ordinary tourists, and there were some business types too. A few people were standing on one side waiting for the elevators.

As soon as their feet hit the marble floor of the lobby, a man extracted himself from the group waiting by the elevators and came towards Jim and Dorothy.

"Mr. Mitchell?" He asked. Jim knew darn well he was not mistaken about who he was, so he felt it was not necessary to dodge that question. He was an American, Mitchell was sure of that. Dressed in the latest designer business suit, he didn't appear to pose a threat to Jim or his family.

It did not seem necessary to reply, because the man continued, "I've been waiting for you since early this morning and I hope I won't interfere with your plans, but I must talk to you. It's rather urgent."

The well-dressed gentleman had a decided Brooklyn accent and as most Americans who live in states other than New York think, it seemed abrasive. Unless you get to understand Brooklynites, you will never get over the idea that they are pushy, loud, and irritating. It was certain that this guy did not intend to give Jim that impression. He tried very hard to be courteous, but his voice nettled Mitchell to some extent. So Jim strove to treat him with some civility.

Without hesitation the man offered Jim his passport as

I.D. The passport was Israeli, his name was Martin Stein, age 45, and his address was Tel Aviv. Mitchell was 100% sure that he had an American passport somewhere on his person. He had dual citizenship.

Jim was always of the opinion that it was unfair that some folks could have allegiance to two countries. As a proven true red blooded American, the colonel could not conceive of anyone being true to two countries at the same time. Personally, he would never consider it for one second. His country was the good old U.S., the country that he fought for and for which he shed some blood.

The passport in itself did not give him any right to ask any questions and Jim told him so. The Israeli then pulled out a business card which gave the name of an obscure organization. The institute was called "FIND" and he was Chief Investigator.

Stein explained that the purpose of their organization was to look for war criminals. Their search was never-ending and they were uncovering information on former Nazis all the time. The process was long and time consuming. They had achieved some success and had some prosecutions. Now he was looking for one man in particular and was hoping that Colonel Mitchell would be able to help.

"No," Jim said, "I don't think so. I never met a Nazi war criminal and I am under the impression that they were all caught and prosecuted at the Nuremberg trials."

He shook his head in disbelief. "Do you really believe that? Only some of the top leaders were tried and punished, but many hundreds escaped to other counties throughout the world. We are funded by the Jewish people and the Israeli government to track down these criminals and bring them to justice."

They were still standing in the lobby. James, Jr. and Judy were standing on one side anxiously waiting to go to the dining room for breakfast. They must have been starving, because they made faces and rubbed their stomachs indicating that they wanted to eat.

"Kindly wait in the lobby, Mr. Stein, and I will be glad to talk to you after my starving Armenians have their breakfast." Jim motioned towards his children.

Stein nodded agreement and walked over to a plush chair that faced the entrance to the dining room and sat down.

"Well, Mr. Stein," Jim thought to myself, "Maybe you can help me, too!"

Not being hungry he chose a continental breakfast, a roll and coffee. The others had good American style waffles and bacon. Jim had too much brewing in his head to be tempted by great smelling food. He was a bit anxious to continue his interview with the representative of "FIND."

Dorothy's quick mind had caught the drift of the conversation with Stein and she wanted to know how he knew them, and how did he find them, plus a whole lot of other questions.

Jim answered by repeating the words he heard children say, but he twisted it around like this, "It's for him to know, and me to find out!" She understood and laughed.

Dorothy was going to be Jim's partner and help ferret information from the Israeli investigator. Two against one, that would be fair.

After having a second cup of coffee Jim felt ready for whatever the day was to bring. All had finished the morning meal to their satisfaction. The children were going to go out and check the area near the hotel. They would wait nearby until Dorothy and Jim were through with Mr. Stein, THE MAN FROM FIND.

CHAPTER THIRTY NINE
The Man From "FIND"

As Dorothy and Jim seated themselves across from Stein, Jim asked the question that had been bothering him since their encounter at the base of the stairs to the lobby.

"Who told you about us, and told you where to find us? And why do you think I know anything that could help you?"

"Hold it, hold it, not so fast! I'll tell ya whatever I may be permitted to tell. I'll try to be honest with ya, but foist I'd like your cooperation."

Stein had unconsciously lapsed into street talk. He must have been overly excited and anxious. Cooling his heels for an hour while the Mitchell's had breakfast honed his appetite for new information that he thought would be forthcoming.

Mitchell still hadn't made that phone call to the Valentes to inquire about the accident on Route 65 involving the Cavelli van. That would have to wait until he was through interviewing Mr. Stein while the Israeli was thinking that he was interviewing the Mitchells.

"Chief Gabrielli told me that you were here. I spoke to him on the telephone last night and he said that you had checked into this hotel." Stein had opened up a small notebook and was looking at its contents. Just like the cops in the movies.

"It seems," He went on, "That Gabrielli seems to think that you have the key to the matter that we are now pursuing."

"How could that be?" Jim hastened to correct him. "I told the Chief everything I knew in answering his questions. In addition to that, I haven't the slightest clue about what he was after. Can you enlighten me?"

Mr. Stein rubbed his chin and looked thoughtfully at the floor before replying. He took a deep breath, straightened his tie, and reached for his notebook that rested in his lap. He then leaned towards Dorothy and Jim in order to say something in confidence.

"Please do not repeat what I tell you to anyone. I am violating a strict rule of "FIND."

He cautiously looked around to see if anyone was within earshot. The lobby was quite empty, except for one man who was reading a newspaper in one corner.

Satisfied, Stein continued by saying, "I'll give you one name and I'd like you to tell me if it registers, it might jog your memory."

He was watching Jim closely. Then with high expectations he dropped the name. "JAKOB MANDIL!"

Mitchell sat there expressionless, waiting to hear more. He faced Stein squarely, "Anything else?"

The Israeli agent had bombed out. Jim could give him nothing. That name meant nothing to him and the Chief Investigator of "FIND" realized it. His hopes were dashed but his search would continue in other directions.

CHAPTER FORTY
The "Palestinians"

In reacting to the stunned silence, for a moment Jim felt a bit sorry for the guy who seemed to be chasing a ghost.

"Why did you think I could be of any help to you and your organization?"

Jim was sure that Gabrielli had filled Stein in on everything that he knew; yet the FIND agent thought that it was important enough for him to find out things for himself.

"It's no secret that in our (FIND) files in Tel Aviv we have your dossier with all your vital statistics, photos and info about your term as commander of the Modena refugee camp." Martin Stein smiled and continued.

"All the data on you has been corroborated by many who passed through your camp. You'd be surprised at the thickness of your file."

Stein seemed assured of Mitchell's confidentiality.

"Gosh," Jim began, "I never realized that I was so important. I was only a little guy doing a big job under orders. I personally don't have a single scrap of paper from the military that could prove that I was in Modena in 1945!"

Then he added, "Please send me copies of your file that I could include in my service record and 201 file." Jim laughed because he knew that it was an impossible request.

Martin Stein joined in the laughter. They were bonding.

"Our files on Mandil dwarf yours. We traced him to Italy. It is believed that he wormed his way among the refugees with forged papers, however we are not sure. Nor do we know the alias he used. We think that posing as a Jew with fresh tattooed numbers on his arm he could go anywhere ---- with or without papers."

Stein halted to catch his breath.

"You are right," Jim responded. "Most of the Jewish refugees posing as Palestinians that were processed by us had no papers at all, or did not choose to show them."

Then he ventured with, "What makes you so sure that he isn't in Israel living as a Jew?"

"We've looked into that aspect and have investigated many reports of sightings in Israel, but we blanked on all of them. Besides, this guy hated Jews so much that he would not be able to bear living with us for the past twenty five years."

"Now tell me something," Jim pushed, "How did Gabrielli know that I was staying at this hotel?"

"Oh, don't you know? He had you tailed all the way down here. When you arrived and checked into the hotel, Gabrielli called me at the Hotel Fini. I quickly drove down last evening and checked into this hotel so that I would be sure to see you this morning."

Dorothy came up with a question, "In the first place, why were you in Modena?"

"Israeli agents in Rome heard about your impending arrival from informants in Modena, so the information was passed on to us. I got to Modena three days ago, but played it cool because Gabrielli was on your case. I did not want to complicate matters. I'm sorry I didn't contact you in Modena, it would have saved me a lot of time and energy."

Stein hesitated a moment before continuing: "Incidentally, Colonel Mitchell, do you remember a guy named Sam Eisen who was in Modena as a representative of the Joint Distribution Committee?"

"Yes, yes, of course, I remember him well! We argued sometimes when he came into my office to make some nutty demands for the Jewish refugees he represented. But we had some good times together too. He was the only American civilian around at that time. We needed each other's company."

"Well, he's in Israel, married and has a family. He works for our Institute. So you see there are no secrets!"

"Hey," Jim exclaimed, "When deluged with incoming refugees, I called on Sam to help in registering, maybe he interviewed this guy, Mandil."

"No, we've been all through that with Sam years ago. He was no help there. We pinned our hopes on your memory."

"Oh, come now, I registered only a few people during the first few days of my appointment as commandant, and that was only to acquaint myself with the system. I must admit this; I spoke in Arabic to a lot of people, including all the rabbis, hoping to find a true Palestinian. I only found about six real honest-to-goodness Palestinian Jews who wanted to go to their homeland. All the other Jews eventually got to their "homeland" too."

Stein snickered, gave Jim a low Bronx cheer, and laughed. Dorothy and Jim also laughed. What Mitchell had just told Stein was an open secret, but for a long time it was an Israeli "state secret".

Stein took his leave in good humor. He went away with nothing, while Jim and Dorothy gained a lot of information, which at some time might be helpful.

CHAPTER FORTY ONE
Intrigue

"Golly," Dorothy said softly to her husband when they had returned to the privacy of their room. "Here we were in Italy and in the center of something intriguing and also frightening. Gabrielli must have known more that Stein would admit."

Jim agreed, and suddenly remembered that he had to make that phone call to Modena and fast!

"Pronto, pronto!" He could hear Mario Valente's voice on the other end of the line. His call finally got through after many attempts by the hotel operator. Phone service wasn't that great in Italy.

"Mario, come sta? This is Jim Mitchell. This is Jim," He repeated the last, there was some interference on the wire, "How is your family? And Mama Elena?" It was not polite to be quick and to the point, as he did at home. One had to go along with the small talk and ask how everyone was. Then a person had to listen for, "tutti bene" before continuing the conversation and getting down to business.

"Any news in Modena?" As soon that question was put to him, there was dead silence for a moment and then Mario's voice came back loud and clear, "Si, si! How did you know? Cavelli's camion (truck) had a terrible accident and two of his men were killed! It's in the newspaper this morning and on top of the front page. And pictures, too. It was very bad, that highway should be condemned. It is too dangerous for a big truck. I should know, we're in the trucking business and we don't use Route 65 unless we absolutely have to, and then we are very careful. It's a mystery why they were down that far, it is out of their trading area."

All of that gushed out from him without taking another breath, or so it seemed. His words swept over Jim like a torrent of icy water. It left him cold, and for good reason. It proved the legitimacy of his concern for the lives of himself and family.

Mitchell asked no more questions. Mario told Jim that the Valente families wanted them to come back to Modena because they considered the Mitchells as part of their family. They would always be welcome. Jim thanked him and hung up. He needed time to think.

Now he was sure that Gabrielli either had his own men watching, or was relying on the Florence police to do the job. When Jim went down to the lobby to rejoin his family, he noticed the same man in the corner reading the same newspaper. He had to be a detective, and he knew he was right, because as they moved out of the lobby to go out to the street, he dropped his newspaper and pulled himself out of the deep cushioned chair.

Jim allowed his family to lead the way to some shops nearby. As he followed them through narrow streets, he would occasionally glance back to see if their shadow was still there. Somehow, he felt safe knowing that a protector was close by.

It was about two o'clock, and time to have something to eat and drink. Dorothy and Judy had maximized their purchases and Jim was loaded with their packages. Jimmy only bought a couple of cheap souvenirs. Mitchell bought nothing.

Their man was still around. Only Jim knew that. His family was totally unaware that eyes were upon them all the time.

A doubt filtered into Jim's mind; maybe this fellow was not on their team. Perhaps Gabrielli only had people follow so that he could tell Stein where we were and nothing more. Maybe he pulled his men off and left them wide open for the "other side" (whoever they were).

Having convinced himself that it was the right thing to do, he was determined to "ditch" their shadow. To do this, he would have to tell his family something but not everything, in order to get them to cooperate. He thought it would be easy.

The streets were still crowded with tourists and with so many shops in the area, they could walk into one store and out the back door before anyone would notice. But first, they had something to eat, then after a little explanation, Jim revealed his plan.

"Sure," They said. "Let's do it!"

They did, caught a taxi, and got to home base fast.

★   ★   ★

Reaching his room, Martin Stein took off his coat and readied himself for some work.

But first, it was time for Stein to make his phone call. Gabrielli answered on the first ring. "Pronto," He said without identifying himself.

"Mr. Gabrielli? This is Stein. I just finished my meeting with Mr. Mitchell and his wife, Dorothy."

"Did you find out anything new?"

"No, sir. Not a thing. He appears to know nothing about the man we are seeking." Stein sneezed. "Excuse me." He reached into his pocket for a handkerchief.

"Don't catch cold this time of year. You will have a hard time getting rid of it."

The Chief was quick with his advice. He caught colds easily.

Then Gabrielli asked, "Did you say anything to him about the other thing?"

"Oh, no. I'm saving that for the time my partner comes."

"Well, that's fine, but that information might prompt the comandante to tell you something that is critical to our investigation. We will cooperate with you, if you think that way is best to achieve your goal. Good luck." The Chief hung up.

Stein paced the floor for a few minutes after his talk with Gabrielli. He was gathering his thoughts on how to proceed further. The arrival of Sam Eisen would make things easier. Two minds were better than one. It was best to wait.

CHAPTER FORTY TWO
The Private Detective

After a good night's sleep and an early breakfast, Jim sauntered into the lobby of the hotel, and looked for the detective whom they had outwitted the afternoon before. Sure enough, he was there as usual, hiding behind a newspaper. His family had returned to the suite, so he thought he'd have a little fun. Bravely walking up to the mustached gentleman, Jim stood squarely facing him. The man did not stir and kept his face hidden in the folds of the paper.

Daringly, Mitchell reached out and rattled the paper a bit to get the man's attention. Putting the paper aside, the man looked up and glared.

"Perche?" He asked as his face reddened. No doubt about it, he was furious and Jim was enjoying it.

"Why are you following us?" Jim countered, "You lost us yesterday."

He wanted to make that person squirm.

"I don't know what you are talking about." Still sitting, the man responded, playing with his thin mustache. "I'm not following you or anyone else. I'm a business man."

With that he pulled out a card and handed it to Jim.

He was a salesman for a ceramic company in Sassuolo, a town about nine kilometers southwest of Modena. His name was Dominic Conti.

Signore Conti stood up his eyes glaring, picked up his paper, and without another word walked toward the elevators.

Good cover, Jim thought, these undercover people know their jobs. He figured that their shadow was embarrassed at being caught. Going up in the elevator to prove that he was a guest was redundant. Mitchell was sure that he was not registered. The manager of security at the hotel probably knew him and that is why he was able to get on the elevator without being challenged. They had tight security in the Hotel Montebello.

To feel secure in his assumptions, Jim walked over to the concierge whom he was sure saw the episode of his confrontation with the 'detective'. Mitchell showed the business card to the concierge and asked if he knew him.

"Yes," He replied. "He checked in here a day or so before you arrived. I remember asking him if he had any samples of his factory's ceramics with him, because we are making some changes in our kitchen in my house. He said that he did not bring any."

Did Jim make a boo-boo? No, he still didn't think so. But he did follow them. Of that he was sure. He did not identify himself as an officer of the law. Maybe he belonged to Interpol. That seemed far out. Perhaps he was one of Stein's men. But then, if he wasn't a real Italian detective, whom was he serving? The more questions that came up, the more confused Mitchell became. He had to find out about Conti and what he was doing there.

He went upstairs and directly into the room that he and Dorothy occupied. Picking up the phone, Jim asked the operator to get Signore Conti. "Conti?" She asked. "We have no Conti here in this hotel."

"Are you sure?" "Certamente!" She hung up.

Puzzled more than ever, Jim sat in the chair feeling helpless and wondering what to do next. Meanwhile, his family was tiptoeing around, anxiously waiting for him to go out with them. He felt that they were under no one's protection. They had to fend for themselves. At that moment, he was inclined to leave immediately for one of Rome's airports and get out of the country. His wife and children were ready to spend the day sightseeing in Florence and were looking forward to enjoying two days in the Eternal City before leaving for the United States.

What a quandary! There was a possibility that he was blowing up everything out of proportion. Could he be paranoid for no reason at all? He could enumerate reasons, but they did not seem to be sound enough. Best idea was to wait and see.

CHAPTER FORTY THREE
The Plot Thickens

As Jim stood up, ready to go out with his family, he plunged his right hand into his pants pocket to make sure that he had the room key. His hand came up with Conti's card. He immediately went to the phone and asked the operator to get the ceramics factory, and he read the phone number to her. He hung up and waited for the operator to ring back after getting his connection. Thirty seconds later the operator called.

"No factory by that name, sir, but I reached a store called "Cavelli's," a liquor store, I believe. Shall I try again? Do you have a name that I can ask for?"

"Yes, yes," Mitchell answered, "Ask for Dominic Conti and let me know what happens. Thank you." He put the phone down.

A minute later he snapped up the phone when it rang only to hear the operator say, "Sorry, sir, no Signore Conti there and they hung up on me!"

"Coincidence?" Jim thought not. His musings continued. "Someone made a mistake in putting Cavelli's number on that card, or was it done purposely? Did someone in the Cavelli organization hire this man Conti? And did Conti put the Cavelli number on the business card so that his informants could reach him there? Did I trip him up in the lobby and cause him to blunder into giving me a card and not taking it back?"

As they say in some mystery stories: "The plot thickened."

Mitchell was getting nowhere. Best thing to do now was to get out into the August sunlight and spend time with his family. Picking up the movie camera, he said softly, "Let's go."

Now he was sure of one thing, someone was interested in knowing what he was doing, and it was not the police. Gabrielli had given up on Mitchell in his investigation. So, apparently, had Stein and his organization, FIND. Or so, Jim thought.

He was quite wary as they wandered the streets of Florence, visiting churches, Museums and, of course, shops. No one followed them that day. It was not necessary, because they had to go back to the hotel. They weren't going anywhere. Neither was Jim getting anywhere in his search for answers.

Upon returning to the hotel, for lunch and some rest, the Mitchells literally plopped themselves down on a large leather couch in the lobby before going to their suite. After a minute or two, Jim arose still clutching some packages of the day's purchases and walked over to the concierge's desk. He was busy with another guest for a moment and then turned to face the American.

"Yes, Mr. Mitchell?"

"Do you recall that you told me that Signore Conti was registered at this hotel?"

"Yes.

Then Jim hit him with: "Well, he's not! He is not a guest at all! I checked."

"Oh, I am sorry," The concierge whispered, looking around to see if they were being overheard. "He gave me a big tip the day he stopped here and that was before you arrived. He wanted to impress some clients and asked if he could sit in the lobby to meet with them. At his pay level, he said that he could not afford to stay here. I believe he was registered at the Anglo-American Hotel, which is near here. I'm truly sorry if I inconvenienced you in any way."

He was truly apologetic and was forgiven.

A concierge, if tipped enough, will do almost anything for you, including going along with a charade. This one did his job well and Jim wanted him on his side if he chose to pull off something.

CHAPTER FORTY FOUR
Rome

The following morning, Jim called the desk and asked that their car be brought around because they were going to check out right after breakfast. While walking down the stairs, he scanned the lobby to see if his 'friend,' Conti, was in sight. He was nowhere to be seen. The few people that were seated in the lobby looked like American tourists.

The members of the Mitchell family were good travelers. All the luggage was packed and locked before they went downstairs for breakfast. But to get someone from the hotel staff to bring your luggage to your car is something else. The first bellhop will get a cart and come up for your luggage and take it to the desk while you are getting your bill. You give him the tip that you have ready and turn around to pay the tab. After receiving your receipt, you turn around and the bellboy is gone. Then you get the desk or concierge to get another bellboy to take the luggage to your car. So you have to tip him too. There are tricks in every trade.

*   *   *

The drive to Rome was uneventful. The Mitchells enjoyed the larger car and the air conditioning. Dorothy didn't dare drive so Judy drove while Jim took a short nap. It was refreshing. This time he was positive they were not being followed.

The Mercedes pulled up to the entrance of the Hilton, which is situated on one of the Seven Hills of Rome. From there you could get a good view of the city. After moving into their rooms, the Mitchells decided to forego sightseeing that evening.

Judy and Jimmy wanted to use the hotel swimming pool before dinner. Dorothy and Jim decided to just relax and watch local television. Needless to say, both dozed in their chairs.

Tomorrow was going to be the one full day that they were going to spend in Rome. At two o'clock the following afternoon they would be on their way home. Jim was looking forward to leaving Italy with the same intensity that he had wanted to go to Italy. It was hard for him to figure that out.

On the way to the dining room they passed through the lobby and Jim noticed nothing out of the ordinary. He was not sure what he was looking for anyway. At least, neither Conti nor Stein was there. Was there a third person to look for?

From the lobby it was necessary to go down another floor to the hotel restaurant that the children had chosen. They were served a fine dinner and were about halfway through eating when they heard loud noises coming from the kitchen. Then three or four waiters came running out of the kitchen, spilling all over each other. The cook was on a rampage. Their waiter told them that a customer had insulted the cook's presentation of his specialty. The cook was yelling a word that they had heard not too many days before, "SCIOPERO! SCIOPERO!" (STRIKE!) He probably was going on strike. Thank heaven; the Mitchells already had their dinners. It was like watching a floorshow. Very enjoyable and memorable.

Later in the evening, Jim telephoned Mario to inquire if there was any more news about the accident. He was happy to receive his call and hoped they were enjoying their holiday.

"Si, si," he added, "Cavelli has been cited by the police by being delinquent in repairing the trucks for inspection. The brakes were faulty and Cavelli will have to pay a big fine, maybe prison, too!"

Jim wondered if Cavelli had to go to trial. Would the prosecution bring up his prison record? There was nothing Mitchell could do to help him. He was on his own.

Tomorrow they would enjoy Rome to its fullest. Dorothy had made arrangements to meet a priest, Father Hutta, who was going to show them around the Vatican. They were to meet at the Obelisk in Saint Peter's Square at seven o'clock in the morning. It was early to bed that night, for Mom, Dad, and the children. Jim phoned the desk and asked for a six o'clock wake up call.

CHAPTER FORTY FIVE
Fr. Hutta, Chocolate Bars and The Vatican

Father Hutta arrived at the Obelisk just as the Americans were pulling up to park. He was perched on his Vespa with his coat tails flying. His vehicle was a small, motorized bike that was very popular in Italy. With the price of gas very high, it afforded good transportation. The motor was not much bigger than that of a lawn mower and got about 60 or more miles per gallon, or in European terms about 96 kilometers per gallon.

The priest was from Czechoslovakia, behind the Iron Curtain, and he was in charge of a nunnery and some grottoes situated in the suburbs of Rome. He had reserved the day for the Mitchells and for that they were grateful. This man of the cloth opened up every gate of Rome to them. He knew everybody in the hierarchy of the Vatican who was worth knowing. The Swiss guards opened up the gates and they drove into the Vatican City.

Father Hutta presented the guards with chocolate bars. The family walked into the Pope's garden and saw where the Pope took his walks. At that hour of the morning, the Vatican was closed to the public, yet they were inside. The large salon where the Pope greeted heads of state and dignitaries was opened to them and all took turns sitting on the Pope's chair. They snapped pictures to prove it.

Dorothy opened up a large door to an adjoining room and she gasped in amazement because it was the Sistine Chapel. No flash bulbs allowed in the chapel, so said the brochures they had read.

"Go ahead," said Father, "Take all the pictures you want!" He had given that guard a bar of candy, so it was O.K.

They saw the Vatican Treasures, a magnificent wealth of gifts of gold and silver encrusted with precious gems. That room left them breathless; there was so much to see.

The Pope was going to go to his summer palace in Castel Gondolfo that morning and they observed his personal aides packing his robes in the room where the vestments were kept. The trunks that were being used for the trip were very old and timeworn. They were probably used for a century or more.

It was an unforgettable experience and they enjoyed every precious minute of it.

The Mitchells returned to the Vatican square shortly after eleven o'clock, and although exhilarated by what they had seen, they were hungry. St. Peter's square was crowded with humanity from all nations. Busloads of people came from all parts of Europe. It was difficult driving through the crowd in order to get to Father Hutta's Vespa. Father asked Jim to follow him and he would take them to a restaurant that he recommended.

At first, they drove through some narrow streets, then onto a wide avenue. The Mitchells hung on to Father Hutta's trail as he zigzagged through the traffic. He took them to an area with a name like "New City" and it looked like it. The street was lined with modern buildings, probably the financial district. Hutta pulled up to the curb in front of a modern restaurant. Jim followed and parked.

The interior of the deli, Dorothy recognized it as a delicatessen, had a long counter and refrigerated display case with every kind of processed meat or cheese of which one could think. The large rolls were fresh and with a hard crust. The Americans were all ready for that kind of meal by that time. Each of them picked up a tray and ordered a sandwich to suit the appetite of the day. Jim had lots of salami in his with cole slaw and pickles on the side. And a coke. Dorothy had corned beef and a coke. The children, Jimmy and Judy, had ham and cheese on rye. And cokes.

They were not too far from Father Hutta's place of residence. He had to return to his duties, which included raising funds for his "Cause." His mission was to help his people who were under Communist rule. Jim gave him a generous donation for which he was deeply thankful, claiming it was too much. Dorothy prevailed upon him and made him accept. Earlier, while having lunch, Father drew a map on a napkin showing Jim and Dorothy how to get back to their hotel.

110

CHAPTER FORTY SIX
The Raging Partners

Mandelli was pacing the floor in his home. He was going over the confrontation that he had with Cavelli the day before. The job that he was supposed to do in eliminating the comandante was botched. Cavelli had roared into his office and raged until he had exhausted his vocal cords. It was the first time that Mandelli had ever feared Cavelli.

"You damn fool, you idiot! Do you know what you have done? The damage you have incurred will never be recovered. You have played with people's lives and we have lost two of them. Do you realize that? These crazy games must stop. Either way we were going to be the losers. If you succeeded, my friend would be gone. And you would have lost the man who once saved your life. We are the losers anyway. It is now YOUR duty to see about the bodies and to console their families........"

To Mandelli, it seemed that Andrea was spilling out the hate that had accumulated in him over the years. Cavelli's voice was harsh in his chastisement of Mandelli and his cohorts.

Andrea left Mandelli's office without giving his partner a chance to respond.

In any case, Mandelli had no answer for the accusations and charges that Cavelli had made. He was speechless, not only because of the outcome of his plan, but also for the repercussions that were soon to come down on his head from his superiors in their organization.

It was incumbent upon him to make that call to the others in northern Italy. He had to telephone as soon as Cavelli exited and took his rage with him.

Still shaking, Mandelli dialed and held the receiver to his ear. He was dying for a drink.

"I should have had a strong drink before I dialed." Mandelli thought as he waited for the phone on the other end of the line to be picked up. "Damn, damn.....stupid me...."

"Ja, ja." His party had answered the phone.

In a quavering voice, Mandelli responded in German.

* * *

Mandelli could still hear the guttural voice bearing down on him because of his failure. He could make no excuses because they were not accepted nor were excuses expected. Blubbering to himself a day later in the sanctuary of his own home did not make it easier. He still felt the pain and could only look forward to more of the same.

"Cavelli's right." Mandelli acknowledged to himself. "It is going to be our undoing. We should have left things as they were." He continued to berate himself.

His head ached and he was tired. He needed time to think and rest.

"That louse in Ivrea....." Mandelli slouched in a chair and closed his eyes.

CHAPTER FORTY SEVEN
Out of the Blue – The Chief!

Upon returning to the hotel from their tour of the Vatican, Jim found a message waiting for him at the desk. It was from Stein. His message said that Eisen was arriving in Rome in two days and could Mitchell manage to see him?

Jim never returned his call because he was still angry. How in the world did Stein know where to reach him? He could whistle "Dixie" for all Jim cared! Besides, they would be on the way to the States the next day.

The Mitchells rested in their rooms for a couple of hours. Judy and Jimmy decided to go down to the pool. Dorothy and Jim thought it best to go out for a little while by themselves.

Instead of going towards the center of Rome, they drove towards the suburbs on Viale Angelico and soon arrived at a forum that was once called Foro Mussolini. Jim told Dorothy that he had spent a week there in 1944 when it was a rest center for the Allied forces. They walked around a bit admiring the statues that surrounded the arena.

While returning to the hotel, Dorothy spotted some shops that looked interesting. Evidently tourists did not frequent that area. Very few people were on the street and they looked like natives. Jim parked in front of a small gift shop because a beautiful cobalt blue bowl in the window had attracted his wife's attention.

They walked into the store and browsed a bit. The main course was in the window and Jim asked the clerk to get it so that they could get a closer look. She obliged. It was gorgeous and all that Dorothy was worried about was how to get it home without breaking.

It would be their last purchase, so they asked the lady to wrap it carefully because they were taking it to America. Jim paid for it and said that they were going to the bar next door and would pick up the bowl later. That would give her the time to do a good job of packing.

Almost every block in every village, town, and city in Italy has a bar. These bars serve coffee, soft drinks, chocolate, beer, wine, and whiskey. Continental breakfasts are served there; coffee and a roll. They stood at the counter, which was only two feet or so in from the sidewalk.

As they were sipping their drinks, Dorothy turned around to face the street. "Look," She exclaimed. "There's the Chief of Police across the street! I'm sure that's him. I saw you talking to him a couple of times."

Mitchell spun around to look, but the man had turned his back and was walking away. Quickly putting his cup on the counter, Jim stepped out to the curb and called, "Signore Gabrielli!"

There was no response. Then Jim moved to the center of the street and called again. This time, the Chief slowly turned around and fa:ed Jim as he reached the other side. It was easy to see that Gabrielli was embarrassed.

"Oh, Signore Mitchell, how nice to see you again." He shook Jim's hand.

"What are you doing in Rome?" Mitchell asked, slyly.

"Just for a short holiday."

Looking around as though seeking something, Jim asked, "Where's your wife, is she shopping?"

The Chief understood what the American was trying to get out of him. He gave up immediately by throwing up his hands and with a grin answered, "My wife's at home doing her housework and I'm here doing my job."

"Were you following us all the time?"

"No, no, not all the time. After I heard about the accident on Route 65, I went to the scene. I talked to the police who had been there and gave them your description and the auto you were driving. One of them recalled speaking to you as you were passing. It wasn't hard to learn that you were staying at the Montebello from the Firenze police. They told me you changed cars to a Mercedes and I got your license number. Stein got that information from me and immediately left to find you. I had to get here to find out for myself what Stein needed to know. Besides," he added sheepishly. "I wanted to see you safe."

So Jim was right most of the time. They were in danger. But who? Why?

Mitchell invited Gabrielli to go across the street with him for a drink. He graciously accepted. After politely greeting Dorothy, he gave his order to the bartender, "Espresso."

Jim waited until the Chief took his first sip before asking any more questions. Meanwhile, Dorothy went to the shop to pick up the package.

"What was your man Conti doing in Firenze, Signore Gabrielli?"

He looked at Jim intently, "I know of no one with the name Conti."

Handing Gabrielli the card that he still carried in his pocket, Mitchell asked, "This is the Conti I want to know about, what is his real name? I think he was one of your men."

The Chief's eyes widened as he read the card. "He's not one of ours. What did he look like?"

Jim described Signore Conti as best he could and added that the man had the habit of playing with his mustache when under stress.

Gabrielli nodded his head. "I believe I know who he is. A private detective with a dubious record. He has an office in Bologna. May I keep this card?"

"Certainly," Jim answered. "But first you must tell me who he is working for and why you think he was following me."

"I do not have the answer yet, but I guarantee you that I will find out."

At that point Dorothy was returning carrying a neat package. It was time to go, and there were no further questions for the Chief. They shook hands again with Gabrielli and took their leave. On the way back to the hotel, Jim noted that a car was following. It was O.K. Mitchell knew they were in good hands.

CHAPTER FORTY EIGHT
Mystery of Sorts

Going down to dinner that evening, Mitchell took his usual look around the lobby and sure enough Gabrielli was sitting in a soft chair facing the entrance to the hotel. He was on the job and Jim still did not know why. He was certain that he would not see or speak to the Chief again, since they would be going home the next day.

Dorothy brought up the subject of Gabrielli a few times during dinner. She thought it was a remarkable coincidence that they would meet up with a friend of the Valentes so far away from Modena. Jim agreed with her.

Somehow, his answer did not satisfy her in the least bit. She felt that something was amiss. Her reasoning was that since northern Italy was Communist and Jim was a retired American officer, they were keeping an eye on him because they suspected him of being a spy. Or something, or other. Jim placed his bet on "Other."

While flying back to the United States, Mitchell tried to put the pieces of information he had together and form some kind of answer. It was a jumbled mess. A lot of parts, but none seemed to fit with any other part. A mystery of sorts? Yes, but there had to be a part that held all the pieces together. At that point, Jim possessed many pieces of which the Chief knew only what he chose to tell him. Gabrielli was aware of parts about which Mitchell knew nothing. Stein figured in on this and he probably knew some things that neither Gabrielli nor Jim knew.

Perhaps a day would come when all three could sit down together and fit the myriad of pieces together!

CHAPTER FORTY NINE
Back to Italy in 1973

Three years had passed since the Mitchell's last visit to Italy. Now they were on the way again. Judy had just completed her third year at Muhlenberg College and Jimmy would be a sophomore at Princeton in the fall.

Since they left Italy in 1970, the Valentes phoned the Americans at least once a month and then again on major holidays. Every time it was the same litany: "When are you coming back to Italy? Our house is your house. You are always welcome!" And when their calls were returned, they got the same questions and invitations over and over.

Their requests wore Mitchell's family down, and they decided to go once more. This time Jim was hoping that he would not be burdened with all that nonsense about a war criminal, and fending off Gabrielli and Stein. This trip was going to be different. They were really going to see more of the country. Jimmy had planned an itinerary that covered most of Italy. Maps of Italy and all its major cities and points of interest were piled in their den for weeks prior to the date of departure. They resolved to stick to their plans. The visit to Modena and their friends, the Valentes and Cavelli, was sandwiched between Pisa and the seashore. Cavelli's daughter, Carla, was going to make reservations for the American family at a seaside hotel in Milano Marittima (on the Adriatic side). The Mitchells intended to use that hotel as a base to go to Ravenna to the north, and Rimini to the south.

The whole family was satisfied with the way Jimmy laid out the schedule. He had spent a lot of time on it and as far as Jim was concerned, it was perfect. Naturally, his sister was not perfectly sure, but she was satisfied. Dorothy would go along with anything her children wanted to do. After all, they were grown up now and they had ideas of their own. James Mitchell could not and would not contest that line of reasoning at all.

In July, he received a packet from a General Barbolini who was now the Comandante of the Accademia Militare. It contained a commencement program of the graduating class of 1973. It was a nice gesture on his part, which Jim appreciated very much. A brief note was included inviting Colonel Mitchell to visit him and the Academy whenever he was in Modena. It was quite flattering to see that he had written the name on the envelope as "Comandante James Mitchell" and then his address. Jim hadn't planned to go there on this trip, but if he had the time and opportunity, he just might take General Barbolini up on it. Oddly enough, Jim had never met this general, so he assumed that his predecessor, Colonel Giannangeli, had told him about the Mitchells' visit three years earlier.

Jim still had the copy of the commencement exercises of 1970 in his possession. It was filed in a drawer in the den with other papers and memorabilia of Italy. On the day that he received the 1973 program, he went to the file drawer and opened the envelope, which contained the one from 1970. The comparison proved that both were beautifully done. The two had great colored photos of the Academy, some of the classrooms and other facilities.

In replacing the 1970 program into its envelope some papers fell to the floor. Other souvenirs, Jim thought, as he stooped to pick them up. Some were hotel and restaurant bills that had been charged on his American Express Card. Among them was the note that he had crumpled three years before. It seemed like yesterday when he had read: "GO AWAY, DON'T STIR THE POT". Jim put all the slips back into the envelope except the one with the warning. For some unknown reason, he tucked it into his wallet.

CHAPTER FIFTY
Uncustomary Customs Agent

The 747 Jumbo Jet carrying the Mitchells and other passengers arrived at the Fiumicino Airport on time.

With passports in hand, carry-on luggage strap tearing into his right shoulder, James Mitchell approached the custom booth and shoved all four passports through the glass opening to the officer. He eyed Jim intently after glancing at his passport and then turned his eyes downward at what was apparently a sheet of paper. His eyes seem to narrow as he read something written there. He quickly brought his head up and with a half smiie asked, "Why are you coming to Italy?" Mitchell was taken aback by the question. He wasn't asked that in the other countries they had visited. They were always ready to welcome American tourists. American dollars were needed everywhere.

Nervously, Jim responded by saying that he and his family were coming to tour Italy and see the sights. The custom's officer glanced at the Mitchell family of four and saw that a long line of people was forming behind them.

The officer took a look at the paper again, shrugged his shoulder, stamped the passports and shoved them back to Jim. Not another word was said. He just waved them on, but his face had a puzzled look as he reached for the phone. His eyes followed the Americans as they made their way to the exit.

Everyone is always in a hurry to get away from the customs area and the Mitchells were no different. However, Jim did momentarily wonder what was in the officer's mind while he held them there. He reasoned that he probably had some English words written on that piece of paper and was going to put them to practice. Mitchell forgot about it immediately after he remembered that he had to pick up a rental car at that Roman airport.

His worries about the car were soon realized when he saw the autos that were available were not Mercedes Benz, or any large car for that matter. He had to settle for a small station wagon and their luggage had to go on the roof. Not in the style he had imagined!

That was their second trip to Italy. That was the year 1973 and they had been there in 1970.

The hotel reservations were for the Cavalieri Hilton, the same Hilton of the Mitchell family's 1970 stay. The children were hoping to see the high-strung chef in action again. But first they wanted to use the swimming pool and then have a late dinner. Dorothy and Jim wanted to unwind, take showers, and hopefully, a little nap.

Driving to the hotel wasn't too bad until they came to a traffic light that was out of order. A bus coming from the west was stopped in the middle of the intersection. The Mitchell car was going west and several cars away from the cross street. Horns were blaring. The leading autos coming from the south were stranded in front of the bus. And to make it worse, the truck leading the pack going south was blocked by the bus.

The din was awful, many people got out of their vehicles and congregated under the traffic light. They argued with each other, arms moving in all directions to get points across. Evidently, no one was listening, and no one offered to make the first move. It was gridlock at its worst. Fifteen or twenty minutes went by before a policeman appeared. He made his way to the center of the dispute and put in his two cents. After five minutes or more of debate, the policeman took matters in his own hands and directed traffic to everyone's satisfaction.

While all that was going on, Jim got out of the car like the others. He spoke to the driver of the auto behind his for a minute or two. Each of them deplored the situation. Then Jim asked the Italian autoist if he knew a short cut to the Monte Mario area where the hotel was located. Certainly, he knew the way well. "Just stay on this street to "il fondo" (the end) and then turn left and go "diritto" (directly) to it." When you get directions like that, Jim knew enough to disregard them. It only meant trouble. It also meant that the guy hadn't the slightest idea of how to get there. It is a face-saving device that Italians use, because, heaven forbid, that he should admit he hadn't the least idea of how to get there. Jim drove the long route to the hotel.

*   *   *

120

The concierge recognized the Mitchell family but he could not recall their name. Jim gave him a big tip and told him to keep his car parked as close to the hotel as possible. He made sure that the concierge would not forget his name by giving him a carton of cigarettes that he bought in the duty- free shop at Kennedy Airport.

They had their drinks, they had their showers, and they had their naps. All in that order.

Having dressed for dinner, they were preparing to go down to the children's favorite restaurant, the one that had the temperamental chef, when the phone rang. Jim was in no mood to answer any calls at that moment. "That better be the Pope." He said as he picked up the receiver. It was the wrong number, probably an in-house call. One hotel guest trying to call another guest. They left their rooms for the stairs to the lobby.

Reminiscent of the first time at the hotel, they were given rooms on the second floor. As the lobby came into view in their descent, Jim looked over the folks who were seated or standing. He had reacquired his habit to check.

CHAPTER FIFTY ONE
Mandelli's "Black Satans"

It was the first day of August 1973 and Mandelli and Cavelli had their monthly meeting. The last three years had strained both of them. The rift of 1970 had not healed and there was no evidence that it ever would. The scars were deep. Cavelli had been deeply wounded by Mandelli who in turn was deviled by his superiors. In his mind, Mandelli had termed the members of his organization as "black Satans."

The 'silent partner,' Mandelli, had softened his demeanor and more often than not, acceded to Cavelli's wishes in their business dealings. Andrea was running the show now and was doing very well. Mandelli, together with his cohorts, had tempered his demands somewhat to Cavelli's satisfaction.

It was Andrea who broached the subject. "He is in Italy." It was a broad statement with many implications.

Quietly, Mandelli said, "I know."

"Promise me that there will be no bad occurrences this time."

Hedging, his partner responded. "I'll see what I can do. I do not wish to cope with another mess. We are still not out of the woods caused by our last fiasco. It haunts me still."

It was a confession that Cavelli was glad to hear. Mandelli had never opened up like this before. He was getting soft. Perhaps he had a conscience.

"I'm glad you feel that way." Andrea was forgiving. "My family is going to spend time with them at the seashore. Carla had made the reservations at a nice German hotel. I, too, wish to make amends. Il comandante was my friend in 1945 and he remains my friend today. Business is business. Let's let it go at that."

Mandelli reached for his hat. "I'm leaving for the mountains tomorrow. I'll be in touch. Have a nice vacation. Buon giorno." He added some niceties for a change.

Cavelli was pleased with his partner's attitude.

CHAPTER FIFTY TWO
Pasta A La 1944

The hotel chef handled himself well that evening. Especially so because the vacation month of August had begun and it is the time for workers to be itching to get to the mountains or the beaches. The food was excellent and there were no tantrums. Judy and Jimmy were disappointed in that respect. Pasta was Jim's favorite food and he was determined to have it every day while in Italy. Each region has its own way of cooking pasta. In the deep south, the sauce is red and hearty. As one proceeds north the sauces have subtle changes and upon reaching Bologna, the sauces are creamy, white, and very delicate. Dorothy and Jim liked all kinds and being adventuresome, they were going to try them all.

*　　*　　*

During World War II, Lt. Mitchell and three of his men came upon a small village that their forces had just liberated. It was a warm day and as they drove by a small farmhouse in their jeep, Jim saw a woman and her husband walking towards one of their small outbuildings. The soldiers were hungry and they were aware that the Italians were too. The lieutenant had a great idea.

Ordering the driver to halt, Jim dismounted, called to the couple, and motioned to them to come. They cautiously moved in the soldiers' direction and at the same time two children came out of the house. These poor people, who only hours ago had been under German jurisdiction, were still afraid for their children's safety. They were assured, however, when the men reached into their pockets and offered the kids candy.

The only thing Lt. Mitchell wanted was to ask the wife if she could make some pasta if they furnished the flour and whatever else she needed. She was delighted, and she had the tomato conserve.

The driver turned back to find the supply vehicle, with orders to get a five-pound bag of flour. The others rested in the shade. Within a half hour the jeep was back with the flour plus a few other goodies that he thought the Italian family would appreciate.

The husband brought out a wooden table and put it in the shade. He put some benches and chairs around the table. Then as his wife was making the pasta from scratch, he brought out the china and silverware, which was a luxury to the famished troops.

It was the best pasta in the world! The noodles were homemade and cooked perfectly. The Italian family sat and ate with them. The Americans ate heartily and their Italian friends ate with gusto. It was a pleasure watching the little boy and girl hungrily eating everything that was put in front of them. All of the men left some of their rations with the family. The leftover flour and the cans of food that the driver had brought would keep that family fed for the next two weeks or so. Lieutenant Mitchell and his men left there well fed and the Italian family was content.

Jim also remembered going into the Grand Hotel in Rome shortly after the city was under Allied control. Lt. Mitchell and a fellow officer walked into the restaurant, but they had nothing on the menu. In fact, they had no food to serve. The officers opened their musette bags and pulled out cans of hash and gave them to the cook to see what he could do to improve the taste. They were surprised what some onions and spices could do to hash! They enjoyed that meal with a tin of biscuits. Cigarettes and money were left for the cook and the waiter. In 1973 that hotel was as grand as ever. Mitchell just looked in once and did not recognize anyone, as if he could!

CHAPTER FIFTY THREE
Another Warning

The Mitchell family left the restaurant and walked up to the lobby. Every time one passes the reservations desk one must ask if there are any messages, even though one knows that there shouldn't be any.

This time it was a shocker. There was a message. A handwritten one at that. They hadn't told anyone where they were going to stay except their closest relatives at home, and naturally, Jim and Dorothy's office. But no one in Italy.

Jim tore open the letter as they crossed the lobby floor towards the stairway. It was in the same handwriting as the warning note that he had received three years before at the Hotel Reale Fini. This letter was hand delivered which indicated to him that the person who wrote the note was in Rome. Maybe in the same hotel!

"PLEASE DO NOT COME TO MODENA. DON'T HURT YOUR FRIENDS." That was it!

It bore no signature. Just that German script. It didn't come across as a warning this time, more like a plea. But it didn't compute.

Jim had really been convinced that the mysteries of the last trip to Italy had played themselves out. The idea that someone had tried to kill them was completely erased. It was now resurrected. The note did that.

What was the motive? Seemingly, the case of the Nazi war criminal was closed when Jim's family left for the United States three years earlier. There was no apparent reason for including him in the investigation at that time, except for the remote possibility that he might help in some way. It was proven beyond a doubt, as far as Mitchell was concerned, that he could not be the key figure for which the investigators had hoped. Was this trip going to be fouled up with all that nonsense again?

On the elevator, Dorothy wanted to know what the message was about. Jim said that he would show it to her later. At that point, he decided that he should confide in her and let her know what was going on. Of course, Jim would also have to tell her the truth about the events of three years ago. Deep down, he knew that if she knew the facts of the 1970 trip, she would not have approved of this one in 1973.

After entering their suite, James Mitchell went directly to his briefcase and pulled out a small package that contained the memorabilia of the war years in Italy. He had packed them again this time, hoping to have the prospect of seeing other friends that he hadn't seen previously. Jim also took out his wallet and removed the first note of 1970 that he had determined was written in German script.

Carefully placing them side by side on the table he asked Dorothy to look at them. She pored over them for a minute or so and then said, "They are written by the same person that's certain, and in foreign handwriting, but not by an Italian."

"That is German script," Jim explained. "And you're right, they were written by the same person. We received this first one three years ago when we arrived at the Hotel Fini in Modena. I never showed it to you, because I didn't want to alarm you. Nor did I realize its seriousness until the final few days of our stay in Italy."

Jim then proceeded to relate some of the happenings of the last trip and of which she was totally unaware. The incident involving the Cavelli truck, he left out deliberately. No sense worrying her on that score. She was totally unaware of the conversations that went on with, Gabrielli, Franco, and Conti, the detective.

Dorothy was amazed that all of that was kept from her and she was close by all the time! Jim proudly concurred.

"What are you going to do about this?" Dorothy prodded, referring to the second note.

"I don't know, but I am sure as heck not going to change our plans because of it."

Oddly, she agreed, then added. "Let's sleep on it."

Before turning in, Jim went one step farther and got out the postcard that he had received from Lake Garda twenty eight years earlier. It was the one with the signatures of some of the service personnel of the refugee camp and the signature of one Yacob Klein. Remembering ...... that he had compared his signature with the first note probably with the idea of enforcing his thinking that it was written by a German. Since Yacob was a German Jew, his handwriting would be German script. By doing that Jim was sure it was written by a German, nothing more. He was not a handwriting expert by any means.

Curiously, he compared the second note with the Yacob's signature and was startled to find that the letters "a,c,o,l,e,i, and n" matched almost perfectly! He checked once more and came up with the same answer. The clincher was the capital letter "M" which Yacob Klein had started to write in place of his surname and had stricken it with an "X". The "M" was clear enough to match with the letter in "Modena" which had been capitalized. Was it possible that this guy whom he had thrown out of the kitchen many years ago was corresponding with him. No, that was too far fetched. It was a German, but not Yacob, of that he was sure!

While lying in bed, Jim compared the tenor of the two notes. The first one was threatening, but the second didn't appear to be menacing. The writer was concerned about hurting his friends. How would Mitchell harm his friends? Was it a veiled threat after all? He did not wish to put anyone in jeopardy. The message seemed to indicate that by merely going to visit Modena, he would imperil his hosts. That possibility seemed remote.

CHAPTER FIFTY FOUR
"Friends and Others"

The following morning the Americans visited the church and underground grottos of the Capuchin monks. Monks of that order were buried underneath the church for centuries. The bodies were in placed above ground in alcoves. The cellar was littered with bones. It was not fitting for an early morning outing.

The church was only a short distance away from the American Embassy and the Excelsior Hotel where Jim had some pleasant memories from the time it was a Rest Hotel for officers. He still had a pastel chalk drawing of himself that was made by an Italian artist in the lobby. It cost about 50 lire (fifty cents). The embassy and the hotel are on the famous street: Via Veneto. Everyone who goes to Rome winds up there one way or another.

Naturally, they had to go to St. Peter's. Judy was an art major in college and wanted to see the many things that we had missed during their first trip. Many students of art spend months in the Vatican Museum studying the magnificent works of talented and famous artists of the past. The architecture of the Basilica, the marble statues and works of art contained therein boggle the mind.

The note and its contents were still in the back of Jim's mind. He did not wish to worry about it. But it seemed to leave him no choice. Time and time again, his thoughts would shift to that subject. Trying as hard as he could to become interested in the sights as they moved along, his brain would pick up that subject again. He just had to deal with it as best he could. It was not going to go away.

Neither Gabrielli, nor Stein knew about the original note. He toyed with the idea of showing the first note, and possibly the second note, to Gabrielli. He could give them o his crime laboratory for analysis. At least, that's how detectives handled clues in the movies and television. Consciously, Jim was very careful in handling the note he had received the night before. As soon as he saw the handwriting, he was cautious to the extent of only touching the edges.

Jim and Dorothy only examined it as it was positioned on the table. Afterwards, he picked it up with a tissue and carefully placed it in the envelope. The envelope was then wrapped in tissue and placed in a pocket of a suitcase. It was going to remain there until Jim found a way to put a handle on the situation.

Later that day Mitchell decided to telephone Efrem Valente and let him think it was only a courtesy call to inquire about his family's health, etc. Possibly he would say something that would give Jim an idea as how to proceed.

After several attempts, the operator got through and Jim heard Efrem's, "Pronto, pronto."

It was a weak connection and Jim hung up. He called the operator once more and asked her to try again. This time Efrem came across loud and clear. After a couple of minutes of small talk and finding out that everyone in his family was fine, and conveying to Efrem that the Mitchells were all in good health too, Efrem said that he had some good news about his "work" and he would explain and "show" them when they came to Modena. He did not volunteer any other news or mention anything else that would make an impact or revelation. Being excited over his job was not a major bit of news. Not then, anyway.

That evening, Jim took a sheet of hotel stationery and made a list of "his friends." He had to look at it the way the writer of that note considered who his friends were. Mitchell's list should contain only those with whom he had been in contact on their last trip. That was obvious. It was going to be a short list, and he began to write slowly and deliberately.

In less than five minutes James Mitchell had written the following:

FRIENDS AND OTHERS

Efrem Valente	Gabrielli
Mario Valente	Stein
Renzo Valente	Col. Giannangeli
Camille (Valente) Caselgrandi	
Andrea Cavelli	
Franco DiMarchi	

The "Friends" names included their immediate families.

Naturally, they had met and seen many other acquaintances and relatives of their "Friends." Jim did not feel that he needed to put their names down. Besides, he had forgotten most of the names and they were not relevant.

He could not, under any circumstances, figure how he could hurt his "Friends" by just seeing them.

Consider Efrem and his brothers -- they were hard working truck drivers. They were honest and had wives, children, and their mother to support. They were only young boys when Il Comandante was at the Academy and he never had any dealings with them. He had visited the Valente farm a few times and saw them there. Jim had to deal them right out of the picture and cross out their names.

Then there was Camille. Jim had never hired her because he was under the impression that she was only sixteen and too young. Lady Raus of the British Red Cross hired Camille after Mitchell left for America. She was out of the mix also.

Next he considered Andrea Cavelli. How could he hurt him? He was well off and in a lucrative business. Although the Valentes snickered whenever Jim mentioned Cavelli's success, they never elaborated as to why they gave each other knowing looks. In one instance, Mitchell was told by Efrem that Cavelli had a silent partner named Mandelli. He was ready to discount Cavelli as the candidate, when he had a thought that brought Andrea right smack dab in the middle of the picture.

"The German," as he named his unknown correspondent must have known about how close they were to being casualties when the accident on Route 65 occurred. He knew Cavelli's truck was involved and surmised that when Jim and his family got to Modena, the subject would come up again!

How right "The German" was! Jim was going to ask how the case against Cavelli was adjudicated. There were other questions on his mind that he wanted to clear up and the only way to do it was to ask questions of the right people.

That had to be it! The only way James Mitchell could hurt Cavelli and his organization was to delve into the court case and find out some facts on his own. He would need help and he had decided to use Erus Caselgrandi's niece who had a prestigious position in the Modena government complex. Jim had decided to do some of that fact-finding long before they left the United States for Italy. At that time, he only wanted to learn the outcome of Cavelli's court case and to find out if they used his prior conviction against him. He was not going out to destroy anyone, only to get the facts for his own satisfaction.

Mitchell drew a line through Franco's name, because it was without a doubt that it would be Cavelli who was on The German's mind when he wrote the note. What was The German's interest in all this? He must have a big reason if he came to Rome in order to leave a note. Something big must hinge on his actions in trying to keep the former Comandante away from Modena.

In his first note, he warned Mitchell to "GO AWAY, DON'T STIR THE POT."

"POT" meant money to Jim then and still did. Big money must be involved in this deal!

CHAPTER FIFTY FIVE
Anzio Beachhead

Upon awakening the next morning, the sheet with the names was on Jim's night table. He tore it into tiny bits and flushed them down the toilet. He needed no reminders of the quandary he was in. His sub-conscious mind would work things out for him as it had many times in the past.

For that day, August 3rd, they had planned to go to Anzio and the Sicily-Rome Cemetery located in Nettuno, and nothing was going to interfere with that visit. James Mitchell had lived on the Anzio beachhead for three months in 1944, and had lost many comrades there. He wanted to visit their graves and pay his respects. It was already twenty-nine years since their deaths in that hellhole that was the beachhead.

★　　★　　★

The Allies held that Anzio beach for several months. It was eight miles inland at its deepest point and about nine miles long along the Tyrrhenian Sea. The enemy was on all sides and the Allies' backs were toward the sea. The Germans were on the high ground and in the mountains. The American positions were in the flat lands where their every movement was observed by the enemy. The same was for the friendly troops who were there with them. The troops lay in their foxholes all day and only came out after dark in order to take care of nature's calls.

At night Jim's platoon went out on patrol and set up their mortars at a site far from their permanent positions. They would then fire their mission on selected targets, then pick up their equipment and leave immediately for their original site. In that way, the enemy would be confused as to where the mortars' positions were. In retaliation, much enemy cannon fire and machine gun fire would focus on the positions that they had left a few minutes before.

Knowing that the Allied troops would be moving about under cover of darkness, the Luftwaffe would become increasingly active and would strafe and bomb the Allied lines intermittently. This type of activity went on all night long and every night. Cannon fire went on day and night. Anzio Annie, one of the largest cannons in history, was located on a railroad car in the mountains to the front of the Fifth Army. When the Germans fired it, everyone on the beachhead would hear the boom as the projectile left the muzzle and a moment later it could be seen and heard. The 561 lb. shell as it tumbled towards its target sounded like a locomotive and was very frightening. There was no defense against that weapon. One certainly could never dig deep enough, so one held his breath and prayed. Praying also was the only defense against other bombardments.

One sunny day in April while the 34th Division was still surrounded on the beachhead, some German fighter planes were strafing the front lines when one of them was hit by the Allied anti-aircraft batteries. The plane came tumbling out of the sky crashed about a hundred yards from Lieutenant Mitchell's position. It struck ground with a "pouf" and black smoke floated up from the wreckage.

Suddenly, machine guns and rifles were being fired upwards by troops who were mostly under Jim's command. They were not firing at the enemy to the front, but up into the air where a German pilot was floating down in his parachute.

Lt. Mitchell yelled, "Cease firing, cease firing," until they stopped.

At that time of day when visibility was excellent, it was not wise to jump out to capture the pilot because positions would be exposed. Instead, Jim picked up the phone and called the battalion headquarters and told them that they were about to get company because the Jerry pilot was going to land in their back yard. Sure enough, while they were still on the line, the men of Headquarters Company hauled the prisoner into the Command Post (C.P.).

At dusk, Lt. James Mitchell slunk over to the headquarters to see the prisoner. The command post was in the basement of a bombed out farmhouse. Jim noticed that the prisoner was holding his left upper arm and was very glum. Unfortunately for him, they had to keep him in the cellar until dark for obvious reasons, and there was no way to safely get a doctor or medic to treat his injuries. So this poor guy had to hold his arm which had been broken by a bullet coming from ground fire.

The German pilot spoke to Lt. Mitchell in perfect English. "You Americans don't fight fairly. Your planes chased me and shot at me, then when I got here, the anti-aircraft guns hit my plane, and then when I parachuted your men shot at me as I was coming down. You don't fight fair."

Jim did not respond to him directly, but he learned from the sergeant in charge that the medics were on their way to take the wounded German pilot back to the field hospital. Incidentally, that hospital where he was going was often shelled and bombed by the enemy. He would be safe as anyone could be on The Anzio Beachhead. There just was no place to hide. The large Red Crosses on the tents were just aiming points for the Nazis. They were also used as reference points for the artillery. By doing that they could deliberately fire at any point with fair accuracy.

CHAPTER FIFTY SIX
The Lord's Intervention

From Rome the Mitchell's drove along the Via Appia Nuova then down past Aprilia towards Anzio. Anzio was a new city, there was nothing left of it after the war. The next town was Nettuno where the Sicily-Rome Cemetery is located.

As they approached the cemetery, Dorothy read from a pamphlet: "The cemetery site covers 77 acres, rising in a gentle slope from a broad pool with an island and cenotaph flanked by groups of Italian cypress trees. Beyond the pool is the immense field of headstones of 7,862 of our military Dead arranged in gentle arcs that sweep across the broad green lawns beneath rows of Roman pines. The majority of these men died in the operations preceding the liberation of Rome."

The Mitchell family was very quiet as they drove into the cemetery and parked.

Jim had tears in his eyes and his throat was choked. He could not speak for several minutes as they walked towards the chapel. The sight of all those Crosses and Stars of David was overwhelming. What a loss! Thousands of young men were buried there and Mitchell knew some of them. Quickly glancing at some of the stones, he could see that officers and enlisted men were buried side by side. Rank had no privileges in this cemetery.

Upon entering the chapel they again were overtaken by a feeling of great sorrow when they saw the engraved names of some 3,094 Missing, whose remains were never recovered or identified. Their names were on the white marble walls. Very impressive, but heartbreaking. The Mitchell family stood there in silent tribute for some minutes and then Jim went over to the information desk to get the location of Lt. Kneece's grave.

First Lieutenant James Mitchell knew very little about 2nd Lieutenant Kneece. He came to Anzio as a replacement about the middle of April 1944. He was commissioned when he graduated from the Citadel. His home was in the Carolinas, Jim couldn't remember whether it was North or South, and he was soft spoken and with a heavy southern accent. Lt. Mitchell couldn't understand everything he said, but they got along fine because there was another officer, nicknamed "Chesty," (his surname was Morris) from Charleston, who acted as interpreter. They did not see much of each other because they were dug in along the Mussolini Canal, and as said earlier, they only ventured from their holes only at night. Actually, they did not "see" each other, but recognized one another by voices. They only spent a few minutes each night with each other for briefings, or other official business, and to receive orders for the next day's operations.

Since Kneece was new, he was assigned to a mortar section of the heavy weapons company. Jim was in charge of another section.

On the evening of May 22, 1944, orders were received stating that the 135th Infantry Regiment was to team up with some units of the 1st Armored Division (tanks) to form Combat Command B. The big push to break out of the Anzio Beachhead was set for "H Hour" which was 0600 the following morning. The next day was to be First Lieutenant James Mitchell's 28th birthday.

That order reared its ugly head like a bad omen to Jim, and he could not picture himself living past the 23rd of May. He recalled thinking to himself that if he could survive the big battle that they were going to face, he would make it though the rest of the war.

A wall had arisen between Mitchell and life, a barrier that had to be overcome that day. If he got past May 23rd, he would be o.k. It was purely a mental bulwark that his subconscious had erected. To him it was very real.

Tomorrow, he would face that test!

At "H Hour," Lt. Mitchell was to lead his men and follow the tanks to the objective that was about two miles behind the present German

An hour or more before dawn, the tanks moved up to Co. H's area and took their positions in front of the company. In doing so, one of the tanks ran over a sergeant's foxhole and ground the sergeant's shoes to bits. Fortunately, the sergeant was not wearing the shoes at the time. He had placed them beside his hole while he slept. Jim didn't remember how, but he got Sergeant Reagan another pair of shoes in time for him to participate in the attack.

Under cover of darkness, the tank companies with help

from the engineers, put together sections of bangalore torpedoes which when completed were about a hundred yards long. The tanks pushed them forward until they went under the enemy's barbed wire fortifications.

Five minutes before he was to lead his men to the Line of Departure, Lt. Mitchell received an order on his walkie-talkie to remain in position and join the reserve units when they reached his area. Lt. Kneece's unit was to proceed and take the route that had originally been designated to Jim Mitchell.

Precisely at H hour, every Allied artillery piece began firing. Naval guns off the coast also participated in the bombardment of the German positions.

The bangalore torpedoes exploded as scheduled and the smoke enveloped the advancing soldiers like a black fog. Soon the sky was also black from the barrages of projectiles fired into enemy territory. The morning had been bright and clear, full of sunshine. In a few minutes, raindrops fell. It was not a hard rain, just a smattering of drops. The sun was still up there in a cloudless sky, but it rained because of the hot smoke and the dark clouds that had formed from the thousands of explosions.

Jim's theory was that the ascending hot smoke reached the cooler air and formed rain clouds. Hard to believe? The lieutenant firmly believed that it was the truth!

The tanks moved forward and Lt. Kneece's men followed in the first wave. No more than five minutes later, Lt. Mitchell's followed the tanks that were in reserve. It would seem that being in that position would be safer, but that was not true. Enemy artillery will always focus on the reserve personnel and supply trains following the front line troops. The enemy infantry and tanks are left to handle the attacking forces.

The German Panzer (Tiger) tank, which was armed with an 88-mm. cannon, was a terrifying piece of equipment. The "88" was far superior to the weapons that the Allied tanks carried. The high velocity weapon's projectiles could easily pierce the armor of the Sherman tanks. The "88' could be used as a weapon against tanks, as an anti-personnel weapon when used with timed bursts, and as anti-aircraft against low flying attack planes.

The Panzer's "88" had a significant sound of its own. Once a soldier heard it, he never forgot it. The sound was terrifying.

The First Armored tanks did not run into German tanks until later in the day. The enemy was completely surprised by the attack that morning. It would take them a day or two to marshal their forces and bring up their reserves from the vicinity of Rome and beyond.

The beachhead had many miles of underground catacombs, which twisted and turned in every direction. The Christians had used them to hide from persecution and while living there improved them. This time the Germans occupied the caves and used them to every advantage. The Allied troops rooted them out and the Germans who surrendered were sent to the rear under escort.

Lt. Kneece's troops came upon a cave that was being defended by the enemy. When the German leaders saw that they were surrounded and there was no way out, they held out a white flag indicating that they wanted to surrender. Rising from his prone position, the Lieutenant gestured to the enemy soldiers to come out.

As Kneece was rising, Sergeant Garner, his second in command, yelled, "Stay down, stay down!"

At that moment, a German soldier emptied his machine gun into Kneece and the Lieutenant fell over mortally wounded.

Sgt. Garner then took over by crawling back out of sight of the cave-bound enemy and getting one of the tanks to fire a round into the cave. A few seconds later white flags appeared once more and the Germans filed out leaving their weapons behind.

Jim Mitchell arrived there a few minutes later and saw the body of James Kneece, his blue eyes still open, his left hand on his stomach where he had been hit. His graduation ring from the Citadel was on his left hand. Lt. Mitchell instructed the sergeant to take off the ring so that it could be sent to Lt. Kneece's family.

Jim was very shaken by that sight. But by the Grace of God, that would have been him! In all probability he would have made the same mistake and his worst fears would have been realized!

Standing beside Lieutenant Kneece's grave, Jim related to his family how by some quirk of fate he was still alive because orders were changed almost at the last moment.

Still more eerie is that the company commander who reversed the order was an officer who was not admired by his men, nor did Jim respect or care for the man at all. Lt. Mitchell did not like the Captain from the moment that he met him. He was crude, loved to drink, and when the action was heaviest, he sought the safest and deepest cover. The officers and men seldom saw him.

Leaving the cemetery, which held almost eight thousand bodies of American soldiers, the Mitchells hardly spoke. Jim was deep in thought thinking of the days they fought in this same area. He had the same contour maps that he carried with him in combat. The positions they occupied in those days were clearly marked, as were the enemy emplacements. Jim was determined to show his family the exact spot where he had dug his foxhole, and the places on the beachhead where they had taken positions from time to time.

He was able to locate where they had lain during those days while under constant fire. The area was now a vineyard, so they couldn't get to the Mussolini Canal. He was satisfied that at least he had taken his family within a few yards of where he had taught himself Italian.

From where they were standing, he was able to point to the hills and mountains to the front where the enemy was located and watched the Allies every move.

On the way back to the hotel, they passed Castel Gondolfo, the Pope's Summer Palace. During the war it was used as an observation post by the Germans. The enemy could see the seaside "resort" of Anzio very easily from that vantage point.

CHAPTER FIFTY SEVEN
Gabrielli Returns

As usual, upon entering the lobby of the hotel, Jim Mitchell went directly to the desk for messages. Surprise, surprise! There was one. It was short and cryptic. Written in Italian by the operator, Jim knew it would lose something in the translation. He was to call Gabrielli at once! Something important! Then a telephone number.

Jim was not in the least bit inclined to call The Chief right away. He was taking them back to three years earlier when they parted with each of them thinking that there was no sense in continuing the investigation regarding the so-called "War Criminal." It was of no concern to him anymore, or to Gabrielli. The way Mitchell now felt about it was to let Stein and his organization, "FIND," pursue the matter. The Israeli government would give Stein all the resources he needed.

"Deal me out." Jim said to himself, "I don't wish to go through that crap again." But he did use harsher words.

After having a good dinner, including pasta, Jim felt a little better inclined to make the call to Gabrielli. It was late in the evening, close to ten o'clock , when he picked up the phone. It was then that he realized that the telephone number written on the message was a local number. If Gabrielli was in town why didn't he wait in the lobby for their return, instead of phoning and leaving a message? Especially if it was that urgent.

Jim placed the call with the operator and waited for her to call back. In a few moments Gabrielli was on the line. Desiring to waste no time, Jim asked him bluntly to tell him what he wanted and why he was in Rome. Before the Chief could answer, Jim also demanded to know how he learned that they were in Italy.

He answered the last question first. "Cavelli told me you were coming. Then I telephoned someone I know in Dogana (Customs) and he found out that you arrived a couple days ago. I arrived this morning but with a very bad cold and fever. Waiting for you in the lobby was impossible. I was too sick. Now I am in bed with whiskey and tonic. Maybe I'll see you tomorrow. I can't talk to you over the phone about my business here. Domani (tomorrow)!"

There was no further conversation.

Jimmy and Judy wanted to spend the following morning at the pool, so they made no plans. It was going to be a restful day for Jim and Dorothy.

In the morning Dorothy said that the swimming pool looked so inviting she decided to join the children. James Mitchell sat in the room and read the complimentary copy of the London Times that was left at the door. He tried to watch television but gave up after a few minutes.

Going back to the Times, he noticed a little item about a war criminal that was abducted from his home in Glifada, Greece, and taken to Israel by a private jet. The jet took off from the American Air Force Base at Hellenikon without the knowledge of the Greek authorities. Could that be the man that Stein was looking for?

Jim took out his 1945 notebook and found the page that read: "Greeks to be sent to Bari on or about 12th Aug." Was the war criminal one of them?

CHAPTER FIFTY EIGHT
The Chief Knows

At eleven o'clock the following morning the phone rang. It was Gabrielli. He said that would wait in the lobby for Mitchell. As usual, Jim scanned the lobby as he walked down the stairs. The only person recognizable was Gabrielli and he was holding a handkerchief to his nose. He withheld offering to shake hands.

"Germe." He coughed. Jim preferred not to pick up a cold in summer either.

James Mitchell motioned towards the bar and the Chief immediately understood the gesture.

"Certainly, I will welcome a drink of brandy. Thank you."

The two sat at a small table in a corner and waited for the waiter to take the order. Jim ordered cappuccino for himself and a brandy for the Chief.

Gabrielli did not speak until he had taken a sip of the brandy. "To cleanse my throat." He explained.

Still holding the London Times in his hand, Jim pointed to the item of the kidnapped war criminal and said, "Was this the man they have been looking for the past three years and more?"

It took Gabrielli a few minutes to digest the story because his English was not that great. He said that the Italian Government had received the information about it from the Greek authorities that angrily deplored the fact that the United States aided the Israelis to kidnap a Greek citizen.

"No, that's not the same man." Gabrielli added.

"Oh," Jim breathed. "Are you sure?"

"Certainly, if he was the man, Stein would have let me know to drop the case."

"You mean that you are actually still on that case, I thought you dropped it three years ago? You were up against a stone wall then."

His eyes red and teary from his cold, Gabrielli forced a smile. "Not stone, my friend, maybe wood - -even paper. We'll find him, if you help us."

"Me, me! How in the world can I help? you know everything that I do! Where do I fit in this time?"

"Non so," The Chief lapsed into Italian, then recovered. " I don't know, but you figure in it somewhere. I am sure you do. But you yourself do not know if you do. We'll find a way, you and me, and maybe Stein."

Up to that day, the only piece of information that Mitchell never revealed to the Chief was the first note with the German script that he had picked up at the Hotel Reale Fini in Modena three years earlier. He never believed that it had any bearing on the case that 'FIND' was working on. Figuring that it was his own private affair and not one for the Italian authorities, Mitchell had kept the note and it's warning to himself.

For a moment, Jim was tempted to tell Gabrielli about both notes that he now had in his possession. He discarded the idea thinking they were not relevant to this investigation. It would be best to talk about them when they get to Modena. Perhaps by then the Chief would have more time to evaluate and probably process the notes through their laboratory. Jim decided this was not the right time to bring the notes into their investigation.

Gabrielli finally came to the point about his trip to see him. First, he wanted to talk to Mitchell in person before any of his friends did. He did not explain why, and Jim did not ask.

Secondly, he thought it would be best if they went over all the questions he had asked three years ago with hopes that Jim would add something to some of the answers.

Thirdly, he seemed to think that the Mitchells still needed protection in light of what had happened in 1970.

James Mitchell was baffled with this last statement, because he did not recall mentioning how close they were to the crash of the Cavelli van to Gabrielli or anyone else.

The Chief was an astute person. He was toying with Jim in a way that would possibly elicit some answers!

To the best of his knowledge, Mitchell answered every question that Gabrielli put to him with the same answer that he had given three years before. He was actually grilling Jim in a way that was not offensive. It was conversation-like. Give and take, with pauses and with small talk about things that had nothing to do with the case. In between, the Chief sipped on more brandy while the American had espresso.

Later, during a short break in their talk, Jim casually handed Gabrielli his notebook. It seemed that he leafed through its pages with polite detachment. Only when he saw the notation "Greeks to be sent to Bari on or about 12th Aug." did he express any real interest.

Even at that, Gabrielli said, "I understand why you thought that the kidnapping in Greece was umportant.

After reading th following page, the Chief looked up at Jim saying, "Here you have written that 600 were to go to the Adriatic during August."

That probably did not seem important to him at all. But did it? This guy was cute!

When he got to the page with Adam Weksler's name on it and his concentration camp serial number, Gabrielli was a bit excited.

"I know this man, he is employed at City Hall and handles foreign mail and communications. He speaks several languages and has an important position. We use him often when we take foreigners into custody!"

"I didn't know that he remained in Modena after I left. I was of the impression he was going to return to his homeland. He was a prisoner of the Nazis in a concentration camp where they also had Jews. I believe that when they evacuated Dachau, they sent Weksler along with the Jews to the refugee camp in Modena. Adam was one of my interpreters. I am so glad to hear that he is in Modena. Now I will make it a point to see him." Mitchell felt happy at the prospect.

The Chief finished his brandy and put down the glass. Obviously, he was feeling better or the drinks were affecting his composure.

"I wish to speak to Signore Weksler, too."

He was still fiddling with the notebook. When he got to the page with the list of bakers, Gabrielli thought it was important enough to take out his own notebook and carefully enter their names.

Noting that there was no reason to copy anything else, he returned the notebook to Jim with a word of thanks.

Upon completing the interview they parted with a friendly "Arrivederci!"

CHAPTER FIFTY NINE
On To Pisa

At midday, Judy insisted upon going to Piazza Navona for lunch and then walk around that area for an hour or two before returning to the hotel. Meals away from the hotel were something to look forward to. While having lunch at the Piazza Navona, the children made the decision to go Trastevere (Across the Tiber River) for dinner. There were some excellent restaurants in that area and Jim's gourmet family decided to dine at one of them that evening. He, too, was game because he'd order pasta. The other three would try exotic entrees.

At home James Mitchell was a meat and potato man, or pasta. Why should he be any different in Italy? Since he was aware that Italy's restaurants are not noted for their steaks, he opted for pasta every time. His son, Jimmy, loved pasta, too. Three years earlier while they were in Florence, Jim took Jimmy out for breakfast one morning and the boy ordered pasta! He was older now and able to make better choices.

That evening, at one of the most famous restaurants in Rome, while waiting to be seated they watched clams in a bowl squirting water. One could tell how fresh the clams were by their activity. It was a curious sight. They had never seen clams displayed in that manner in the United States. In seafood houses one only saw lobsters in tanks with their claws tied. Jim had pasta with white clam sauce that evening.

Early next morning the Mitchells were packed and ready to leave for Pisa. After breakfast, they found that their luggage was already in the lobby. Jim looked around and saw no suspicious looking persons. Their car was parked at the front door and he noticed that the concierge had efficiently corralled a bellboy to transfer their baggage to the vehicle.

While his father paid the bill at the desk, Jimmy was busy supervising the loading at the curb.

Jim shook hands with the concierge and tipped him on the way out. Jimmy took care of the bellhop. They were ready to leave on schedule, according to his son who had efficiently taken over the job as traffic manager.

Judy drove, Jimmy rode shotgun, and Dorothy and Jim rode in the back with one piece of luggage on the seat between them. They had heard about Ostia, a seaside resort, situated about twenty kilometers west of Rome. It was pleasant riding on Via del Mare (Avenue of the Sea) towards the coast. After going twenty kilometers they saw a sign indicating that Lido di Ostia was another eight kilometers. Judy stepped on the gas when reminded her that they were losing precious time, since they were traveling southwest instead of west as Jimmy had calculated. Upon arriving at the beach, they were surprised to see that the so-called sand was jet black. It was pulverized lava from many centuries past. Walking barefooted on the hot "sand" was an impossibility. Sandals had to be worn. Judy and Jimmy had planned to take their shoes and socks off and wade in the salt water. They gave up on that idea when they saw the beach and realized what they were up against.

With Jim driving they turned back four kilometers and then picked up the coastal highway that would take them to Pisa. In less than an hour they reached the port city of Civitavecchia.

CHAPTER SIXTY
A Deserter And his Just Deserts

About June 7th, 1944 after Rome was seized by the Allied forces, Lt. Mitchell's group came upon the railroad yards adjacent to the port Civitavecchia and saw Anzio Annie in all her glory sitting on a railroad flat car. That was the weapon that was used to inflict terror and damage on the military forces on Anzio and its port. It would never be used against anyone again.

Jim climbed up on the flat car and then straddled the barrel that was 70 feet long. That cannon had a range of 36 miles. The weight of Anzio Annie was 218 tons and it spewed shells that weighed 561 pounds!

*   *   *

Continuing on their journey, the Mitchell family arrived at the town of Tarquinia. Jim recalled bivouacking near there one June night in 1944 and awakening to find that they were ensconced in a beautiful olive grove.

The Third Battalion was to rest in the olive grove that day and pull out when darkness fell. While sitting in the shade early that afternoon with his eyes half closed, and enjoying the peace and quiet, Jim noticed the shadow of someone stop in front of him. It was one of his men who had disappeared on the day of the big push to break out of the Anzio Beachhead. His name was DiNardo and he came from Brooklyn. He stood at attention, saluted and stated that he had come to report to the lieutenant and explain where he had been.

DiNardo was missing for more than two weeks. He was unaccounted for from the minute his unit jumped off in the attack. All the men of his squad were not complimentary in making remarks about his disappearance. He was a known malingerer and a screwball.

It was every officer's duty to screen and censor his men's outgoing mail. The letters would be handed to Lieutenant Mitchell unsealed, he would read and seal them, and then write the word "censored" on a corner of the envelope and sign his name.

This guy, DiNardo, wrote the god most awful lies in his

letters. He told how he would go out by himself behind the enemy lines and kill Germans with his hunting knife. Reading his letters made you think that he was a one-man Army. His letters were consistently that way, day after day. There was nothing to censor in his letters because he was never privy to anything secret. Jim had to O.K. every letter including the one where he stated that he knocked out a German machine gun nest with his chrome-plated pistol! The pistol that he wore was not G.I. issue, neither was the knife.

"Get rid of them!" Lt. Mitchell ordered.

DiNardo was a lousy soldier, lazy and shirked his responsibilities even to the point of endangering himself by not improving on his foxhole, or keeping himself clean. Even on the Beachhead, Mitchell insisted that the men shave whenever possible, change their socks, and bathe. Bathing meant putting water in a helmet and washing one's body as far as possible and also washing "possible." DiNardo never met these criteria. He was a menace, not only to his fellow soldiers, but to himself!

Every soldier in Company H knew that DiNardo was a deserter and hoped that he would be punished for it. First, Lt. Mitchell had to listen to the lying alibi: how he got lost in the attack, floundering from one unit to another looking for us for two weeks. He told Jim about his near death experiences, pinned down by enemy fire, and how he had to scrounge for food from soldiers in the field. He lied and lied and lied. There was no evidence of lost weight from hunger and his uniform was clean! That deserter remained far behind the lines until the heavy fighting was over and he could hitch a ride to his unit. He never attempted to report to any American officer to tell him of his plight. If he had done so, he would have been with his company in 24 hours, or less. He chose not to do so and remained A.W.O.L.

Private DiNardo was Number One in composing letters of his heroic deeds, but he was less than a man in accepting his real responsibility as a soldier. Because he chose not to be with his squad, the other men had to tote extra equipment and share in carrying out his duties.

There was only one course of action First Lieutenant James Mitchell could take. He placed DiNardo under arrest and recommended court martial. An investigating officer came to the same conclusion. More than a month later Jim was advised that the deserter received a sentence of five years in the stockade. Sometimes Mitchell thought that's what the man wanted. To him, it would have been better than fighting in the front lines.

Sgt. Heinz

CHAPTER SIXTY ONE
The Massacre

The Mitchells had stopped in Tarquinia to get something to drink and while sitting at a table on the sidewalk, Jim told his family about DiNardo and his fate.

My son, Jimmy, made the remark that, "If that happened now, in the 70's, some organization would demonstrate in his behalf and he would go home a hero." How true!

It was Jimmy's turn to take the wheel and Jim sat beside him. Judy joined her mother in the back seat with that one piece of luggage between them.

Upon reaching the northern part of Tarquinia, Jim noticed a road sign with the arrow pointing to the right and with "Viterbo 42 km."

Seeing the name of that town, the father instinctively shouted, "It was in Viterbo that I had that lady make pasta for us. I'll never forget that!"

His little notebook gave the date of the pasta feast as Monday, June 12, 1944.

Traffic was getting heavy as they approached Grosseto and it was time to change drivers. They halted near a small restaurant, which was open for the vacationing seashore customers. After entering and being seated the Mitchells ordered toasted sandwiches and cokes.

While sitting there eating his "toast," Jim was wondering what other surprises were in store for him in Modena. He couldn't help but wonder if Gabrielli was able to gather any additional information from him while they had that cozy chat in the bar. When leaving, the Chief appeared to be half drunk and with the sniffles. Jim was a bit inclined to conclude that the head of the Surete had failed in his mission.

On the other hand, realizing that the Chief was not the type of investigator who would leave without achieving some success, Mitchell was forced to assume that he did gain something with his persistence. Jim was certain they would meet again and at that time he would find out whether that meeting paid off.

Judy insisted on driving. She just loved the stick shift. In an hour they passed through the town of Cecina where the 3rd Battalion of the 135th Infantry Regiment fought for three days before capturing the town and the heights beyond.

★   ★   ★

One of Lt. Mitchell's men, Pvt. Lingle, was killed there on the 30th of June which was the first day of the attack. Cecina was taken on July 2nd. It was during those three days that the Germans counter attacked against Co. H's heavy machine gun platoon and overran the American positions. Five of the men surrendered and one man faked death.

The Germans had the five stand against a fence and mowed them down with machine guns. The uninjured soldier who was lying there was left for dead. When H Company regained the position, they heard the whole story from the only soldier who survived.

The battalion commander wanted to court martial the survivor for not turning his machine gun against the enemy, and in addition make that soldier pay for the loss of the machine gun that the enemy had captured.

It was a sorry day indeed when Lt. Mitchell and his men learned that their comrades were murdered in cold blood. Jim was on that position when the colonel was there and heard him griping in his guttural German accent. He was a reclaimed German soldier!

151

CHAPTER SIXTY TWO
Two GI's and A Panzer

When the word got around to 3rd Battalion troops about how their colonel had carried on, their morale went down to a very low level. They could not understand how an officer could carry on about a captured machine gun when five men who were executed lay at his feet. Lt. Mitchell couldn't understand either, even knowing that any weapon is valuable. The men muttered to themselves and fittingly called him a Nazi because of his German accent. Jim never found out what the colonel's credentials were and he was not going to ask.

After four more days of heavy fighting for Rosignano, Lt. Mitchell got a reprieve in the form of a five day pass to Rome. When in combat the moment a soldier received a pass he took off for the rear as fast as possible. There was no sense in staying in harm's way and getting killed the next minute. Jim got out in a hurry. The war would still be there when he returned to duty.

When Mitchell registered at the American Officers Rest Hotel which was the Excelsior, he happened to see an officer whom he knew sitting behind the desk. Allowing that officer to be nameless is necessary because the last he had heard of his whereabouts was that on May 23rd at "H" hour he was hightailing to the rear. He was scared stiff. All were scared but did not run. There he was, the manager of the best hotel in Italy, wearing a dress uniform resplendent with medals. He was well rewarded for shirking his duty! While in conversation with him, he showed Lt. Mitchell the Legion of Merit medal that he was wearing. A general awarded that lieutenant the medal for meritorious action in running the hotel. The Legion of Merit is a higher award than the Bronze Star, or Purple Heart. Jim had the latter two medals, but was never awarded the Legion of Merit.

While returning to his unit after the five-days pass, Jim was hoping that the troops would be beyond Rosignano. No such luck, they were practically in the same positions, and the fighting was still heavy. Lt. Mitchell had returned on July 12, 1944. Forty-eight hours later they were going to attack in the direction of Leghorn which was an important port strongly defended by the enemy.

On the 14th of July, the battalion attacked and took the town of Gabbro, which was located on hills overlooking Leghorn. That night the rifle companies moved into the hills to the north of Lt. Mitchell's position. Once they were in place and secure, the heavy weapons were to follow and lend support. Jim and his fellow officers were in radio and telephone contact with those forward units. At about 2:20 P.M., Lt. Mitchell was told that the rifle companies were pinned down by German machine gun fire and that he should go forward alone, locate the enemy machine gun nest, and direct artillery and mortar fire on the enemy machine gun positions.

In a minute, Jim put on his pack, picked up his carbine and walkie talkie, and started to follow the telephone lines that would show him the way to the forward units. A rifleman, who was nearby called out, "Sir, may I go along with you? I'm looking for my company."

"Sure," Jim said, "Follow me."

The first fifty yards beyond Mitchell's foxhole was an open field, then they encountered a draw that was quite deep and was fed by a stream. The two slid down the steep hill, which was wooded and came to the water's edge. It was the 15th of July. The day was very hot and their canteens needed replenishing. The soldier kept his distance. One never bunched up under any circumstances while in a combat zone.

First Lieutenant Mitchell called to his companion and told him to fill his canteen.

"You're going to need the water. You won't have a chance like this for a while." The lieutenant advised.

The stream was flowing on a flat rock base and the water was clear and inviting. The men were about twenty feet apart and stooping to fill their canteens when a missile exploded between them. Jim felt as though someone had hit him with a baseball bat on the back, and he also felt a sharp sting on his left leg.

Lt. Mitchell looked to see how his friend-in-arms was doing and asked him in a loud voice, "Are you hit?"

"Yes," He heard the soldier yell back.

"Where?"

The rifleman laughed, yes, he really laughed before replying.

"In the ass!"

At that moment more shells were exploding all around them..

"Let's get the hell out of here." Jim shouted as he screwed the cap on his canteen.

"I have to find my piece!" The G.I. cried.

"To hell with your goddam gun, let's go!" Lt. Mitchell ordered.

His leg was bleeding profusely, but didn't care about that. It was his back that hurt. The duo tried to crawled back up the hill as fast as they possible could. A German Panzer (Tiger) tank sitting on a bridge overlooking the draw continued taking pot shots with its 88 in their direction. The sound (whizz bang!) of the missiles was as terrifying as the explosions themselves. As the two wounded soldiers reached the top of the draw and safety, they fell to the ground exhausted. They were covered with dirt, blood, and grime.

At 10:30 that night Lieutenant James Mitchell was operated on at a field hospital. His cot was in a tent and he was kept there for one more day. On the 17th of July, he was flown to Rome and placed in the Hospital of the Good Shepherd (Ospedale di Buono Pastore). The Army called it the 6th General Hospital. An operation had been performed on his left leg. Shrapnel had pierced his thigh near the knee. His back was bruised where he had experienced the pain when the shell exploded.

Most certainly if he had been in an upright position instead of stooping to fill his canteen, he would have died on the spot. A large piece of shrapnel skipped over his back, giving him a hard blow but not penetrating his body. The nurses told him that the black and blue area was the size of a baseball. Jim never saw his partner after leaving the first aid station, prior to going to the field hospital in an ambulance.

CHAPTER SIXTY THREE
Tracked Down By "FIND"

The highway on which the Mitchell family was traveling towards Pisa was well marked with signs pointing to the villages and towns. At one point, Jim asked Judy to slow down as they approached a road that branched off to the northeast. As he suspected, the arrowed sign read " Gabbro 6 km." and Judy turned right and they were off to see the spot where he had given some of his blood for a good cause.

Since Gabbro was rather small and there was only one little stream, they soon found the spot where James Mitchell had been wounded. The streambed was almost dried up. There was no marker to note the battle that went on there some 29 years earlier. But the draw was now a dump. All kinds of refuse, tires, bottles, etc. were strewn all over the place.

Jim shook his head sadly after seeing the result of his and the young private's sacrifice. The Mitchells joked about it at the time. And they also noted that many of the National Monument Parks that are in the United States are trashed just as badly, even worse.

It was shortly after five o'clock when they arrived at the outskirts of Pisa. They stopped and asked for directions to the hotel several times, and as they wound their way around the narrow streets Jim observed that a large black car was making every turn they made.

As Judy parked the Fiat in front of the hotel entrance, Mitchell noticed that the black car halted and parked a hundred meters behind them. Coincidence? Maybe. Jim sincerely hoped so. After checking into the hotel and seeing to their comforts, they decided to take a short drive to an area near the Tower of Pisa. It was still daylight so they could take some photos. The next day they intended to visit the Baptistery, the Cathedral, and the famous Leaning Tower.

The first time Lt. Mitchell visited the Leaning Tower, the telephone wires that the Germans had used were still lying on the stairs, running from the top to the bottom. The staircase smelled strongly of urine, attesting to the fact that the Tower was used as an observation post. Since the Tower was so high and had no facilities, the observers let nature take its course on the steps. In 1973 when Jim visited the Leaning Tower with his family, the odor seemed to be there still.

155

They walked about the grounds near the Tower and took some pictures. Jimmy had a great idea. He held the camera while in a crouched position and had his father stand with his right arm outstretched so that the picture would show Jim leaning on the Tower of Pisa. Then Jim took a picture of Jimmy holding up the Tower. They had some laughs in envisioning what the photos would look like when they were developed. Judy and Dorothy did not get involved in those shenanigans.

On their way to the Tower, they had seen several inviting restaurants. During the drive back they decided to explore the possibilities of one of them that served meals on a raised verandah. It was cooler up there and they could observe the street and the people who were strolling on the sidewalk.

The vacationers had taken over the town and their smiles and laughs while having a good time were contagious. That attitude spilled over into the restaurant, and in a short space of time, and helped by the wine and good Italian food, the strangers became friends. One table would "SALUTE" another and the glasses would clink amid laughter. And so it went from table to table.

The Americans could not tolerate wine like the Italians who drink wine every day with their meals. In turn, the Mitchells would raise their glasses, clink them and take a sip. Their new friends at the adjoining tables would take a healthy drink. It was very pleasant indeed. They had made a good choice. At least, Jim thought so until he saw the big black car pull up to the curb.

Jim had paid the check and the waiters had cleared the table, save for their wine glasses that they would bring to their lips intermittently to show the new friends at the adjacent tables that they were Italianized, at least for the evening.

Two men were standing beside the black car as if deciding whether to have dinner or not. Then Jim was distracted when a man at a distant table stood and began to sing an aria from an Italian Opera.

Dorothy said, "He has a fine voice and knows his opera. Perhaps he from Modena, they have some great singers there."

While the tenor was entertaining, two men were standing at the doorway leading to the verandah. They politely remained there until the song ended and the applause had subsided. Like football players, they wove their way between several tables until they stopped beside the Mitchells' table.

The first man was Eisen, who represented the Joint Distribution Committee in 1945, and with whom he had argued and fought with regarding policies Comandante Mitchell adhered to in administering the refugee camp. Stein was the second man.

"Sam," Jim arose to greet him. "You old son of a gun! What are you doing here?"

Mitchell knew damn well what he was doing.

"Seeing the sights, Jim." He answered with a laugh. "You gave us a real Cook's tour today. Tell me, what's with the dumps?" He was referring to Gabbro.

Jim came back with, "My son is an ecology major and I wanted him to see what an Italian dump looks like."

Mitchell also shook hands with Stein and introduced his family. Dorothy had met Stein once three years earlier.

Then Jim took the bull by the proverbial horns and gave them this warning: "Look, you guys, I am not going to let you make me take time away from my family to answer your questions. I know what you are here for. And you know darn well, Martin Stein, that I gave you all the cooperation possible three years ago."

Softening a bit, Jim then asked, "I assume you are still pursuing the same man?"

Sam and Martin answered in unison: "Yes, the same guy, but we are getting closer."

"If you are getting closer, what do you need me for?"

"Probably for assurance," Eisen replied.

"I'll make a deal with you fellows," James Mitchell offered. "We'll be in Modena day after tomorrow. At the Reale Fini. Get in touch with me there and we'll talk about old times. What do you say?"

Stein hesitated for a moment and then confessed, "We've been following you since Rome. Sam and I were afraid we would lose you once you left there. Not knowing your itinerary, we hung on your trail. I'm sorry we intruded. Gabrielli called me and let me know where you were. Our lines of communication with the Modena police have always been open. I got the impression from the Chief that he was through asking you questions. He caught a bad cold in Rome." He chuckled. " Maybe he blamed that on you." Then turning to Eisen, "Let's go, Sam, we'll see Jim later this week."

They were gone, but Mitchell was left with the problem of explaining to his family the reason for that odd visit.

Military Academy at Modenna

CHAPTER SIXTY FOUR
Back In Modena Again

All went to bed immediately upon arriving at their rooms in the hotel. Jim was tired and hopeful that for a day or two no one was going to interfere with their holiday. In addition, he silently resolved not to look for cars or people who could possibly shadow them.

The following morning as they were going to the dining room of the hotel for breakfast, Mitchell noticed that the boys from Israel had already checked out and were going out the front door. They were going to be true to their words. It was the thirteenth of August and he was certain they would see him on "Fra Agosto," the 15th, which is a religious holiday in Italy. In other parts of Italy the holiday was termed "Mezz-Agosto."

They enjoyed the day in Pisa immensely. They visited the Baptistery and the Cathedral. Judy and Jimmy climbed to the top of the Tower of Pisa and waved to their parents as their father took movies of them. Between seeing the sights, they enjoyed some fine dining. Later, all had a mid-afternoon nap in their air-conditioned rooms, and then returned to the restaurant with the verandah where they met and toasted more new friends who sat at adjoining tables. A nice time was had by all.

Jim did all the driving to Modena the next day. Getting to the Autostrada was easy. They went north along the coast for a short distance and then turned east to Lucca, then passed Montecatini and Pistoia. A few miles north of Florence, Jim picked up the Autostrada going north to Bologna and then veered west to Modena. He drove fairly fast, but every car on the road passed their Fiat. He was driving at the speed limit, but the Italians don't believe in signs. No one was arrested for speeding on the Autostrada. They arrived in Modena at two or three o'clock having had only one stop for fuel at a Pavesi rest area, and at that time, picked up sandwiches and a drink.

At the end of that trip, they checked in at the Fini, despite the protestations of the Valente family. The Mitchells enjoyed their hospitality in 1970 but did not think it advisable to take advantage of them this time. They probably would have, if they were able to reciprocate in some way. If only some of them would go to America, then the Mitchells would extend them every courtesy. Dorothy and Jim invited them time and time again. Their home would be the Valente home in America. The Mitchells used the same Italians words in their offer.

★   ★   ★

About five o'clock, Marcello (also called Mario) called up from the desk and invited the Americans to his home for the evening meal. "Mama Elena is making something special for you. I have come to take you."

"I guess we have to go," Jim said to Dorothy. "This is like a command performance. When Mama says you must come, you must obey. Her children never dispute that fact, and neither will I."

"Mario, we'll be down in ten minutes, piacere (please)." He would wait.

When they arrived at Via Tardini and entered Mama's apartment, the Mitchells found the whole clan there and were kissed by all of them, men, women and children.

Mama made a special lasagna with a delicate white sauce, which Dorothy was not able to duplicate at home even though she got the recipe from the "horse's mouth."

Dorothy noted that the Valentes' families were small. Only Renzo had two children, his brothers and sister had one child each. It seemed to be the trend in northern Italy. In the south, families were larger.

Jim figured that Renzo had two children because the first one was a girl. The second was a boy. All of Renzo's siblings had boys first, then no more. Italy was well on the road to population control.

As Mario drove them back to the hotel, he reminded them that the next day was a big holiday and every business place would be closed, so they must go to his apartment for dinner at noon. He would not take no for an answer. The Americans were locked in again!

It was then that Jim wondered if he would be able to accept because of the visitors he was sure to have the next day. Dorothy made up their minds. She said, "Si, Grazie." By doing so, she took the matter right out of her husband's hands.

CHAPTER SIXTY FIVE
Mandelli's German Ties

Giacamo Mandelli was anxious and troubled. It was only two days before "Fra Agosto," the national religious holiday. Mandelli was not religious but he acceded to his wife's wishes in celebrating that festive day. They had come to their mountain retreat in Rabbi, a small town near Trento and noted for its spa and the natural mineral waters.

The air was cool and refreshing where Mandelli sat on the verandah which overlooked the wild water roaring past the old flour mill. It was soothing watching the white, foaming waters of the rapids. The sight made one feel cooler than it actually was and it was often necessary to use a lap robe in summer.

The altitude was discomforting the first two days until one became accustomed to the thin air. Mandelli and his wife, Marissa, had already overcome that hurdle.

Nevertheless, Mandelli dreaded his scheduled meeting with his associates in Ivrea. It was a meeting that he could not postpone using the holiday as an excuse. That group of men, of which he was a part, did not believe in religious holidays either. They worshiped power and money. Their agenda was fixed and exact. No deviations were allowed.

Mandelli was going to leave early the next morning for Ivrea. It was going to be a long ride. From his position on the porch, Mandelli could see his driver washing the car and preparing for the trip. The meeting was going to be very trying on this man who was growing in age and who began to change his values and aims in life during the last three years.

He was appreciating Cavelli more and could now see his partner's view of their problems. Their ties to Mitchell monetarily did not hurt them personally, however the syndicate thought differently. Mandelli was preparing himself to push his case on the morrow.

*　　*　　*

Giacamo Mandelli was sweating and the only one remaining seated. The other three members were standing and facing him. It was an old trick, looking down on the person

161

being interrogated. It gave them a feeling of superiority and they were using it to its fullest.

However, Mandelli having seen the light and with the feeling that he had 'religion' by changing his attitude, was holding his own to some extent. He eyed his tormentors with contempt. Quite a change from their previous meetings when he had rigidly adhered to their principles. Their ideas seemed to have been washed away from his mind as swiftly and solidly as the rushing waters of the stream in Rabbi.

The meeting was conducted in German. The leader was a tall blond man, hair tinged slightly with gray. He held a gold headed baton in his gloved right hand. Mandelli could never understand why the man wore gloves all the time and he did not question it.

"This man, Mitchell, is a threat to all of us and yet you deny it. A few years ago you realized the danger that he posed to our organization. Why the change in your thinking?" The end of the baton slapped the palm of the leader's left hand as if to punctuate his question.

"I strongly urge you to believe that the 'comandante' is not here to hurt us. He has his family with him and they are here in friendship and to enjoy themselves. I firmly believe that and hope that I can convince you of that."

A second man countered with, "How can you be sure? Previously, you all gave me the feeling that he was our worst enemy. I cannot shake off the idea that things have changed so dramatically and the courses of action that are under discussion should be shelved. We must adhere to the principles of our organization. If we do not, we will surely lose. How can we turn our backs on the facts? Payments have been made to him regularly for the past twenty-eight years. Why? Because he knows of us and what we are doing.....and more"....

The third man interrupted, "I agree. There is no assurance that he will remain quiet. The Jews are following him. They must know that he knows. It is simple at that. Sooner or later, he will tell them everything. We must stop him, or we will all go down."

Mandelli's pleadings did not move the formidable three that now felt that their invulnerability was short lived by the presence of the former commandant in Italy.

The leader spoke to Mandelli with finality and force-

162

fully, "We three will handle matters in our own way. You are now our weakest link. This problem is out of your hands and we will not let you know of our plans. If you are ever questioned you will know nothing."

Turning towards the other members, the leader said, "This meeting is adjourned." Then peculiarly he added a nicety. "Auf wiedersehen."

CHAPTER SIXTY SIX
The Refugee Files

All were up early on 'Fra Agosto' and, rather than waste the morning, Jim decided to call General Franco Barbolini at the Military Academy. It was only 8:30 and he knew the General would be up and around at that hour, if he was the type of military person that would be in command of that facility. Sure enough, he picked up the phone at his operator's first ring.

"General," Jim began, "This is Colonel Mitchell from the United States. I was hoping that you will have some time for me this morning." He spoke in English, since the invitation that he had received was written that way.

The response was crisp and clear, "Yes, of course. Colonel Giannangeli spoke highly of you. Please come, most of the students and staff have gone on holiday. It would be a good time for me and for you."

"Thank you, General." Mitchell paused, then continued, "If I may, I would like to ask a big favor of you. Three years ago we were unable to see the apartment that I occupied in 1945, the Princess' rooms, because of work that was being done. I'd like my family to see it."

"Certamente," Lapsing into Italian, then quickly recovering, the general was gracious in his response. "Certainly. That is my apartment now and I will be privileged to show it to you."

"I can't thank you enough, sir. Will 9:15 be too early?"

"Not for me." General Barbolini replied. "I will tell the guards at the entrance to permit you to pass."

Dorothy searched through one piece of luggage that contained gifts for their Italian friends. Most of them were silver plated items. She selected a tray that was in a velvety bag with a gold drawstring. It did not need to be gift-wrapped. It was a good choice.

The Mitchell family presented itself at the gate at precisely 9:15 A.M. The guards saluted them and one escorted them to the General's office.

He greeted them cordially. Jim was impressed with the improvements to the same office that he had once used. It was now air conditioned, furnished with the best leather covered furniture, and had oriental rugs on the beautiful marble floor. It was the same floor Lt. Mitchell had, but it was now cleaned and polished to perfection.

General Barbolini was in his sixties with graying hair, about 5'10" in height, and without an ounce of fat. His uniform was immaculate, and ribbons and medals were displayed on both sides of his chest. He was what Mitchell would consider a perfect example of a man who should be in command of a national military academy.

The general graciously accepted the gift that Dorothy had brought and put it on display in a large curio cabinet.

"Come," The General said invitingly, "I will show you my quarters." Then he turned and addressed the children. "It is the same apartment that your father occupied when he was commandant."

The apartment was magnificent by any stretch of the imagination. The high ceilings and its borders decorated with gold leaf, and the large windows with shutters made by artists of a bygone era were exquisite. When Jim occupied those same rooms, he was not impressed as much. The bedroom and the adjacent sitting room were furnished with antique chairs and couches that were reupholstered with tapestry.

Dorothy stated that the furnishings were breathtaking and asked the General where they had come from. She pointed to the bed and said , "Like all the other furniture, this must be centuries old."

The General smiled and replied, "Most of these were stored in the sub-basement during the war to protect them from bombings. Works of art, especially paintings, and our archives were kept there for years."

The kitchen was ultra modern, and the dining room fascinated the Jimmy and Judy. It was very large with murals on the ceiling and the frescoed borders were painted with gold leaf. The table Comandante Mitchell's dined on many years ago was still being used. Its massive legs were hand carved, and it was very wide and long, longer than Jim had remembered. It was one article of furniture that could not be hauled down to the sub-basement. Jim sat down on the chair at the head of the table, the same spot where he was served many meals. And it was at that moment that Mitchell recalled what the General had said earlier about "archives" being stored.

165

Looking up at the General, he asked, "You mentioned something about storing records in the sub-basement, what types of files are still stored there?"

The General thought for a moment, pursed his lips, and said slowly, "When I was an instructor here in the late 1940's, we would punish cadets by sending them down there to file records and papers that had accumulated during the war. It was a dusty job, and over the years, we have been able to restore the archives in some semblance of order."

He paused for a moment, then added, "We even have the records that you kept when the Academy was used as a refugee center."

That was very interesting! Very, very interesting!

Jim followed with, "Will it be possible to see some of the refugee records? They aren't secret."

"Later. I'll take you down to the records room personally."

Judy wanted to see the princess' bathroom that had been described to her. In 1945, the bathroom was equipped with an electric hot water heater! The room was very ornate and with all the newest plumbing. The vitreous fixtures were pink and the tub had a shower. It was great for the American commandant, because he had spent the past two years living in the field with no facilities.

Although newly decorated and painted, the bathroom still retained the same fixtures of 1945. Judy was enthralled! It was still fit for a princess.

On their last visit to the Academy in 1970, Jim had told his family about the dungeon that was on the floor beneath the apartment. This was his chance to show it to them. He cautiously led them down the narrow staircase to the floor below. There was a bedroom on one side where the body-guards slept, and another short stairway that led to the "dungeon". It was actually a jail cell that appeared like a cage in a zoo, with metal bars from floor to ceiling on two sides.

On the far wall of the cell two pairs of iron rings were cemented into the wall. The comandante had been told that the room was used to torture prisoners during interrogation for centuries, and had been used by the Fascists in the 1930's and 1940's. Dorothy and Judy did not spend much time looking at the cell, but Jimmy was intrigued. The General stood by watching with amusement.

166

Then the General took charge once more and led them down to the ground floor and a room that opened up to the courtyard.

It was Jimmy's turn to ask about something. "I remember, Dad, about the jail that was in this courtyard. Is it still there?"

"Come on, I'll show you, it's right over there." Jim pointed to a far corner of the courtyard, and all walked towards it. It was still there, but unoccupied. The Comandante had made good use of it only one time. Two Italian soldiers half dragged and half carried a drunken refugee into his presence one day and asked what to do with him. He was making a nuisance of himself by bothering the women. It was Yacob.

"Throw him in jail!" Lt. Mitchell had ordered in disgust.

It was about a week or so later that the Captain who was in command of the Italian Guards came to see me about the disposition of the prisoner.

"Oh, my God!" Jim moaned. He had forgotten about him!

The pressures of his job as Commandant were so great at that time that Lt. Mitchell had completely forgotten about the prisoner. Jim only meant to sentence him for an overnight stay in the jail to sleep off his drunkenness. He never forgot the injustice of it!

General Barbolini looked at his watch. He had been very patient and cooperative. He said, "I have some things to take care of at this time. Let the ladies go up the stairs to the balcony and see the beautiful works in marble that are displayed."

Then he faced James Mitchell. "Colonel, I'll have a member of my staff take you down to the sub-basement and show you the files of the refugees that are stored there. I'll join you later."

Jim thanked him for his courtesy. Dorothy and Judy walked up the wide marble stairway to the balcony, while Jimmy and his father waited for their escort. A lieutenant appeared in a few minutes to show them the way.

Comandante Mitchell had been down the two stairways in 1945 when basement and sub-basement were dark, damp and airless. He did not spend much time exploring them.

CHAPTER SIXTY SEVEN
The Purloined Records

The basements were cluttered with large boxes and statues and statuettes that were covered with dust. Jim Mitchell recognized no value in them at that time, but now he realized that he was vastly mistaken. Some of the art treasures stored there were priceless.

The basements were transformed with modern electric lighting and Jim could see that they were clean. The sub-basement was partitioned, there were many cages along one wall, and each was clearly marked. Many of the cages containing file cabinets were padlocked which meant that they were off limits. The lieutenant led them to a far corner, and Mitchell could see that the cage had a faded sign that said: "Evacuation Camp No.24". The gate was not locked.

Reaching that section, the Lieutenant showed some interest, and he let me know that he had spent many hours in that cage filing. Jim laughed and said that he must have been a bad boy. He nodded and joined in the laughter. Saying that he would leave them for a while, their escort turned and walked towards the stairs.

Mitchell wasted no time in going to the file cabinets and reading the inventory cards that were inserted in front of each drawer. There were ten file cabinets in all, but they held the vital statistics and records of the many thousands of refugees that passed through the camp. The cadets had done a neat job of filing despite the fact that the cards and papers had deteriorated with age.

Jim was mainly interested in the registration cards. After searching through them, he was going to look through the correspondence files. He wasn't sure what to look for, but he was willing to take a stab at it. Jimmy was going to help.

They went to the registration cards first. Upon arrival at the camp, the refugees were given cards to fill out. Interpreters and clerks were on hand to help them. Most were literate and could write their names and country of origin. The office also needed their vital statistics, age, height, weight, etc.. Former addresses were requested, but the Jews never filled in that portion except to write "Palestine." Jim took out his notebook and gave Jimmy the name: Josef Gelbart. Jim looked for Leo Friedmann.

They found the two cards quickly. The cadets had done a marvelous job of filing. Soon they found Schaumann, Goldberg and Nussbaum. It was too good to be true!

Jeolic and Weksler were assigned to Jimmy. Jim was going to search for Mandil and Klein.

Searching through the M's for Jakob (or Jacob) Mandil, Jim found many Mandels, but not a single Jacob. Mandil's card was not in the file and Jim doubted if it ever existed.

Jimmy had no problem completing his assignment and handed the cards to his father. There were now seven cards in his possession and Jim shoved them into his inside coat pocket. He would read them later. The Academy would never miss them. Mitchell and his son were probably the only persons who ever searched those files for data.

Having only to look for Yacob Klein's card, Jim asked his son to look for correspondence regarding Jacob Mandil or anyone close to that name.

Yacob's card was easy to find and he immediately put it with the others. Jim then moved over to the correspondence and searched for Klein. He found no correspondence, but did find a memo with Klein as the subject. It was dated August 10th, 1945. That found its way into a pocket, also.

Jimmy was unsuccessful in his search for Mandil.

Then they turned to the files marked 'Imbarco' (Shipment). They were filed by dates of embarkation. Jim looked for August 1945 and found six manifests that were typewritten with hundreds of names and their destinations. Stuffing them in one pocket would have been a dead giveaway, so he folded them hurriedly and distributed them to other suit pockets and one set in his pants pocket. It was perfect.

The only name they did not find was 'Mandil.' If he were a war criminal, he certainly would not use his name. Getting new identity papers would have been a snap. Money could buy anything during that period, but not with German marks!

The young lieutenant returned and asked if he could help in any way. Mitchell thanked him and said they were satisfied.

"Very interesting," Jim said truthfully as they went upstairs.

Judy and Dorothy were at the bottom of the stairway to the balcony. They commented about the art that was displayed, then all followed the lieutenant to the General's office. General Barbolini had a visitor, but came to the open door when he saw the Mitchells approaching. They thanked him for his kindness and left him to his duties. They had taken up more than two hours of his time, for which Jim was deeply grateful.

CHAPTER SIXTY EIGHT
The Israeli Duo (Agents)

Noon was approaching and the Americans had a dinner date with Mario and Ada, his wife. Their son, Fabrizio, would be there, too.

Ada outdid herself that day. She had soup with angel hair pasta to start. Then cheese ravioli with the cream white sauce that Dorothy and the children liked. Jim always preferred red sauce, except when he dined on pasta with clams.

After the ravioli Ada brought out a meat platter containing what Jim recognized as pork, and something that looked like chicken laden with garlic sauce. He tried the pork, the others tried the 'chicken.' Judy loved the taste. Jimmy thought it was O.K., and only Dorothy knew what it was. It was rabbit!

Efrem dropped in and joined them. They saluted each other with their wine glasses. As usual, Jim added carbonated water to his 'vino.'

They were sought out by Efrem because, as he put it, "I want to show you my work."

Dorothy and Jim decided to decline for that day, at least, because it seemed that he wanted to show them his new "job".

"Domani (tomorrow)." Jim replied. That made Efrem happy.

On the way back to the Hotel Fini, the Mitchells wondered what his "work" could be. They decided that if it was that important, it was only proper that they go with him.

As Jim parked the car, it occurred to him that he had subconsciously forgotten about the promise that he had made to Stein and Eisen. They were supposed to meet on the 15th of August.

"Lots of time," Jim thought. "It is only three o'clock."

And there they were, Stein and Eisen, waiting in the lobby. Fortunately, Jim had stuffed all the papers, purloined from the archives of the Accademia, into the glove compartment of the car. Also, by good luck, he had completely forgotten about them. He would look over the stolen files in good time. Meanwhile, he had to handle the Israeli agents.

The Mitchell family walked towards the elevators but Jim peeled off towards Martin Stein, the Brooklynite, and Sam Eisen, from Philadelphia, who were now Israelis with dual citizenship. Mitchell motioned to them to go to the bar.

CHAPTER SIXTY NINE
Jim's Swiss Bank Account

"Hi, gentlemen! Have you been waiting long? I'm sorry if you have --." Jim was interrupted by Stein before he could finish.

"Not long." He lied.

"Well let's sit down over here in the corner, and have something to drink. I'm going to have a nice cold beer."

A waiter loomed over them as they were seating themselves. He was about 6'4".

"Get me German beer and a glass with ice in it." That was Mitchell's standing order in foreign countries because the drinks were never cold enough to suit him.

"Sounds good to me." Came from Eisen.

"Me too!" Echoed Stein.

It appeared to Jim that they were not at ease. Eisen looked at Stein to begin talking. Then Stein would look towards Eisen to start. It was up to Jim to take the initiative.

"Bring me up to date on the case of the man you are looking for. I believe that you must have recently picked up some new information on Mandil, or you wouldn't be here in Modena. When I left here three years ago, the trail was ice cold, just like the beer we are going to drink. Tell me, what did you find? If it is top secret, just say "no", and I'll shut up."

They both squirmed as though they were trying to screw up courage, and each one was reluctant to respond to the question.

The cold beer arrived in time to give them a break, and to give Jim time to take a long drink.

It was Eisen who spoke first. "Jim, for many years we have been investigating some Swiss banks that we know has accounts belonging to holocaust survivors or their families. We have been successful to some extent, but we have never received the honest cooperation from the banks. Our investigators uncovered one strange account recently, and that's why we are here. Our auditors were permitted by court order, despite the Bank's protest, to check the names against the private numbers that are issued for the accounts. Whenever a name on the rosters appeared to be Jewish or of German origin, the account with its number would be examined for dates of deposit and other information."

He paused and sipped his beer. It was an interesting story.

Now it was Stein's turn and he said something that was stunning. "One of the names was that of a "James Mitchell"!

"You're kidding!" Jim exclaimed. There was a long silence, then he said, "But mine is a Christian name. Explain that!"

Stein opened his mouth to continue, thought better of it, and was eyeing Mitchell's every move.

With some hesitation and embarrassment Stein answered Jim's query.

"Understandably our agents went over the line and looked for your name in their searches. Possibly on a hunch. I don't know. But we have found an account in your name." His last sentence was in a hushed tone.

Continuing, Stein said, "The initial deposit to that account was made in August 1945, and there have been regular installments ever since. Quite a sum of money has accumulated there including 28 years of interest."

"Now, Jim," Eisen began. "Tell us your side of the story."

"What side of what story?" Jim countered. "That's not my bank account. There are a lot of James Mitchells in this world. Just pick up any city phone directory!"

He took another long swig of beer. It needed more ice. Jim beckoned the waiter and asked for a refill and lots of ice in a separate glass. He was in no way prepared for what came next.

With a half smile, Martin Stein startled Mitchell by saying, "I acknowledge that there are a lot of James Mitchells. But this one lives in Allentown, Pennsylvania!"

"You're full of shit!" Jim cried angrily. "Now talk sense. If you can't handle your beer, keep quiet!"

"Take it easy, Jim," Stein hastened with assurance. "Now we can see by your actions that you know nothing about that account. We had to make sure. The only person who has access to the account is the one who has the secret number."

Mitchell calmed down a bit. They had been testing him.

"What was the home address listed for that account?" He asked.

Eisen had his notebook at the ready. "Fullerton Avenue."

The American laughed hard and long. "I haven't lived there since 1951. That was 22 years ago. I certainly would have changed the address for something that valuable. Tell me something else, where did the deposits come from? What city, what country?"

Stein took a drink, wiped his mouth with his napkin, and with great deliberation, began, "That's the main reason why we thought you were not in the picture. The money came from Italy through an anonymous person. The Swiss bankers never ask questions of anyone who deposits money. We know the deposits were made with American dollars, but they were transferred through Italian banks in Florence and Milan."

"Wow, the person who figured that out must be a smart cookie! Can you give me a ball park figure of the amount?"

Again it was Eisen with his notebook, "Over a million."

"A million lire? That's chicken feed!"

Sam and Martin laughed out loud, then in unison: "Bucks!"

"Holy cow! Can you give me the number of the account?" Jim asked with a laugh.

"Not on your life." One of them responded. They all roared. The ice was broken. They were friends once more.

Jim noticed that the two Israeli investigators from FIND were relieved, and so was he. He knew that it was going to take a long time before they would follow the money trail to its origin. Italy, with all its bureaucracy, was going to make their attempts to get answers very difficult. With bribery and political pressure, the agents could possibly make progress. The process was going to be very slow. He could foresee that.

It was his turn again. "Does Gabrielli know about this?"

"Of course." Stein answered. "We keep him up to date on everything we learn and he reciprocates. It is a pleasure to work with him. Other departments in Italy are not as cooperative."

So Gabrielli has known about this all along, Jim thought to himself, perhaps that is why he has tried to be protective.

Martin Stein and Sam Eisen rose to leave. Jim assumed that Gabrielli had reported what little, if any, information he got from him. They had no more questions, except one.

174

It was Eisen who needled Mitchell with, "Find any more dumps lately?"

Jim answered by punching his arm.

"I'll pick up the tab," He offered, "If you give me the number."

"No, thanks." Answered Stein, as he made his way to the bar to pay the check.

Jim left the tip on the table.

CHAPTER SEVENTY
Is It In The Cards?

Without having to ask the men from Israel another question, Mitchell knew that there was a common denominator between him and the man they were looking for. The investigators tied him in with Mr. X, because the bank account was started in August 1945 and he was in Modena during that period.

"It had to be someone who knew me rather well, since he used my name and address." Mitchell thought to himself.

In thinking it over, as he made his way to their rooms, he realized that this friend was somehow linked to the source of the deposits. "Follow the money" was going to be the agents' motto.

Jim was going to try to beat them to it. After reaching his floor, he returned to the elevator and pressed the 'down' button. He went to the car to retrieve the "purloined papers."

While the rest of his family napped, Jim picked up the registration cards and carefully looked them over one at a time:

Gelbart, Josef   Born 1895 Poland   Catholic
Shipped to U.S. Dec. 12, 1945

Friedmann, Leo   Born 1897 Palestine Jew
Shipped to Bari Nov. 15, 1945

Schaumann, Bernard Born 1901 Palestine   Jew
Shipped to Bari   Nov. 15, 1945

Goldberg, Berisch   Born 1893 Palestine   Jew
Shipped to Bari Nov.15, 1945

Nussbaum, Wilhelm   Born 1897 Palestine   Jew
Shipped to Bari   Nov. 15, 1945

It appeared that the four bakers remained together for the trip to their "Promised Land." Palestine.

Gelbart, the cook, went to America. That was his dream.

Jeolic, Anthony Born 1906 Czechoslovakia   Catholic
Weksler, Adam   Born 1908 Czechoslovakia   Catholic

There was no record of Jeolic being shipped. Therefore, Jim assumed he also remained in Italy like Adam Weksler.

m/Klein, Yacob Born 1904   Palestine

Here again, Yacob had written an "M" and crossed it out. In 'Yacob," Jim noticed that a faded 'k' was under the letter 'c," Freudian slips, he presumed. Surprisingly that part under "Religion" was left blank. There was no date of being shipped to Bari, which was the embarkation point for Palestine.

He carefully unfolded the memo that had Klein's name as the subject. It was dated August 10, 1945.

The body of the memo stated: "Klein, Yacob - taken to Milan hospital by Cavelli and DiMarchi on 8 August. Permission given by Comdnt. Mitchell." It was signed: Franca Zanoli. She was a clerk in the office.

Permission was given to Cavelli for a couple of days off to have an outing with his family. Franco was given time off for "whatever." Their 'official' time off had no connection with Klein, or the hospital in Milan.

The little packet contained a wealth of information. Like a jigsaw puzzle, if they could match all the pieces, Jim was sure they would come up with an answer.

He pulled out the postcard that he had received from some of the service personnel. It was dated 15 August, yet Yacob Klein's signature was on it. Cavelli and DiMarchi did not take him to Milan. They took him to Lake Garda.

The distance to the lake from Modena was roughly half of what the distance would be to Milan. Klein probably met the others accidentally at the lake and spent time with them. At least, Jeolic, Schaumann, and Weksler accepted him as a fellow refugee and not as "SS" as accused by others.

It was unnecessary to go through the Shipment files for August 1945. It would be too time consuming, and Jim doubted if he could learn anything more by poring over the hundreds of names they contained.

Three years earlier, when he had some conversations with Martin Stein, he had reminded Jim that the way they had traced the war criminals was by the "money trail" that they left behind. In fleeing, they carried works of art, gold, and precious stones with them. They sold pieces along the way when they needed money to bribe or buy their safety. "FIND" would trace the jewelry, stones, and art.

Most of the items were accumulated by the German leaders during the war. They were stolen from museums, banks, jewelry stores. The Nazis looted all the occupied countries and shipped trainloads of art and artifacts back to Germany. Of course, much of it found its way into the coffers of the high-ranking officers including Goering.

Jim crossed the room to the sofa and stretched out. Sleep came easily.

His nap was not without dreams. He was in the courtyard of the Academy, and amidst a rush of humanity he saw a man running for his life. He had his arms outstretched and was reaching for the comandante. Jim put his arms out to help, but he could not touch him. And the man kept running and running, terrified and screaming. Jim still could not reach him. It was Yacob Klein. As the mob enveloped him, he was looking over his shoulder and screaming for Lt. Mitchell to help.

Jim woke with a start.

As he dwelt on the dream for a few minutes before sleep overcame him once more, it was reminiscent of the day he went to Cavelli's shop, and saw a man glance to his rear as he was running for the exit. His sub-conscious mind brought him to the realization that the man in the store was none other than Yacob Klein!

So far, he knew that Yacob, Adam, and Anthony never left Italy. Adam was positively in Modena, so was Yacob, and he knew Anthony would make three.

Time and time again, he looked at the "puzzle pieces" (as he called them). The two warning messages were still in an envelope that he intended to give Gabrielli for analysis in his crime lab. During the Chief's visit while they were in Rome, he was distracted both by his cold and his intrusion. He completely forgot to give him the envelope. Jim was certain that Gabrielli would call on him again. Actually, the American was looking forward to it.

The second note ended with: "DON'T HURT YOUR FRIENDS." At that rate he would have to add Wexler and Jeolic to his column of "Friends." Where would Klein fit? Did he consider Jim as a friend, because he once saved his life? Or should he be placed under "Other?" That question was debatable.

*　　*　　*

178

The Mitchells ordered room service that evening. Jimmy and Judy liked the novelty of it and it suited Dad because he had taken off his shoes and tie. Dorothy went with the flow.

It had been a long day. It was still Wednesday, August 15, 1945, "Fra Agosto"! Jim wondered what surprises were in store for him the next day. Although he was not a detective, he felt that he was making some progress. He was still holding the premise that if FIND, Gabrielli, and Mitchell would sit down at one table, they could put all their pieces of information together and come up with a final picture.

*   *   *

Just before eight o'clock, the next morning, the phone rang. It was Gabrielli. He was most irritating some times.

"Don't you ever sleep?" The American asked with some acidity.

"Not if I can help it." Was his reply.

"I'm still in bed." Jim protested. "Call back at a reasonable hour."

"I'll wait for you to come down. We'll have coffee together. Take your time, I'll read the 'giornale' (newspaper). Be 'informale'."

He meant that Jim did not have to wear a coat and tie. The Chief was getting to him -- dictating how he should dress. Gabrielle was some character, but on their side.

CHAPTER SEVENTY ONE
Dreams

Mitchell took his time, shaved and showered, and put on casual clothes, including shorts. The children were still asleep, so he told Dorothy to call room service when they were ready for breakfast. He left for the dining room to have a continental breakfast with Gabrielli.

The Chief looked a lot better than when seen last. His cold was gone and he seemed to be in good spirits.

As usual, they took a table in a corner of the dining room. A buffet table was laden with rolls and buns of all types, some fruit, and juices. Jim opted for a plain roll, a pat of butter, and a small glass of orange juice. The waiter had already filled their coffee cups. Mitchell had chosen American, Gabrielle had espresso. The Chief picked up two large sweet rolls that he eyed hungrily. He had been up early and had no breakfast.

Taking the offensive, Mitchell opened the conversation by asking why he was not informed about the million plus dollars in a Swiss Bank.

"It was of no concern to you. After seeing the report, I concluded that it was not yours. Every transaction took place here, and you were away for twenty-five years. It did not make sense. Someone had to be using your name for his own ends. I told Stein and Eisen the same thing, but they had to find out for themselves. I saw them yesterday after your meeting. They were embarrassed for not taking my advice and wasting two or three days looking for you."

"Thanks for your confidence in me, Chief." Jim handed him the envelope that contained the two warnings. "Here's a present for you. Be careful with the contents. You may want to check them for prints, and do whatever else you detectives do with clues." He ended with a laugh.

Carefully opening the flap, Gabrielli blew into the envelope to make it expand, and tried to see what it contained. He then let the notes fall on to the tablecloth.

Gabrielli then took out tweezers and carefully picked up one of the notes. "What does this mean?" He read: "Don't stir the pot!"

"I'm not sure," Jim answered. "I believe 'mind your own business'. It's a threat and three years old."

"I'm sure it was a threat." Said the Chief as he nodded his head. "I knew about Cavelli's truck, but I could not prove anything because the driver and helper were killed. That was not an ordinary accident. You and your family were very fortunate."

He took a deep breath and added, "For what reason were they trying to kill you? We will find out some day."

Gabrielli had just verified Jim's worst suspicions, and it disturbed him greatly.

Mitchell did not have to translate the second note.

The Chief pondered over the latest note, then said, "I cannot understand how you could hurt your friends by going to Modena."

"I received that note at our hotel in Rome."

At that, Gabrielli rubbed his forehead.

"These must be powerful people if they have the resources to get information about your whereabouts. I have Italy's entire network of police and other government agencies to work with, and it is still difficult to get the data I need. There are people in high places helping the ones who were looking for you. I must investigate this! These notes were obviously written by a German or an Austrian. He knows the English language and maybe other languages, too."

He was spilling out words as though talking to himself.

As Gabrielli went on, Jim nodded in agreement.

"Now," The Chief continued, "We must put the Swiss account in the pot. See, I used the word 'pot,' just like the note. It's money that this is all about. It is possible that the writer of the notes is afraid that you would get wind of the bank account and try to lay your hands on it. It has to be someone who knows you now or knew you in 1945 when you were Comandante. One person in the thousands that passed through!"

"You are right about that. Many thousands did pass through our facility, but I personally only knew relatively few."

Taking out his notebook, Jim tore out a page, and copied all the names that he had on the list of "my Friends" list and "Others." While he was copying, Gabrielli was wolfing down another sweet roll.

Handing the list to the Chief with a flourish, Jim said, "That man, Jeolic, is a friend of Weksler. When you see Weksler, ask about him."

The Chief looked over the list carefully. "This Yacob Klein, where does he fit in? You don't have him listed as "friend," or "other." You put his name on one side, by itself. Why?"

"He was no friend of mine. He gave me some problems sometimes. I saved his life once. I am not sure where he fits, but I have a crazy idea that came to me after I had a dream." Jim said apologetically.

Gabrielli raised his eyebrows at the last sentence. "Tell me about your 'crazy' idea and dream."

Mitchell went on to relate the dream he had on the afternoon of Stein and Eisen's visit. How he couldn't reach Yacob no matter how he stretched, and he couldn't get to The Comandante because of the mob, and how he was finally going away from Mitchell and casting a terrified glance backwards. Then Jim continued by telling of the odd impression he had when he awakened, and likened the dream with the man running in Cavelli's store.

"I have a hunch that the fleeing man in the store was Yacob Klein. The dream finalized that point for me." Mitchell concluded with a sheepish grin, thinking that the Chief of the Surete would not accept his weird line of reasoning.

He was surprised when his breakfast companion agreed by nodding gravely. "The sub-conscious is a remarkable tool in solving problems. Sometimes I dwell on something for days, and suddenly I find an answer. There must be something to your dream. I will look into the matter of Yacob Klein."

It was then that Jim decided to get the "purloined papers" and show his conclusions. But before doing that he told Gabrielli of his family's visit to the Academy and how they learned of the archives in the sub-basement. That last caught his attention.

"I don't think that anyone in our administration knows that! There must be a wealth of information there! I must make a note of it and inform my superiors. The Italian Government should take charge of those files. They would be informative and historical. Thank you." He clapped his hands.

"Wait," Jim put up his hand. "You must not tell anyone that I stole some of the files. I have them upstairs and I will turn them over to you. Promise me immunity!" In jest, he put both hands out as though to surrender himself for arrest.

Gabrielli chuckled. "I'll put you in protective custody."

They laughed in unison at his remark.

CHAPTER SEVENTY TWO
The Bottomless packet

Jim excused himself and left to get the papers. The Chief ordered another espresso.

On his return to the dining room, Mitchell stopped at the desk and procured a large envelope. Arriving at their table, Jim handed Gabrielli the envelope and plopped all the "purloined papers'" on the table.

The Chief's eyes opened wide as he grasped the import of the registration cards, shipping manifests, and the memo.

"You've accomplished a lot, and I am glad that you brought these papers to me. I am sure they will be helpful."

He picked up the papers, one by one, looking at each in turn and placing it into the envelope.

When he was through, the Chief arose, shook Mitchell's hand, and said; "I'll see you soon. Give my regards to Donata and the children."

He turned away to leave, then suddenly spun back and said, "Comandante, one more thing! About the Swiss bank account - THE ADDRESS WAS CHANGED THREE YEARS AGO - after your last visit to Italy!"

"Than only means one thing!" Jim almost shouted. "That means that the person in charge of the account knows me well!"

"Yes, yes, Comandante, that is so. We were surprised as much as you."

"The men from FIND - they did not tell me."

"I told them not to. I wanted to see you and tell you myself."

Containing himself no longer Jim said, "You kept that to yourself until the end of our conversation, why?"

"It's my training, I could not help myself. Please excuse me. Arrivederci!"

Jim was darned sure he would see him soon. He always popped up at the most unexpected places. Meanwhile, there was a lot of figuring as to what course of action he should take with the other materials he had in his packet. It would take a day or so to make a decision. He had to look them over one more time.

CHAPTER SEVENTY THREE
Franco

It was only 9:30 A.M., Jim had plenty of time to go to Cavelli's place of business. Intending to make it a surprise visit, he sought some sort of excuse. Remembering that Andrea and/or his daughter, Carla, were to make reservations at a seaside hotel, he could say that he just wanted to confirm that they had the right dates and name of the hotel.

Jim's family was just finishing breakfast when he entered the suite. He sat down with them for coffee and a finger of the funny looking Modenese bread that looks like a fat man's hand. He used both butter and jam.

That morning, Dorothy and the children were slow getting started. Jim asked if they had any plans for the morning. They said not, and added that they would walk over to a street nearby that had all sorts of shops. At lunchtime, they said, they would discuss the plans for the rest of the day. That was fine with Mitchell. He had made his own plans and was going to implement them.

Some time was lost in getting the car from the parking lot. The bellboy couldn't find the keys for a few minutes and then he couldn't find the car. The concierge gave him hell and described the car. "The one with the Roma plates." He said.

It was then that Jim recalled the time in Florence when he got rid of a car with Venezia plates because they were being followed. He was not going to try that this time. His life was an open book. It was impossible to hide. He found that out by getting many visits at the most inopportune times. Meaning, of course, The Israelis, Conti, Gabrielli, and there must have been others whom he never saw. They were there, nevertheless.

Cavelli's "Magazzino" wasn't far. It took less than ten minutes to get there. Jim parked and walked across the street to the main entrance. Business was slow that morning, because of Fra Agosto (holiday) the day before. It was now Thursday, the 16th of August. He could see the date on the calendar that was displayed behind the cashier's desk.

He walked towards Cavelli's office, hoping to surprise him. Instead, he found Franco on the telephone. He was sitting behind Andrea's desk. That did not seem unusual, since Franco was a trusted employee. Jim seated himself and waited.

Completing his call, Franco cradled the phone and came towards the Comandante with outstretched arms. He embraced Mitchell and kissed him on both cheeks. Franco was happy to see his visitor.

"Where is Andrea"? Jim asked, after a couple of minutes of small talk and questions about each other's family's health.

"Cavelli's at the seashore with his family, but he left directions and telephone numbers for you. He thought you might stop by. They are right here."

He handed Jim a sheet of paper and a hotel brochure.

Feigning idle curiosity, Mitchell ventured, "Signore Mandelli, where is he? Is he here? I would like to meet him. I understand that he is a modest person and a great philanthropist."

Franco DiMarchi was thoughtful for a few moments and his hands were fidgeting.

"He's not here today. Mr. Mandelli only comes in two or three times a week. He doesn't stay long. He relies on Andrea and me to run the business."

"He must be a very nice man to get along with. Since he knows how trustworthy you are, he can depend on you. That way he can do other good things with his time. I certainly would like to see him before we return to the United States."

Then he added, "Do you have a photograph of all the company employees, or a picture that was taken when you were having a party? I'm sure Mandelli would attend those affairs."

Franco shook his head, "Signore Mandelli is very shy about having his picture taken. He never permits it, even when he receives awards about his gift giving to the schools and churches in Modena. Yes, Comandante, he is very modest."

Then, as an afterthought, he reached for his wallet and removed a small photo.

"This is a picture of my son, Giacamo, and Mandelli at my son's confirmation."

Jim slowly and deliberately reached for the photo, hiding his anxiousness. He took out his glasses and asked, "How old was Giacamo when you took this picture, was he 12? That's usually the age, isn't it?"

Jim focused on the boy's picture first. "He's a hand-some boy, takes after his mother, not so?" He nudged Franco's ribs in emphasis.

Franco laughed and said, "Si, si. My wife is beautiful." Proudly.

"Giacamo is 22 now. When will he graduate from the University? Has he decided on a career?"

He was trying to keep Franco off guard while he took a good look at the man in the picture. Mandelli was the man running to the rear of the store! He didn't look like an Italian, but neither do many people in North Italy.

With a steadied hand, Jim returned the photo. He would have given anything to keep it, but it was only one of a kind and it was treasured by Franco. Keeping it in his wallet did not necessarily mean that he loved Mandelli. Quite the opposite. He loved his son and treasured the ten-year-old picture.

As Mitchell was leaving, Franco gave him a box of Swiss chocolates to take to his family. He remarked that they often received shipments of chocolate to sell in their store. Mandelli would order them when he went to Switzerland on vacation or business.

He than added, "Cavelli goes there about twice a year to buy things to sell. I only went once and didn't like it." Franco, unknowingly, was giving Jim more information.

CHAPTER SEVENTY FOUR
Follow The Money

Long before his family returned from shopping, Mitchell was back in the suite at the hotel. Sitting on the couch, he recalled the phrase: "Follow the Money." Having an accounting background, he had a fairly good idea of how the I.R.S. would handle a case before they actually conducted an audit.

In Italy, it would be different. Everybody cheats on income tax returns. Bribery is rampant. Books are always 'cooked.' There is a huge underground economy. Since almost everyone is guilty of cheating, no one squeals on someone else.

In the United States, the I.R.S. considers the taxpayer's lifestyle in comparison with his earnings. They look at the home, summer or vacation home, and automobiles. Then they look into their bank accounts, especially the checking accounts. That's how the taxpayers spending habits are put in focus. If 2 plus 2 makes 6, then the roof falls in, and a detailed audit is conducted. In other words, they follow the money.

Three years earlier, when he had inquired about Cavelli's success, the Valentes had smirked and made faces. Without saying anything in words, they had given Jim the impression that Andrea's wealth was not a matter of very hard work. He evidently came into some money. Perhaps from Mandelli. And how about Mandelli's wealth? Where did his money come from? He had seen this man before--ages ago.

In one of their conversations Gabrielli said something like "it's all about money, big money." Now Jim was sure he was right!

Among his listing of "Friends," Cavelli was the only one who was really wealthy. He had a Ferrari, a large villa (So Jim was told. He never saw it), a piece of a good business, a villetta (small house) at the seashore, and he took frequent vacations.

The Valentes earned everything by the sweat of their brows. They earned enough to have a roof over their heads and some left over for niceties in life. Camille and her husband were hard working folks. No wealth there either.

The money trail led to Cavelli and Mandelli. In another life, back when he lived at the Ducal Palace and slept in the Princess' apartment, Mandelli was not in the picture. He had never met him. He wondered where he came from and decided he moved down to Modena from northern Italy. Probably Milan, but maybe farther north.

Mitchell was becoming very confused. It did not seem possible that Klein was now Mandelli. That dream put all his facts askew. The dream had superimposed Mandelli's face on Klein's. Jim decided to put things to rest and gather his thoughts in a sensible manner. He was not going to go half cocked and jump to some very wrong conclusions.

CHAPTER SEVENTY FIVE
Desperate Thief or Murderer

Going from one extreme to another, Mitchell reeled back and forth with all the possibilities of putting Yacob Klein and Giacomo (Jacob) Mandelli together.

Yes! Why didn't Klein/Mandelli go to the Promised Land? Because he wasn't a Jew, that's why!

Viewing the postcard with Klein's signature, and then recalling the registration card (Gabrielli had it now) and how it was written, almost proved to him that the signature was not the name of the registrant. On the postcard and the registration card the letter "M" was written unconsciously and then crossed out. In both instances he started to write Yacob "M" and that letter meant something other than Mandelli.

On the registration card, Yacob resisted entering his religion. He could not write 'Jewish' because being German and having been indoctrinated to hate Jews, Yacob could not write the word. Jim tested the waters with this theory:

1. Yacob was a German -- He hated Jews, yet traveled to Italy with them and lived with them in a refugee camp. THAT MEANT HE WAS DESPERATE.

2. He had concentration camp identity numbers tattooed on his arm. --------He must have had that done after the war was over. If he was free and stopped before hostilities ceased, he would have been shot.

3. He was fleeing and hiding -----------From what? The Nazis? No, they were too busy fleeing and hiding, too.

The Allies? Don't know. Doubtful.

Was he a thief or murderer? Gabrielli will check that out.

4. He was once accused of being "SS" (German Elite Troops and high up in the chain of command).

------------A case of mistaken identity.

Desperation will make a man try many things that he will not do ordinarily. Yacob was desperate.

Yacob was supposed to have gone to Milan, yet surfaced in Lake Garda and later in Modena.

Mitchell went on and on trying to put down on paper all the possible angles. Maybe he would come up with the right school solution. Putting his theories on paper placed them in

190

some sort of perspective. He could take them or leave them. For the rest of the day, he left them. His sub-conscious mind would sort them out.

He placed the paper with all its scribbles and scratches, plus his theories, into his little packet. They would keep for a while. At least, until he returned from the seashore. Dorothy and he were also looking forward to exploring Rimini on the Adriatic.

Keys rattling in the door's lock awakened him. He had dozed for a few minutes. His family walked in carrying some packages. They were ready to rest, too. Remaining in his position he fell asleep. His mind needed that rest.

CHAPTER SEVENTY SIX
Efrem's "Work"

The phone rang, Dorothy picked up the receiver, as Jim awakened she looked at him and mouthed "Camille." Jim was always able to read her lips. The conversation was not long.

"We're invited for this evening. She wants us there about three. Eros or Noris will pick us up. I said O.K. It's twelve thirty, let's go down and get lunch."

As they were leaving their suite, the telephone rang again. Jim picked it up.

It was Efrem. They had promised to see his "work" that day.

"Fine." Jim answered politely. "Come and have lunch with us now."

He thanked Mitchell and declined. He already had his "dinner."

"I will come by the hotel at one thirty. Camille told me that she wanted you at her home at three. I will take you there after I show you my 'work'."

At lunch Jim said, "Dorothy, what do you think his "work" is? He seems to be awfully proud of it."

"We'll soon find out." Dorothy said sagely.

While Efrem was driving them to his 'work,' Jim tried to get him to tell them what line he was in, or what trade he was working at. He would only smile and hold up his finger indicating that they should be patient and wait.

"It's going to be a surprise." Jim warned his family. "So be impressed."

They were both surprised and impressed when they arrived at a small plastics plant. It was Efrem's. It was no wonder that he was so proud. It seemed that he bought the factory during the past year. Knowing nothing about plastics going in, he was an expert now. It was either sink or swim. He came out as a champion swimmer. His wife and son were working. He also employed his two sisters-in-law, a nephew and a niece. It was truly a family affair.

The machinery used in extrusion, etc., were of the latest and most modern models. All the extended family members were trained to operate every machine. It was marvelous.

Mitchell was overjoyed and happy for them all. Talk about lifting oneself by the bootstraps, this guy, Efrem, got the prize!

Dorothy had worked for a plastic manufacturer in Philadelphia when plastic was in its infancy; therefore she understood the use of all the machinery. Efrem and his wife, Valeria, were pleasantly surprised at Dorothy's knowledge of the plastic industry. Jim's wife was in her glory as she looked over the molds, and the products that were formed by them.

They looked over the finished products that came out of this relatively small plant. They made the caps for the Bertolli oilcans, and gearshift lever tops of all shapes and colors. The latter were made for the exotic cars that were manufactured in Modena, like Ferrari, Lamborghini, and DiTomaso. Electric insulators of all kinds were made there. Items were made for toy companies. Jim saw bushels of checker pieces and plastic forms used to assemble games. Best of all, they made the bottle caps for Lambrusco wine!

The hour allotted for their visit was not enough. They promised to come back another day. Efrem was delighted with their interest and gave them a few samples of the toys and a catalog of the items they manufactured.

CHAPTER SEVENTY SEVEN
Fresh Pasta and Rabbit

The home of Camille and Eros Caselgrandi was in a rural area and not far from the original family farmhouse. As the Mitchells entered the fenced in yard, they were astounded to see a dead chicken hanging on the fence. Its throat was cut and its head was downward for the blood to drain from its body. Seeing a sight like that immediately drew gasps from Jim's family. He knew that picture would remain with them and most certainly curb their appetites. It was also going to affect him that way.

The house was quaint and with some modern improvements. The walls were very thick and, as a result, the rooms were cool. Camille was very proud of her little home.

She showed the Mitchells her little station wagon parked outside. It was stacked with dry goods of every kind. She sold clothing and linens to the country folk who couldn't go to town often. She was a peddler, and it was evident that she was a good saleswoman.

Camille had to be aggressive. She and her husband had plans to own their own home someday, and it was her way of contributing towards that end. Brava, for her. They congratulated her on her accomplishments. And Eros, too.

Eros had been in the Italian army during the war. For most of that period, he was stationed on the Island of Sardinia. After Italy surrendered, his unit worked with the Allied forces. He showed Jim and Dorothy a letter of commendation that he received from a General of the U. S. Army. Eros was proud of that citation. It was framed and hung in the dining room.

While Dorothy and Jim strolled through the garden, Camille was dressing the chicken. Judy and Jimmy had never seen anyone pluck feathers from a chicken. They were entranced and stood transfixed by the scene before them. Camille's son, Noris, drove up and parked on the street alongside the house. He wanted to show off his new Fiat to the children. Judy went quickly and Jimmy followed reluctantly.

Fortunately, Camille made fresh pasta 'from scratch'. They watched her roll the dough and cut it into strips. Dorothy was intent on getting the recipe for the sauce and watched Camille at the stove. The pasta removed the fearful prospect of being forced to eat the chicken. Jim had pasta and wine. His family followed suit.

Efrem returned and joined them. The Mitchells thanked heaven that the chicken was devoured by Noris and his uncle. It took the Americans off the hot seat.

It was a long day. When Noris returned his American friends to the hotel it was still Thursday, August 16th! Jim was tired and ready to retire. Dorothy and Jimmy were going to watch an American television show that was scheduled to come on at ten PM. Judy was going to bed.

CHAPTER SEVENTY EIGHT
Stirring The Pot

Friday, August 17th. It was important to keep track of the dates. On vacation, one usually does not keep track of the days, until one is reminded that it is time to go home. One day seems to run into another when there is no schedule to keep. But this time it was like having a job. The Mitchells had to keep track of the social engagements, and Jim, personally, had to deal with all the interruptions and inquisitions. How he was able to balance the vacation aspect with the question and answer periods was a mystery. Somehow, it worked out.

During all those days in Italy, Jim had a continuing sense of expectancy. It was the feeling that at any moment, another rider would gallop into his life. It would be someone who wanted more and more or something that he did not possess. He was getting a proverbial headache from all that pressure. His headache was real that morning. Dorothy blamed the wine he had the evening before.

Jim got up from the table while they were in the middle of breakfast and said that he would be right back. He was going to go to the "Farmacia" (Pharmacy), which was right around the corner.

"I'll be back in a minute, Dottie." He said to his wife in parting.

As he walked out onto the sidewalk in front of the hotel, Jim noticed a man standing at the curb who was eyeing him curiously. Jim continued on his way and entered the pharmacy. The man discreetly followed and waited outside. The pharmacist tried to sell Jim some powders that were made on the premises, but Jim insisted on Bayer. He paid for the aspirin and put the package in his pocket. The price was staggering. Bayer aspirin cost almost five times the price paid in the U.S.! However, it was worth the price to get rid of the headache.

As Jim turned to leave the store, he realized that he was probably going to need the pills, because the man was waiting for him.

It was more serious that he had thought. He identified himself as a detective working under Gabrielli's orders.

"Capo Gabrielli wishes me to keep you under protection today. He is serious for your safety."

His English was adequate. He was implying that Jim was in danger. Mitchell wondered how the Chief had arrived at that conclusion. It was highly possible that Gabrielli's intensive investigation had stepped on someone's toes. Hard enough, possibly, that it could touch off a perilous backlash. The Chief figured that Jim would be the one to get hurt, because he was STIRRING THE POT!

Jim shook the detective's hand, asked for his card, and thanked him for his concern.

"Come in and have some coffee." The American gestured toward the hotel.

"Mille grazie." The detective answered. "Thank you, but I must not be seen with you after this. I hope that I did not make a mistake in talking to you, but I thought it best that you be warned. Ciao!" With that, he walked away.

Before turning the corner to the hotel, Jim spun around and ran back to the detective. "Where is Garbrielli today? I'd like to know where I could reach him."

"He's in Ivrea --," he stopped, realizing that he was caught off guard. The detective hastened to say, "Call my office and leave a message, then I will communicate it to the Chief."

He turned and looked into a shop's window. End of conversation.

CHAPTER SEVENTY NINE
The Surrender

Ivrea? Jim remembered the area near that town. Ivrea is situated near the French and Swiss borders. As the crow flies, it is a little more than 40 miles from the Matterhorn in Switzerland.

About April 30th, 1945, the 34th Division captured many thousands of Germans. Whole units were marching on the roads towards the American lines with white flags, as the attacking troops made their way towards the northwestern part of Italy.

Lt. Mitchell's group bypassed the prisoners and continued on to complete their mission. Later in the day, some of the battalion officers were ordered to go to an assembly area where they were massing the prisoners. First Lieutenant James Mitchell was included and, arriving at the coordinates shown on the map, he saw whole units of German soldiers still formed in ranks and carrying arms. It was a scene to behold, and one that he would never forget.

Jim was positioned near some colonels and generals, and was very aware of what was taking place. First, a cease-fire was to take affect by midnight. By the time all the German units could be notified by their commanders that they had surrendered, another day or two would pass. The Americans were all advised of that fact, and therefore all units were alerted to the possibility that they may encounter some German units that knew nothing of the surrender.

At that time the 34th Infantry Division was north of Milan and had heard that the Italian partisans had taken over that city. Many of the German troops had fled farther north and were surrounded, except for those Divisions that were at the base of the Italian Alps.

Lt. Mitchell watched as a regiment of about a thousand "Wehrmacht" troops prepared to disarm. A German officer would march forty or fifty men to the front of the American contingent in single file, and at shoulder arms. Then the officer would order, "left face, order arms." The German soldiers who were still at attention would be told to lay down their arms. The rifles, automatic weapons, pistols were put on the ground in front of them. Then they were ordered to empty their pockets of all sharp instruments, pocketknives, razors, etc. After that, they would step back, face right and march forward to take their places in the ranks of their unit.

Platoon after platoon marched forward and engaged in that ritual until the whole regiment was disarmed.

The German regimental commander, along with his staff, was standing and observing. Upon completion of the disarmament of his troops, he turned to the 135th Infantry regimental commander and asked for a vehicle.

He wanted to ride, while his troops were going to march to the encampment, which was some distance away. That request was instantly rejected. "Your men march, you march!" Ordered the American colonel.

The German Wehrmacht Regiment was ready to march. The German commander and his officers led their regiment away. Without any apparent signal from anyone in the ranks, the tired and beaten soldiers burst into a German marching song. It gave Jim a thrill, and a chill raced down his back. These men were great soldiers to the end and they wanted to show the Americans that their morale had not been dampened or broken by their surrender.

There were many captured trucks parked on one side. The drivers were still seated and they had their rifles with them. The sergeant in charge of the convoy was named 'Heinz' or 'Einz.' He was a blond, good - looking soldier who spoke some Italian.

Lt. Mitchell was ordered to take the German sergeant and his company trucks to an Army depot that was south of Milan. A German Major was to ride in Jim's jeep. He was given one American soldier as a guard, for every truck. One American truck with a driver and assistant driver was to follow the convoy in case of breakdowns. First Lieutenant Mitchell sat in the back seat of the Jeep with the German Major. The driver, Corporal Mohn, and Heinz sat in front.

It was getting dark as they left the assembly area with an armed German and an armed American soldier on each German vehicle that was emblazoned with the swastika.

CHAPTER EIGHTY
Behind Enemy Lines

The German Major was only going to ride as far as the 34th Division Headquarters. He was to be the liaison between Corps Headquarters and the LXXV German Corps. The Major spoke perfect English with an Oxford accent. He tried to brainwash Lt. Mitchell by telling him that the Americans were going to be forced to fight the Russians in the near future. Jim disagreed.

"How could that be possible?" He argued. "The Russians are our allies."

"You'll see." Was his response.

First Lieutenant Mitchell turned him over to the M.P.'s (Military Police) at Corps Headquarters.

The route to get to the US Army depot was leading them right through the center of Milan. It was about ten P.M. when they entered the city. The streets were crowded with people. They rushed the trucks to get at the German soldiers, but the G.I. escorts intervened. It was nip and tuck for a while. At one point, the lieutenant stood up in the jeep with his pistol drawn to protect the German prisoners, including the sergeant.

An hour or more after they had passed through Milan, at Mitchell's command the convoy stopped at a farm where there were several large outbuildings. They parked all the vehicles and ordered the men to go to the barn to sleep. No guards were posted. Germans slept with the Americans, and all had rifles by their sides. The hay was soft, and Jim went to sleep, too. It had been a long day. Tomorrow was going to be longer.

All were up at sunrise. Lt. Mitchell's men immediately busied themselves making coffee in a big pot that they borrowed from the farmer's wife. They had real coffee. The Germans were used to making coffee with toasted grains. The prisoners told the Americans that they did not have real coffee for years. They appreciated sharing the coffee and rations with their guards. They enjoyed a good breakfast. The G.I.s gave them cigarettes, too.

The farmer's young son came over and asked for the used coffee grounds before they were dumped. Lt. Mitchell also gave him some fresh coffee grounds for the use of the barn. He hadn't asked permission. It was necessary to make use of the barn and they did. It was still wartime.

Two hours drive and the strange convoy arrived at the American depot and dropped off the captured vehicles. It was also necessary to pick up some rations and to gas up one truck and the Jeep.

The prisoners, still armed with their rifles, and their American guards were loaded on the truck for the return trip. The sergeant, Heinz, remained with the lieutenant.

They made good time returning to Division Headquarters. The prisoners were disarmed and taken to the German stockade. The American soldiers returned to their units. Heinz stayed in the Jeep with Mitchell.

Heinz was to be taken back to his unit, near Ivrea, where the Germans had set up their line of defense. Why he had to escort one German to his company that was situated behind the enemy lines was beyond Lieutenant Mitchell's comprehension. He was only taking orders. Heinz was going to be instrumental in guiding the beleaguered German troops to the position where the total surrender of all German troops was to take place.

Sergeant Heinz had knowledge of all the routes and was well respected by his superiors. Jim could understand that. It was going to be a drive of about 75 miles according to his map to get to Aglie, which was a few miles south of Ivrea. Averaging 25 miles an hour, it would be possible to get there in three hours. It was already 6 P.M.

The passengers in the jeep were going to negotiate their way through the Allied lines and then enter the German stronghold at the base of the Alps. It was only a cease-fire. Actually, total capitulation was not due until the terms of the surrender were agreed upon and signed.

It was May 1, 1945; it was possible that the next day would be the last day of the war in Italy. Mitchell hoped so. So did Heinz; he was tired of the war, too.

They were still in the Po Valley when they passed the forward American Infantry units. Twenty or more miles of terrain lay between them and the German lines.

Heinz directed the driver, Pfc. Mohn, the way to Aglie. About nineteen miles later, they came across the German

201

outpost that was composed of several vicious looking Panzer (Tiger) tanks. Upon being stopped, Heinz got out of the jeep and walked up to the sentries. He identified himself and explained their mission. As the American vehicle slowly passed the sentries, they clicked their heels, snapped to attention, and saluted. Mitchell gladly returned their salute (and he was pleased with the respect they accorded an American officer). They passed through numerous checkpoints and Lt. James Mitchell always received the same snappy salutes!

Finally they arrived at a house that was the headquarters of Heinz's unit. Carrying their arms and packs, Mohn and Mitchell entered the house with the sergeant leading.

Heinz knocked on a door of a room that was off the entrance hall. The Americans heard a voice say, "Kommen." The German sergeant opened the door and Jim could see by candlelight that someone was in the bed. The sergeant clicked his heels and, with his outstretched hand, gave his captain the German salute. Lt. Mitchell walked in and stood beside Heinz.

The captain spoke English and asked if the lieutenant wished to stay the night.

"Yes," Jim responded. "We are very tired. Thank you."

Still lying in bed, the captain quietly said something to Heinz in German. Lt. Mitchell had studied German in high school and Mohn came from Pennsylvania Dutch country, so they both got the drift. It was, "Get them a bed!"

That's exactly what Heinz did. The Americans stood at the base of the stairs as he went up. Then they heard, "Raus! raus!"

People were moving around in a bedroom and soon came plummeting down the stairs and past the astonished guests. The sergeant had evicted two soldiers from a bedroom on the second floor and it was ready for Mohn and Mitchell. The bed was still warm and the Americans were not squeamish.

Lt. Mitchell put his Colt 45 under the pillow. Mohn put his rifle on the floor where he could reach it easily. Knowing that they were under the protection of a top-notch German sergeant and his commander, the Americans were inclined to feel only slightly uneasy. But they were exhausted. It was best to remain there than to return to the Allied lines in total darkness. Quickly undressed to their underwear, they crawled under the white sheets, and immediately fell asleep!

CHAPTER EIGHTY ONE
The First Americans

Awakened early the following morning by voices that came from beneath their window, the Americans heard: "Zwei Amerikaner......."

The German soldiers were talking about the two Americans and inspecting their jeep. Heinz had told us to leave some of our gear in the jeep. "No one will touch them." No one did. Everything remained in place.

The captain was up and invited the two guests for breakfast. Lt. Mitchell declined, saying that they had to get back to their unit as soon as possible.

Understanding the need for the Americans to leave, the German captain reached for his field glasses. He handed them to Lieutenant Mitchell as a gift. Heinz reached into his holster and pulled out his Luger. He handed it to Mohn. It was a solemn moment. They shook hands to say good-bye and good luck.

As they got into the jeep to leave, with German soldiers all around them, Heinz reached into his pocket and gave Lt. Mitchell a photo of himself standing in front of an armored vehicle. Jim thanked him and waved as they drove off.

It was about seven A.M. and they were riding in bright sunlight. It was obvious that all the check-points were advised of their presence, and Lt. Mitchell was saluted as they passed. The news must have gone out to the civilian population also. Jim was certain of that when he spied a young woman of about twenty running and calling to them as they were passing a villa.

"Stop! Stop!" She cried out in English. Pfc. Mohn stopped the vehicle and the two waited for her.

"Are you Americans?" She was very excited and out of breath. Pretty, too.

"Yes, we are." Jim answered, not knowing what to expect.

"My father would like to see you and talk to you. We live here." She pointed to the villa. "Please, come!"

"Okay, but we can't stay long."

As the Americans walked into the entryway Mitchell spied a baton on a small marble top table. The short ebony stick had a round gold head which was highly polished and engraved with the letters 'J i M.' At least that's how it appeared to him.

The girl walked ahead.

The lieutenant whispered to his driver, "There's a great souvenir. It even has my name on it!"

"No, sir." Replied Mohn. "They are your initials 'JM' with a design between the letters that looks like a dotted 'I'."

The American soldiers followed the girl into the living room where they were greeted by her parents.

The house was beautifully and tastefully furnished. Mr. and Mrs. Anton Vezzetti were overwhelmed.

"You are the first Americans to come here. When are the rest coming?" Anton Vezzetti couldn't get the words out fast enough.

They all sat down in the parlor or music room; there was a grand piano on one side.

Anton was an American citizen and had come to Aglie (a suburb of Ivrea) to retire. After the war started he lost touch with his friends and relatives in the United States. He was hungry for news. Jim could not oblige him for long. He did not have much time to spare.

Lt. Mitchell sent Mohn out to the jeep for some rations to give to the Vezzettis. Meanwhile, he commented about the beauty of the piano and asked who played. The daughter graciously arose and walked over to the piano and began to play after Mohn returned. It sounded wonderful at that time of the morning.

Just as the young lady finished playing, the sound of heavy shoes or boots was heard on the stairway. It was a German officer. He nodded to Jim and said, "Good Morning." With a British accent, no less.

Upon giving it some thought, one realizes that the German teachers of English were taught by the English. Naturally, they acquired the British accent.

The Vezzettis were not in the least intimidated by the German's presence. They continued talking about how happy they were that the Americans were there. Jim told them that the Americans weren't in their town yet.

"We're the only Americans here," Jim reminded them.

The German officer was having breakfast in the dining

room. Lt. Mitchell was certain he heard every word said. There was nothing he could say or do at the time. By the next day, at least, he would be another prisoner of war.

Mohn handed the rations to Mrs. Vezzetti as the Americans rose to leave. It was a tearful, yet happy good-bye for that family. They sincerely did not want to see the two leave.

Anton shook our hands, with tears. His wife kissed the soldiers on both cheeks, and best of all, so did the girl. That short visit was memorable!

In leaving, the baton projected itself fully into Jim's brain and he realized that it belonged to the Nazi Major who was in residence at the villa. He glanced sharply at the golden head and mentally agreed with his driver that the initials were J and M. The letter 'i' did not exist!

Without any more interruptions, they drove back to their unit, and passed many German tanks and roadblocks.

It was later that day, that the formal and full surrender took place. The war was over in Italy! It was May 2, 1945.

CHAPTER EIGHTY TWO
On The Beach

On January 3rd, 1946, Anton Vezzetti expressed the desire to hear from Lt. Mitchell again. He also reminded Jim about his being the first American to visit his town. .

Anton also wrote: "...after a few days we had here in Aglie, a whole company of American soldiers, for about three weeks."

On August 17, 1973, Chief Gabrielli was in Ivrea. He was not there on holiday, Jim was sure. Gabrielli was not one to leave an important job to his underlings. The Chief was a bulldog and would not drop a case when he was close to something. He was closing in, Mitchell was certain of that.

Ivrea was on the road to Switzerland. North on the autostrada, there is Aosta which is 20 kilometers from the Swiss border town of Martigny. That same road continues on through Montreaux and Lausanne in Switzerland. It's a nice and beautiful ride in August. The snow covered Alps send cool breezes down into the warm valleys. Jim hoped that Gabrielli was enjoying himself in the mountains.

The Mitchells were going to go to the seashore the following day. When the Chief returned, he was going to miss the Americans. If he wanted to see Jim he would have to wait until the Mitchell family returned to Modena on the following Monday.

Jim was of the opinion that the detective, who was following us, would report their whereabouts. Still not convinced that he was the target of someone and that something sinister was in the offing for him, or his family, Mitchell was going to rely on their detective protector to handle the situation adequately.

In the meantime, they were going to act normal and try to have some enjoyment the rest of the day.

Early Saturday morning they took luggage enough for a two-night stay at Milano Marittima. The concierge stored the other bags for their return.

By ten o'clock the Mitchells checked into the hotel by the seashore. It was right on the beach and their rooms overlooked the sea. The clientele, Dorothy noticed, was almost 90 percent German. The signs throughout the hotel were in

Italian and German. No English. Nor did anyone speak English. Only Italian had to be spoken by the Americans to the hotel personnel. It was quite a change.

The Mitchells were used to having desk clerks and the concierge speak to them in English. Now the tables were turned. It was a change for the better, in Jim's mind. His family needed to practice Italian.

Jim asked the desk clerk to reserve a cabana on the beach and to charge it to their room. Walking to the cabana was easy since it was not far from the rear exit of the hotel. Mitchell needed the shade and a reclining chair. Dorothy and the children wanted the sand and the sun. All were satisfied with their choices.

While Jim was lying on his chair and dozing under the canopy, Cavelli, with his daughter, Carla, and granddaughter stopped by. Cavelli's villette was not far, but not on the beach. They came down to join the Mitchells at the granddaughter's insistence. Marisa was about Judy's age and knew many young people who summered at the resort. Marisa invited Judy and Jimmy to go for a boat ride with some of her friends.

Carla joined Dorothy. Signora Cavelli was to come by later.

Andrea pulled up a chair and sat with in the shade beside Jim. The beach attendant came along with a supply of towels. Jim asked him to bring drinks for the ladies and two cold bottles of German beer for the men. Mitchell emphasized 'cold.'

Cavelli and Jim sat and spoke in generalities, the weather, etc. , until the beer arrived. Then they talked about and made comparisons of conducting business in the U.S. with business in Italy. Both complained of taxes.

Andrea was still smoking despite the problems he was having with his throat. He claimed that it was a recurring bronchitis, but Jim knew better. Cavelli said that he tried to quit smoking many times.

"It's a bad habit, but I enjoy a good smoke." That ended the smoking portion of the conversation.

While they were sipping their second round of beer, Jim asked, "How do you buy the beer that you sell? Do you have to get them from a distributor, or do you buy direct from the breweries?"

"We do not deal with a middle man, we buy direct. Over the years, we have made contacts with all the major beer manufacturers in Europe. The same applies to all the liquors and wines we deal in. We go to Germany, Holland, Austria, France, and even Russia for vodka. We also get a special Swiss beer that we sell to the better hotels in Italy, but not this hotel." He pointed to their rear, at the hotel where he or Carla had made the reservations for the Americans.

Then he added, "And we get the best 'cioccolata' (chocolate) from Switzerland." His tongue had loosened with two beers, and so had Mitchell's.

"Switzerland, Andrea? Is that where my money is?" The words slipped out of Jim's mouth slowly and of their own accord. He had lost control over them.

Cavelli also answered the quiet questions without hesitation. "Yes, I meant to tell you ...." He stopped, in shocked realization of what he had just said.

Mitchell, too, was stunned!

Andrea turned to look at the comandante. "How do you know? It's a secret! Please, tell me how you found out?"

He was terrified, but not of Jim. It had to be someone else he was afraid of . Andrea's color changed and the beer glass shook in his hand.

"Calm down, Andrea." Mitchell said. "You need a drink stronger than that beer." He motioned for the attendant and asked him to bring a glass of American whiskey for Cavelli.

Jim had inadvertently placed himself in a position that he had not anticipated and of which he was not sure how to handle. Subconsciously, he had formed and asked that question. After the fact, he was not sorry.

Perhaps it would help in his quest.

After downing the whiskey, Andrea asked again, "Who told you? I must know!"

Then he leaned towards Jim and said, "Both of us are now in great danger! We must talk and decide what to do!"

"It's not my problem......." Mitchell began, but he was quickly interrupted by Cavelli.

"Si, si, but it is our problem!"

CHAPTER EIGHTY THREE
Vezzetti and Odessa

The leader of the group in Ivrea was nervously pacing the floor in his villa. The other two members of the society, ODESSA, sat benumbed by the tirade that was being delivered. It was not aimed at them because they were in the inner circle of the tight and impenetrable organization.

'Anton Vezzetti' was railing at the incompetence of their underlings. Now they were in the position of having to implement and direct the dirty work themselves.

"This is not a good position to be in." He complained loudly and bitterly.

"All the other times, in our dealings, we were careful not reveal ourselves. At no time did we handle our problems directly. This act that we are to embark upon must be done by someone who is deeply loyal to us. We cannot brook failure. Our heads hang in the balance. I never believed that this day would ever come. I am going to make a phone call and give the order now." 'Anton' wiped his brow as he looked at the two men for approval.

The two had no choice but to nod in agreement. There were no spoken words coming from them. They were petrified with fear because this was their first direct involvement in a crime that was to be committed in ODESSA's name. The fruits that they had received in the past quarter century now put them under obligation to become major players in this conspiracy.

"Yacob," One conspirator mouthed and then halted in confusion. He could say no more.

The others ignored his attempt to speak. There was only one way to go and they were already on that road. There was no turning back. The decision was final

The implementation was in the hands of their leader, 'Anton', or was it 'Yacob?'

CHAPTER EIGHTY FOUR
The Web of Odessa

Then, finally, it came out.

"It's Odessa! You know about them. I'm sure you've heard of them."

Mitchell had a rather vague idea as to who they were and what they represented, but he was not going to admit it. "No, I know nothing about Odessa. What kind of an organization is it?"

"Fascists, maybe. Maybe Nazi. I'm not sure, but I do know that my partner, Mandelli, is also afraid of them." Cavelli wiped his brow.

"I never met your partner. You never introduced me. I have heard that he is a philanthropist and well liked in Modena." Jim countered.

Andrea swore. "Philanthropist? He paid his way to make a good reputation. I think that at one time he was a bad man, but he's older now and more calm. The priests and bishops love him for the money he gives their churches. The art galleries praise him for his donations. He buys all the politicians and judges with his money. Mandelli pays for protection. He's afraid of Odessa the same way I am afraid. Everybody says that I am fortunate to have such a good man for a partner. How little they know!" He sneered. Then he took a long drink. This time he had a bottle of whiskey. Jim only had beer.

Cavelli seemed somewhat relieved that he had someone to talk to and get that "big load off his back." Listening carefully he heard Andrea talk about Odessa placing people in Italy and using him to obtain false identity papers for them. They used him to sell pieces of art and jewelry on the black market and to funnel the money through local business people and back to the members of Odessa who had taken refuge in Italy. As Andrea performed more illegal acts, the deeper he became involved, and there was no way he could back out.

The network of Odessa members became larger each year for the first five years after the end of the war and then became stable. By that time members were established in so-called legitimate businesses and positions in their communities.

Andrea's speech was slurring and he was rambling. Jim

wanted him to get on track and tell how he got involved in the first place. During a pause, his former comandante nudged him with a simple question, "How did all this start?"

"Oh," he said, "I thought I told you!"

"Tell me again." Jim prodded. "Don't leave anything out this time."

He took Mitchell back to August 1945. While Klein was in the hospital after being hurt by the mob of refugees, he gradually gained Cavelli's confidence. Yacob told him that he owned some valuables and had them hidden. Since he was sick from the beating and in a weakened condition, he needed someone to take him to where his belongings were stashed. He also needed protection, still fearful of being attacked again. Whoever took him would be richly rewarded. Cavelli, who always needed money, took the bait and recruited Franco to go along.

It seems that on that day when Andrea was to take his family on holiday for a couple days, he and Franco took Yacob Klein to Milan instead. Arriving in Milan, Yacob directed Franco to drive to a poor and rundown section of town where foreigners lived. Klein went into one of the homes and after a few minutes came out with a metal box. He asked Franco for a screwdriver and forced the lid open. Cavelli said it was filled with American dollars in large denominations. Thousands and thousands of dollars! Klein gave Andrea about a hundred dollars and Franco about fifty. He was appealing to their greed.

"If you want more, you must take me to another place where I have other valuables." He had Cavelli and Franco hooked!

They bought some black market gas, which had been siphoned from American military trucks. Yacob asked to be taken to Ivrea and Cavelli obliged. Klein was giving the orders and the others were obeying. In the suburbs of Ivrea they stopped at a large and well-kept villa. Andrea said that it must have been the home of a wealthy Fascist. Yacob went to the door and was admitted. In a short while he opened the door and beckoned his Italian friends to come in. He seemed to be very confident in what he was doing. Klein was ready to spring the trap from which they would never be able to escape.

Yacob led them into the basement where a secret panel was opened. They walked into a small room where precious works of art were neatly boxed and stacked. A large safe was in the corner.

Klein opened his arms wide as if to envelop all the items in the room and cried, "This is ours!"

"But it was never ours!" Moaned Cavelli. "It was always his or theirs."

With the revelation that they would share in the treasures, Yacob became very dominant and his demeanor changed. He was the one with the power to do great things for Andrea and Franco. He was playing up to their greed. During those days when poverty was rampant, it was easy to recruit them to his cause.

With confidence, Klein led them to the man who owned the villa and introduced them. The man was a hard-nosed Fascist who had joined the German underground organization called "ODESSA." "Odessa" meant nothing to the Italians from Modena.

They were only interested in furthering their fortunes. Politics did not interest them at all. Andrea and Franco were very willing and ready to do Yacob's bidding.

Cavelli admitted that the one thing that bothered him, but not for long, was why Klein was so important to that organization. At that point, it did not matter as long as their greed was gratified. Andrea acknowledged the latter and said that the question was only fleeting.

Klein took several smaller pieces of art and some jewelry from the safe and placed them in Cavelli's care. Andrea was warned not to touch them or expose them to anyone. Cavelli was to return to work as though nothing happened and wait for further orders.

Yacob was then taken to Lake Garda to recuperate further, while Andrea and Franco returned to Modena.

It was during that period that Comandante Mitchell was contacted by the Committee of Liberation.

In retrospect, Jim thought that he was wrong in ignoring the signals that were coming from the Committee. They probably knew of the potential of Cavelli returning to the business of black marketing. Strangely, they were aware of something that was going on in the Academy. They had informers in the

midst of the camp all the time, and the comandante was totally unaware of it. Mitchell was too engrossed in doing his
job during that period.

CHAPTER EIGHTY FIVE
Entanglement

Cavelli's tongue was on the loose and the words spilled out in a torrent, making it difficult for Mitchell to follow completely.

However, Jim did manage to gather that after he left Modena in November 1945, Cavelli continued in his position until the camp closed in 1946.

In accordance to Odessa's plans, Cavelli started his business with help from Klein. Franco was hired in a managerial capacity.

Not long after that Wexler was recruited with promises of reward and joined their organization. By that time the network had expanded and politicians and judges were on the payroll. Adam Wexler was soon appointed as an interpreter in the administrative offices of the City of Modena.

During the early phases of their black market operations, Cavelli had cunningly informed Klein and his foreign cohorts that Comandante Mitchell was aware of their operations. With their approval and knowledge, Andrea set up a Swiss bank account under the name of James Mitchell and with his address in the United States.

Odessa understood blackmail very well. They were the masters of that art and thought it would be cheap insurance. One small painting or piece of jewelry would cover that small expense annually.

Cavelli said it was too easy. They were confidence men but he conned them. Twice each year he was given money to be deposited to the account in the bank in Switzerland. It was Andrea's job to leave no trace of the transaction. Sometimes he would take the money to Switzerland personally. Even Mandelli handled a few deposits when he traveled on business. Cavelli enjoyed it. After all, it was his account!

Up until that day at the seashore, no one in Odessa was aware that Comandante Mitchell was not involved. Now, Andrea was troubled. He wanted to know how Jim found out about the bank account. That afternoon, James Mitchell avoided answering that question time and time again.

In 1970, when Odessa learned that the comandante was coming to Modena, they panicked and feared that he was coming to join FIND in their investigation. Cavelli protested against any violence and was hopeful that no action of that type would be taken. He was mistaken, and he was sorry about the attempt to run the Mitchells off Highway 65. It was obvious to Jim that Andrea Cavelli knew nothing about the first warning or the second.

During his ramblings, Cavelli was unconsciously using Mandelli's name in one sentence and then Klein's in another. Jim was confused, but did not dare to question Andrea more closely about their relationship. It would be answered sooner or later.

"And now again, today, you are here." Continued Cavelli, "These people think you are working with the Jews from Israel who are in Modena. Odessa knows everything. Both of us are in danger!"

One minute Andrea would be on the verge of tears and lamenting about his and 'our' problems. In the next minute he would flood Jim with more information about the happenings in the last quarter century.

It appeared to Mitchell that Cavelli was terrified of being found out about depositing the 'Mitchell bribe' monies that were never intended for Jim in the first place.

To allay the Italian's fears, Jim calmly said, "Andrea, don't worry, I will not tell your people that you set up the bank account for your own use. I want no part of it."

That calmed Cavelli quite a bit. Being reassured, he began to add to his story when another uniformed hotel employee approached their cabana.

CHAPTER EIGHTY SIX
Attempted Assassination

As Mitchell listened to Cavelli's droning words, he closed his eyes for a moment. Then he heard a thud and the sound of a bottle breaking and then felt pieces of glass and a fluid splatter over his body.

Jim opened his eyes in time to see the hotel attendant fall at his feet. Andrea was standing and clutching the neck of the broken whiskey bottle. He was white as a sheet and trembling. He was cold sober in that instant. The man lying on the sand had a long thin knife in his right hand and a very severe and bloody wound on the back of his head. He was a hospital case if there ever was one.

In a quavering voice, Andrea said, "He was coming for you with that knife. I recognized him. He's one of 'Them'."

In a few moments Gabrielli and his men were there and took charge.

Jim sat there shaken, not moving a muscle until he gathered his wits and achieved some measure of composure.

He owed his life to Cavelli. As Andrea related the incident to the Chief, Mitchell heard him say that he recognized the man approaching and when he saw him take out a knife, he picked up the bottle and hit the assassin as he hovered the comandante. Apparently the man from Odessa was sure that Andrea would not interfere. Gabrielli was impressed and congratulated Cavelli for his quick action.

An ambulance soon appeared and the injured man was taken to the hospital under police escort.

Jim remained sitting on his chair for quite some time while Andrea was nervously pacing back and forth. The Chief came over and sat on a chair beside Mitchell. No words were spoken, but he knew that Gabrielli was honestly worried about the near miss.

Dorothy came to his side, too, and with words of comfort. Jim felt better. It was his family that he was worried about. His children were still out boating and knew nothing of the attempt on their father's life.

Mitchell resolved to get his family out of harm's way as soon as possible and addressed Gabrielli on that issue before he spoke about anything else.

216

"We'll help you get back to the United States as soon as we can conclude our investigation and that will be within the next 48 hours." This reassurance came from the Chief. Jim hoped that he would be true to his word.

Dorothy and Jim waited in the cabana until their children returned a half hour later. It was time to go to their rooms, consolidate their thoughts, and prepare for what was certain to come.

Gabrielli and two of his men walked with the Mitchells to their suite. Two local policemen were placed as guards in the hallway. The Chief was very thoughtful as he stepped towards his room that was on the same floor.

"Keep your doors locked. I will see you in the morning." Those were Gabrielli's parting words.

Meanwhile, Cavelli had returned to his villetta after making his statement at police headquarters. He was also under police protection.

Jim's family had dinner in their suite. Hunger still hadn't returned to the parents, but fortunately, Jimmy and Judy were ravenous.

Dorothy and Jim turned in early. What was the morrow going to bring?

CHAPTER EIGHTY SEVEN
Summit Meeting

Sunday morning while Jim prepared to take a shower, the phone rang. It was Gabrielli. The assassin had died during the night.

Gabrielli was not going to get any questions answered by the killer. The Chief knew where he was going and he would get there fast. Cavelli had given the police the man's name. It was Anthony Jeolic! He was the man whom Jim presumed remained in Italy because there was no record in the Academy files of his leaving the country. He had joined Odessa despite the fact that he was from Czechoslovakia and had been a refugee. Money does strange things to people and causes them to commit murder. He had known Mitchell once as the Comandante, but Jim didn't have a clue about him. He was only one of many thousands who had crossed his path at the refugee camp. Jim could readily understand why he was remembered, but why did he wish to do commit murder?

Gabrielli recalled that Jim had given him Jeolic's name when he turned over the 'purloined papers' to him. Mitchell's hunch was right in asking the Chief to check on Weksler and Jeolic. It was too late to question Jeolic now, but he had better get to Weksler fast! The Chief said he would handle it immediately by calling in the Federal Police, the Carabiniere. He was sure that they were not on Odessa's payroll.

At Gabrielli's suggestion, the Mitchells were not to venture out of their rooms for the rest of the day. All meals were to be brought to them. It was not a sacrifice as far as Jim was concerned; he was still shaken by the event of the previous day. The children groused a bit, but managed to occupy themselves by reading and watching television.

Around noon, the Chief came to the door and asked Mitchell to come with him for a meeting.

"Certainly," Jim said. "How can I help?"

Gabrielli answered by leading Jim to his room.

"Just sit in with us. You may give us some ideas. We are going to make some big decisions this day!" Gabrielli punctuated his remark with a flourish of both arms.

As they sat there alone and before anyone else arrived, Jim told him of Cavelli's confession regarding the Swiss bank account and how he had contrived to make deposits for a quarter century.

"He was very clever to fool the people of Odessa. That organization is very powerful. At least that is what I hear from my counterparts in other European countries and South America. I never believed that they were located here in our midst. We have been wondering who was the brain behind what has been going on all these years. It was baffling and embarrassing to learn from FIND that there were Nazi war criminals operating in my area. They have corrupted many officials in our government. We cannot trust the local judiciary. That is why I am in contact with the law enforcement people in Rome. They may have some solutions. We will also contact Interpol. As for FIND, Eisen and Stein are here and that is why Odessa feels the pressure is on them. The German members must be panic-stricken and fear the worst."

Again Jim reminded the Chief that he felt that Weksler was also involved.

"Bene (good)," said Gabrielli with a smile. "We're taking care of him. I think we are very close.....can you think of any other names?"

"Franco isn't involved in this. Leave him alone. I don't think he knows much. They kept him in the dark."

There was a discreet knock and the Chief hastened to open the door. Martin Stein and Sam Eisen stepped into the room. The investigators from FIND greeted Mitchell and Gabrielli quietly. They sat on the chairs that were readied for them. They were rather grim and appeared to be drawn. They were unshaven and probably deprived of sleep. Jim did not think that they were going to be good company this time.

Gabrielli, being a gracious host, poured coffee for all and offered some biscotti. All four sat in silence for several minutes until the coffee took affect. Then they got down to business.

For several minutes the Chief spoke directly to the men from FIND, bringing them up to date on the occurrences of the last two days. Turning towards Mitchell, he informed them of his investigation that took him to Ivrea. He was certain that he located the villa that was the operational headquarters of Odessa for Italy.

Confidentially, he stated that the local authorities would not cooperate with him. They insisted that the owner was a respected and popular citizen who had his hand in politics, and there was no reason to suspect him of anything illegal.

"It is now up to the government in Rome to act, and I was assured that it will be tomorrow." Concluded Gabrielli.

"We have been informed by our government that our people will be on hand," stated Eisen. "We have been on top of this for days. I'm pooped." Then he turned to the Chief to explain the word "pooped."

Martin Stein looked hard at the American and said, "Jim, every time you come to Italy you stir up some kind of trouble."

"I know what you mean, Martie," Mitchell replied. "Just ask the Chief about the threatening notes that I have received."

You mean the one about 'stirring the pot'?" Stein rejoined.

"Oh, I see you have been informed. I don't have to tell you any more." That put an end to that portion of the conversation.

There was a long pause. Jim ended it by saying that he was afraid that all the activity surrounding him would give the wrong signal to Odessa's people.

The Chief said, "Yesterday's incident on the beach was not in the news -- neither radio, TV, or print-- and would be blacked out until our investigation is over."

Sliding deeper in his chair, Mitchell heaved a deep sigh of relief.

Eisen interjected with, "Gabrielli will have his men pick you up as though you are being arrested."

"But that may lead my enemies to think that I would talk despite the fact that I know nothing about their operations. What little I know is conjecture." Jim objected.

"They probably think you know everything since they believe you've been on their payroll for over 25 years."

"True," Mitchell acknowledged. "We'll go with your plan when you round up everyone implicated. I am guessing that you will move fast and in coordination with all other police agencies."

"Yes," Stein said. "We have a few of our own agents here and we'll have more tomorrow. You can bet the ranch on that." He ended firmly.

Jim arose, excused himself, and then stated with some conviction, "I'm going to take a nap."

He was certain none believed him because he was too tense.

When Jim reached the door, Gabrielli stopped him by saying, "A couple days ago when I was in Ivrea, I spoke to an American citizen who was walking his dog. It was a funny looking Dachshund. The man's accent was different, like an Englishman's and his Italian was fair. I presume accents are prevalent in America, like here, in Italy?"

"That's true. We have 'Southern,' 'Brooklyn,' " Jim winked at Eisen and Stein. He continued, " 'Midwest,' 'Pennsylvania Dutch' ...."

The Chief held up his hand and stopped the American, all the while chuckling, then shot this zinger: "He said he was from Providence..."

Jim gave Gabrielli his full attention.

"....claimed he had an American passport and had retired to Italy. I got all that in the first two minutes and quite voluntary on his part. He aroused my curiosity for a moment, but then I realized that most Americans are very outgoing and not unusual to give their life history in one breath."

At that, Mitchell joined Martin and Sam in a chorus of loud laughter at the Chief's conclusion.

As their laughter died, Jim left them with this tidbit from his past, "In 1941, just before I was drafted, I took a position in Philadelphia. I was very amused with the accent that the Philadelphians had, but I did not ridicule them. I thought I spoke perfect English and with no accent. To my horror, I was told in no uncertain terms by several fellow workers who had atrocious Philly accents, that I had an 'Upstate accent bordering on Pennsylvania Dutch!"

The trio remained in a huddle as Jim departed. Left to their own devices, they were plotting towards the end of their investigation of several years. The boys from Israel were intent on landing one of the many Nazi war criminals that were still being sought. Silently, Mitchell wished them 'happy hunting' with the thought that in some small way he had assisted them in their search.

The Chief possessed the keys, some of which were supplied by the former comandante.

Somehow Jim still had the feeling that his contributions were not exhausted.

For some unknown reason, dinner was served in the Mitchell suite quite early, five o'clock to be exact. They understood why about an hour later when Gabrielli phoned and informed Jim that plans were made for them to leave for Modena at six thirty that evening. It presented no problem for the family. All were anxious to leave the prison-like atmosphere that had prevailed that day.

CHAPTER EIGHTY EIGHT
Mitchell's Arrest

At six A.M., on Monday, the 20th of August, Mitchell's phone rang. The day of reckoning had come! It was Gabrielli.

"The legal machinery is in high gear, the police are in action, and you should not be surprised at anything that happens. Your family has no cause for alarm."

Jim felt that the action included his own arrest.

Breakfast was served in their suite and while they were eating, Jim informed his family that he would be taken into custody as part of an overall plan. His family was not convinced.

At eight A.M. the police arrived and the American was escorted out of the hotel, not cuffed, but with ample security and high exposure to newspaper and TV. Jim clutched his packet of memories, just in case.

At police headquarters, Mitchell was taken to a holding cell where Cavelli and Franco DiMarchi were sitting dejectedly. He was placed in their cell, probably in direct contradiction to standard operating procedure.

Showing great displeasure, Jim greeted Andrea and Franco with, "What's going on? I don't belong here! Cavelli, tell them that I am not implicated in anything illegal. I thank you for saving my life, but somehow I feel that just knowing you has put me in this predicament."

Cavelli had his mouth open, but he was without words. Franco was wringing his hands, looking contrite and yet innocent.

After several minutes of silence, Andrea ventured to whisper to the comandante, "Don't worry, Mandelli will get us out. He has powerful friends. You'll soon find out."

He forced a weak smile towards Jim and Franco.

CHAPTER EIGHTY NINE
The Nazi's Den

In the early light of dawn, the phone shrilled its demanding ring. Signora Vezzetti flung aside the bedclothes and stretched to reach the telephone.

"Pronto! Pronto!" She called into the receiver with some degree of irritation.

The response was immediate and she quickly handed the phone to her husband who was still rubbing the sleep out of his eyes. The Signora left the bedroom for the kitchen. She never allowed herself to get involved in any of Anton's business dealings.

Besides, her husband never permitted it. To some extent, it was an Italian custom; but it was far more reaching than that. There were other implications that she soon recognized in their marriage.

In the bedroom, Vezzetti was standing and wide-awake.

"Mandelli, you dumkopf, you idiot! Why are you calling me direct while the police are there with you? Call the attorneys, that's why we pay them so well. Since you have involved me with your stupid action, I will come to Modena and sit with the lawyers. Do not, I repeat, do not involve any of us with your problem. It will work out - it always has."

"This is bad." Mandelli was whispering frantically into the phone. "I will need all the help I can get. I still don't know what the charges are, but it may have something to do with stolen art. A detective I know privately told me. The police are still here and searching. I think they are going to take me to Modena for questioning."

"Oh, you are in Rabbi? In any case, I'll see you in Modena. Contact our attorneys immediately!" Vezzetti hung up, then picked up the phone and dialed for his driver.

He was now calm and calculating. In his mind, the problem could be handled easily.

CHAPTER NINETY
The Prisoners

An hour passed and a guard brought the prisoners some piping hot espresso. Jim was sure that was not how they treated all the inmates. They were very special and Cavelli and DiMarchi quickly recognized that fact. Their demeanor changed. Both felt much more at ease. No doubt they were thinking that it was Mandelli's influence. As for Mitchell, he knew that it was the Chief's doing.

Shortly after ten o'clock Weksler was placed in the next cell along with three others. He did not acknowledge anyone and kept to himself in the furthermost corner. He was a cagey one and far different than the poor refugee that Jim knew. The portly figure that he carried attested to the life he had been leading.

Noon came and the prisoners were served pasta that was not to Mitchell's taste and obviously not to the taste of anyone else. Their cell was not accorded anything different than the next cell. Gabrielli was too smart to tip his hand by giving comfort to one group while in full view of the prisoners in the adjoining cell. Only iron bars separated them from the next cell. They remained in full view of each other for the next several hours.

Finally, four well-dressed men were shown into the area of the holding cells. Two of them, who were carrying briefcases, were undoubtedly attorneys. Cavelli and Franco leaped to their feet, while Mitchell remained sitting on the bench. In the adjacent cell, all the occupants walked to the front of the cell to greet the approaching men. Jim watched with great interest, wondering what was going to ensue.

Mitchell saw Gabrielli in the background carefully watching the scene that was unfolding before him. Under orders from the Chief, Mandelli was released and placed in the custody of his attorneys. It was a calculated risk and the ploy was being used in the hopes of putting Mandelli and his cohorts off guard. It seemed to be working.

Two suited men, looking like prosecutors, emerged from behind the Chief and walked towards the group of four. Jim did not know what to expect at what appeared to be a showdown of some sort.

"Mandelli," Mitchell heard Cavelli shout, "Get us out of here!"

Weksler echoed that plea from the next cell.

The man called Mandelli came close to the cell, but was kept at arm's length by the guards. He caught Mitchell's eye and with his gaze glued to Jim's, he introduced himself.

"I'm Giacamo Mandelli."

To Mitchell, he was a stranger. He had only seen his picture that was taken ten years previously. He was the man running in the store.

"Oh, you're Andrea's partner." Jim paused, "But I have no connection with you. This is the first time I've met you."

Mandelli licked his lips, "You don't recognize me?"

"No, I don't." Jim said firmly and truthfully. "I saw you for the first time at the store three years ago, as you were running to the rear exit. Nothing more than that."

With a huge sigh of relief Mandelli moved towards his attorneys and whispered something to them.

CHAPTER NINETY ONE
Infiltration

Recalling the confessions of Cavelli and his referring to Mandelli and then to Klein in his ramblings, Mitchell realized that Mandelli and Klein were one person. It appeared that he unconsciously reached the same interpretation when he had recounted his dream to Gabrielli on August 16th.

It also seemed that the visage of the man he pictured as Klein was a montage of the many faces he had seen at the refugee camp. The years had merged many images into one and Jim was unsure of matching faces with names. Time dims and plays tricks on the memory. For the life of him, Jim could not conjure up the image of Klein. He only remembered the bloodied and swollen face of the man who was severely beaten by the mob while they shouted, "SS...SS..."

At intervals, the prisoners were moved singly to be interrogated. Cavelli was the first called from their cell. When he returned, it was Franco's turn. Cavelli would not speak to Jim. He was probably ordered by the lawyers to keep his mouth shut. Franco also remained silent upon his return.

The American's turn came and he was taken to Gabrielli's office in a roundabout way. He had a sandwich and a cup of American coffee waiting for Mitchell.

"What's happening?" Jim inquired, after he took his first bite.

"These people are smart, and they have a lot of influence. They have the best lawyers in Italy and I think the judges are on their side. We must infiltrate and find out what they are thinking and what they know."

The Chief then continued, "They must have a weak spot and we must find out what it is. Also interrogating them in the presence of their attorneys is very difficult. The prisoners we have here aren't talking. We know who the principal suspect is and, as you told me last week, it is Mandelli alias Klein." Gabrielli sighed and wiped his brow.

"Bingo!" Thought Mitchell. "They have arrived at the same conclusion!"

The Chief continued, "Mandelli is so entrenched with the politicians and the church that we cannot accuse him of being a Nazi war criminal. All the official records in Italy have him listed as Giacamo Mandelli. It is impossible to prove that Klein existed in Italy except for the 'purloined papers' that you gave me. Also, our laboratories have come to the conclusion that the writing on the warning notes is Klein's. I saw that you had a short conversation with Mandelli. What was it about?"

Jim related his denial of ever meeting Cavelli's partner and of Mandelli's apparent relief.

"Wonderful!" The Chief clapped his hands in glee. "Now it's your turn to go in the room with Mandelli and his lawyers. See what you can find out. They think that you are on their side. This may give us the break that we are looking for."

Jim gulped down what was left of his coffee and Gabrielli turned him over to a policeman. He was taken in a round-about way to the office where four men sat waiting.

Mandelli, who seemed eager to gain Mitchell's confidence, began the conversation by asking with a smile, "You really don't remember me?"

"Officially, no." Jim replied. To himself, it meant yes or no. To Mandelli, it probably meant yes. The purpose was to have him think that Mitchell/Comandante did know him.

It worked. Without the consent of his lawyers, Mandelli made the mistake of his life.

He whispered, "I'm Yacob Klein!" The fourth man gave a start, but averted his face that was strained.

"I remember the name, but not your face. I don't think you are Klein." Jim was playing the game to the best of his ability.

Continuing on the same track, Mandelli pushed the play farther. "You saved my life from a mob of Jews."

"Now I remember the occurrence, but you don't look like the man we picked up off the floor. Your face was swollen beyond recognition. That is the only way I remember you."

Mitchell had him but Mandelli did not realize it. He thought Jim was going to be his pawn as he thought he was for those twenty some years when he was being paid off.

Mandelli was intent on getting the comandante to recognize him. For what reason Jim was not certain. Perhaps to ingratiate himself, or it had become meaningful to him to gain the comandante's recognition. Like a poor boy that goes into the world and becomes successful, he wanted to be applauded by someone who knew him in the past.

The next sentence that came forth from his mouth hit the brass ring.

"You evicted me from the kitchen when you found me there with the cooks!" He seemed to gloat.

That was it! Jim had picture of a blond haired man in his mind's eye. Klein's hair was dyed black. In order to be Italian, he colored his hair and changed his name. Mitchell put the blond man together with black hair and the answer was positive. It was Klein! Mentioning the kitchen incident struck the proper chord and the answer popped right up in Jim's confused head. The myriad of faces had now merged into the one that only mattered.

Now another question emerged. Was his real name Klein?

Still another question, was he Jakob Mandil, the Nazi war criminal? Let FIND determine that.

"Of course, you are Klein! You jogged my memory, I just couldn't adjust to the black hair!" He could see that Mandelli/Klein was pleased. His ego was satisfied.

At the conclusion of their conversation, Mitchell could see that the attorneys were rather disturbed. After all, they were not sure if the comandante was on their side. Klein didn't give a hoot He was happy with the outcome. The Comandante had finally recognized him. And he probably also thought that Jim was grateful for the money that was passed on to him twice per annum. He was not going to tell Mandelli anything different, but was going to let this encounter play itself out. The fourth man, a stranger, kept his head turned down and away from Mitchell.

Time was up. There was a knock on the door and a guard hustled Jim out of the room before any of the attorneys, Klein, or the other man could complain.

CHAPTER NINETY TWO
To The Enemy's Camp

Gabrielli was waiting for him in his office so Mitchell quickly told him of what had occurred in the meeting with Klein alias Mandelli. The Chief was jubilant.

"Well, we're now sure that he is Klein. With your statement and that of Cavelli, we will be able to hold him legally on some count. Eisen and Stein are here in the building and they have some evidence that may tie Klein to some of the atrocities during the war years. Your past information to us put them on the right track and they have picked up some German SS files that may positively identify him. We dared not proceed before because we were not sure Mandelli was Klein. And with Mandelli's influence we had to stay at arms length. Now we can finish the job!"

"I'm glad I was able to help, but tell me, who is the other person with the attorneys?"

Gabrielli grimaced, "You won't believe me, but that is the man who was walking the dog in Ivrea!"

"Quite a coincidence." Jim smiled. "That happens to us quite often, doesn't it?"

"But this is astounding!" The Chief clapped his knee.

"What is his name and what is his relationship with Mandelli?"

"He is involved in business dealings with Mandelli, other than the liquor warehouse. His name is Anton Vezzetti."

Mitchell felt as though an avalanche had struck him and carried him down a mountainside. They were talking about coincidences and now one had plummeted into his corner like a meteor. Jim was speechless for several moments, then quickly recovered.

Hastily, he reached for his packet, opened it, and dumped the contents on Gabrielli's desk. Rummaging through the papers, Jim quickly pulled out the first letter that he had received from Anton Vezzetti, which was dated January 3, 1946. He handed it to the Chief.

A moment later, he picked out the second letter from Vezzeti, dated September 13, 1946. In that letter Anton told Mitchell that his family was sailing from Genoa on October 1st. They were returning to Providence, Rhode Island, where they had lived prior to World War II. He passed that letter to Gabrielli, also.

"This is unbelievable! Absolutely unbelievable!" Cried Gabrielli.

"Non e possibile! This is not possible!" Jim said in Italian, then English.

"We'll soon find out what this is all about." The Chief said as he hurried out of his office with the letters. He left Jim standing there. Mitchell then sat down to await Gabrielli's return.

That stranger who was with Mandelli and the lawyers was an impostor. What was his motive in taking Vezzetti's name? Jim was hoping that nothing sinister had happened to Anton. There was no communication between them after that last letter of 1946.

Jim realized that he was remiss in not replying to the final letter. It was a time when he was trying to put his world together again. Looking for a job and adjusting to civilian life was a trial and all consuming mission for him in that post war period. It was the same for all his buddies who had served their country.

More than a half hour passed before the Chief returned. He was perspiring and out of breath when he sat in his chair. He waited for a minute before attempting to speak. Mitchell could easily determine that he was very excited and could hardly wait to spill the news. After he caught his breath, he held up his hand and gestured that Jim should wait.

"Relax," he said. "The Israeli boys are coming."

Sure enough, they popped in a moment later, also breathless. Eisen and Stein stood there waiting in anticipation. There was no time for greetings.

"Gentlemen," the Chief began with flourish. "I think we have the Big One right here in the building. The real Anton Vezzetti is in the United States alive and well. The American Embassy in Rome confirmed that. This man has taken the identity of Mr. Vezzetti and used it to his advantage to conceal who he really is. The Italian authorities would never think of bothering a wealthy American living in Italy, and FIND operated on the same premise. We must confront this man today, lawyers or no lawyers. He thinks that he is perfectly safe. We are going to undo all that, and undo it today."

He turned towards the men from FIND. "Do you agree?"

Eisen and Stein declared in unison, "Of course, we're

with you!"

Then Stein added, "He must be an arrogant bastard to come here so brazenly."

Gabrielli buzzed for his assistant and asked him to bring the rest of their team into his office. He wanted to brief them on the latest information.

He then turned to Mitchell and said, "Mandelli's attorneys have been interviewing the other prisoners, one by one. It is now your turn to go back and see what you can learn. I'm sure that they will not get much out of you. You're their ace in the hole, but they'll soon find out that you will turn out to be the Ace of Spades (Bad Luck)."

Not knowing what to expect, Jim followed the Chief's orders.

CHAPTER NINETY THREE
The Gold Baton

Gabrielli decided to accompany and lead Mitchell in the direction of the office where Mandelli was being detained. They had gone only a few feet when a clerk overtook them and handed the Chief a message that was obviously very important. He halted, scanned the sheet and then handed it to Jim with a flourish.

The message was full of information on the bogus Vezzetti: A German immigrant had entrenched himself in the Ivrea area by marrying a cousin of Anton's and thus was accepted into the Vezzetti family. Using the Vezzetti name was no problem because he was highly esteemed for his wealth. (He had achieved the perfect disguise!) Citizens and neighbors alike never questioned his presence. He was a legal and naturalized citizen of Italy.

Mitchell passed the paper back to Gabrielli. They did not need to speak further.

The Chief motioned towards a policeman to take Jim to his destination.

The comandante did not relish going into that lion's den, because he was unsure what the outcome would be regarding his friends, Cavelli and Franco DiMarchi. He did not care much about what was to be the fate of the others. The guard escorted him to the room where Mandelli was ensconced with his team.

While the lawyers were busy writing, Mandelli was sitting back in his chair smoking a cigar, and the stranger was fiddling with his shoelaces. During the previous meeting, Jim had not seen his full face, only part of a mustache and a portion of the right side of his face. He still had his hat on, despite the build up of the temperature in the room. The new Anton Vezzetti was also wearing gloves of fine leather. Mitchell was determined to get a good look at him, one way, or another.

"I think we'll have you all free within an hour!" That greeting came from Mandelli. "They have no case, my attorneys are certain the judges will dismiss them all. We have many friends and they will help us get all of you out of this situation.

"What situation is that?" Jim asked, naively. "I haven't

done anything illegal. I'm only a visitor in a foreign land. The American ambassador is going to help me, I'm sure. We are due to go back to the United States tomorrow. Yacob, where do you fit in the scheme of things?"

"My hands are clean." Responded Klein/Mandelli. "I'm a legitimate business man and haven't been charged with anything. My lawyers do not understand the ridiculous charges against my people. They are being charged with black marketing, which is a silly. The police cannot make the charges stick. You have nothing to worry about."

"This guy still thinks that I was on his payroll!" Mitchell thought.

"Yacob, tell me, who is your friend in the hat?" Jim questioned confidentially. They were now on quite intimate terms. "Please introduce me."

"Anton," Mandelli addressed the man smiling. "This is James Mitchell, the Comandante. He is the man I told you about." Then turning towards Jim, he pointed to Anton and said, "Meet Signore Vezzetti."

The man called "Anton Vezzetti" turned towards Mitchell and extended his gloved hand. He had a firm grip and he looked at Jim squarely and brazenly as they shook hands.

"How do you do? Jolly good to meet you." His Oxford accent had a clear ring.

This man was well educated but Jim could tell that he was not an American, nor was he an Englishman. And most of all he was not an Italian or an American of Italian descent. He definitely was German. The Comandante Mitchell would have reached that conclusion without the information on the sheet.

Mitchell noticed that 'Anton' held a baton with a golden head in his gloved left hand. The head was well worn and it shone brilliantly. The scrolls and initials 'JM' that had been outstanding at one time were not quite as prominent, but it was the same one that Lt. James Mitchell had seen and coveted many years before.

The man that stood before him was the German major who still clung to the relic of his past!

"JM" was indelible in his mind because he recalled thinking the letters spelled "JiM!"

In that instant he knew with certainty that this was the

Nazi war criminal that was being sought by various agencies throughout the world.

"JM" meant "Jacob Mandil!" There was no question there.

Slowly, and with great deliberation, Mitchell faced the two and said very softly, without disturbing the lawyers, "You're not Mr. Vezzetti ."

"No, I'm not," interrupted 'Anton'. "I know that you knew the Vezzettis."

"How did you know?"

He appeared to be smiling, but his eyes belied that point. "I was in the Vezzetti home when you came behind our lines during the cease-fire."

"Oh, you're the German major that was living in their villa! Now, I understand." Jim feigned surprise. "Where do you fit in here?"

"I won't respond to that." He was tight as a clam from then on. He spoke no more, but Mitchell had heard enough.

It was evident to Jim that this German officer had taken advantage of his situation on the day he left the Vezzetti villa. How easy it would be for him to take cover as an American civilian when he was threatened by the Italian partisans and even by naive American soldiers!

CHAPTER NINETY FOUR
Confrontation

There were many Black Shirts who resided in that area at the base of the Italian Alps. (The Fascists were called "Black Shirts" because of the color of their uniforms.) He probably had enlisted their help long before their war was lost. Jim remembered thinking that it was odd that he was the only German living with the Vezzettis.

Usually an officer would have some sort of staff and communications equipment with him. He had nothing with him but his uniform. There were no vehicles parked nearby. Mitchell recalled those points vividly. He apparently was not attached to any unit in the area. He was solo and prepared to go into hiding along with his loot. He was cute! And Yacob Klein was in partnership somehow. Jim was hoping that he would soon find out whether his conclusions were correct.

He was bursting to have the final word and was determined to have it.

Catching "Anton's" eye, Jim expressed his thought clearly and loudly, "You're Jacob Mandil!"

"JM" glared at Mitchell as did his entourage. The attorneys expressed some outrage and showed dismay and motioned to him to speak no more.

His goose was cooked. There was no escape this time. The guards, although in the perimeter, seemed to be aware of what was going on and thus on the alert.

Mandelli was horror struck. He felt betrayed.

Mitchell's time was up and he was removed by a guard and taken to Gabrielli's office where he and his team, together with the Israelis, were planning strategy. The government prosecutors were giving their opinions on the legal issues involved. They, too, were hot to trot.

This was going to be a big day for all concerned, especially after informing the participants in the meeting that he had uncovered the identity of the fake Anton Vezzetti as Jakob Mandil!

There was a hushed cheer by all. The Israeli agents could hardly contain themselves. Mitchell then related to the Chief and the others what had transpired in his meeting with Mandelli and the German major. He stressed how importantly the gold head on the baton had influenced his deduction, which turned out to be an accurate one.

The definite identification of Jacob Mandil boosted the hopes of the men of FIND. They were elated with the prospect that their ages long search was soon to be over.

Armed with the necessary legal papers, the teams left the Chief's office to do their duties as prescribed by law. Jim elected to remain in the office and prepare an affidavit with a notary's help. He waited for news of the outcome. Within a half hour a policeman arrived to escort Mitchell to the courtroom, which was on the far side of the municipal building.

On the way, Jim noticed the office of the mayor. It was the same office where he had confronted the head of the Liberation Party many years before.

CHAPTER NINETY FIVE
Heil!

As he was led into the courtroom, Mitchell heard loud talking before the bench. Mandelli and his lawyers were at it hot and heavy. Something had gone wrong with their plans. They probably thought they had greased everyone up to the top in the judicial system. Stein came to Jim's side and told him that a Roman judge was going to conduct the preliminary hearing.

"I would rather have had my people spirit them directly to Israel, but we did not have the slightest opportunity. We were ready, but the Chief was on to us and watched our every move. He is too honorable a man to let us get away with kidnapping Mandelli and the German officer," Stein said with resignation.

They were interrupted by the silence caused by the judge's entrance into the courtroom. The government prosecutors presented a sheaf of papers to the judge and the attorneys for the defense did likewise. As in all courts, legal talk was bandied about by the judge and the lawyers. Mitchell was only interested in watching the faces of the defendants. Cavelli and Franco were conspicuous by their absence.

The legal team of FIND soon entered into discussions with the judge and the evidence that they had acquired was turned over to the court. Jim remained in the rear of the room and could not make out what was being said, but he had the feeling that things were not going well with the defendant's lawyers. Their arms were flailing through the air in desperation while their clients watched with pale and anxious faces. It was a trying time indeed. No pun intended.

One could sense that the court's decision was going to come fast and with finality. FIND's lawyers were requesting the judge for his indulgence in some manner.

Mitchell heard his name mentioned and then called out loudly. A uniformed man, equivalent to a bailiff, hurried down the aisle towards the American witness. He escorted Jim to a position facing the judge.

The prisoners, with Mandelli and the German officer at the forefront, were to Mitchell's right. Eisen and Stein, with their attorneys, stood immediately behind the former comandante .

It was blatantly obvious to the prisoners of Odessa that Jim was not in their corner, or, frankly speaking, on their team. The change that came over Mandelli's face was shocking. He was glowering, his teeth bared, and his eyes were black with anger accompanied by fear.

The American was sworn in after the judge asked for his name. He came right to the point.

"Do you recognize any of the prisoners standing there?" The judge pointed to my right.

"Yes, sir." Jim replied. "The two men in the front and one of the men to their rear. Yacob Klein alias Giacamo Mandelli, the German officer, named Jacob Mandil and who calls himself 'Vezzetti," and Adam Weksler."

"Are these the affidavits that were submitted by you?" He passed the papers to the bailiff who brought them to Mitchell. They were his sworn statements.

"Yes, your honor, they are my statements." He could see Mandelli and the German seething. They truly thought that he was one of theirs.

Mandelli could contain himself no longer. He shouted at Mitchell. "Comandante! I warned you twice and now you do this to me! We've paid you all these years and this is the thanks we get! I should have ...." He was silenced by the judge, but kept muttering to himself.

The judge excused James Mitchell who then moved to a bench close to the front and sat next to Gabrielli.

Again Klein/Mandelli screamed loudly in Jim's direction, "If you had stayed home, we would never have been in this predicament!" He was sobbing and had to be silenced once again.

The magistrate or judge banged his gavel for attention. In a loud voice he asked the German officer to step forward, then stated, "I have irrefutable evidence that you are Jakob Mandil and are wanted as a Nazi war criminal."

He held the papers high for all to see. "Do you have anything to say?"

The former German officer, Jakob Mandil, clicked his heels together and, as he brought up his right arm to execute a Nazi salute, shouted for all to hear, "Heil, Hitler!"

There was no denying what his answer meant. All was quiet in the court as everyone heard the man's admission of guilt. The Israeli's were expectant and ready to pounce on the prisoner who was going to be theirs.

The judge continued, "In the case against Klein alias Mandelli, there is no proof that he is wanted as a war criminal; however, the government of Italy is interested in his activities in behalf of Odessa while he was citizen of this country. He will remain in custody until arrangements are made for his trial in Rome. As for the other prisoners, they are to be returned to the custody of the local authorities, and to be tried here in Modena "

The attorneys for all parties involved crowded forward to gain the judge's attention. The judge ignored them and made the final decision.

"Jakob Mandil will be turned over to the government of Israel."

A loud "No!" erupted from Mandil.

FIND's men and agents rushed towards the prisoner and cuffed him. They were not going to take any chances. They had a plane ready at the Modena Airport. In five hours they would arrive in Tel Aviv.

Sam Eisen and Martin Stein came to Mitchell's side and shook his hand. Jim was not sure whether he was congratulating them, or they him. They were excited at nailing their prey after all those years of investigation and hard work. The prosecuting attorneys and The Chief also pressed towards him and offered their hands. Mitchell surmised accurately that they all had arrived at the same conclusion – which Il Comandante had helped solve the case in some way.

CHAPTER NINETY SIX
Resolution

As usual, Sam and Martin wanted to know what Mitchell was going to do with the millions that were in a Swiss bank. Gabrielli knowingly smiled at Jim, hoping that he would give them a proper answer. The prosecutors stated that legally the money in the Swiss Bank was Il Comandante's to keep and one of them handed James Mitchell a paper that listed the name of the bank and the account number.

Al Comandante had made a decision quite a while earlier what to do with the money if it ever came into his hands.

This time Martin Stein raised the question. "What are you going to do about the money?"

"I'm going to let the Palestinians have it." Mitchell replied. "They deserve it!"

"Great!" Came from Martin and Sam, simultaneously. They were thinking in the context of the refugee camp at the Academy. To them it meant the pseudo Palestinians who passed through the camp gates. It meant something else to Mitchell because he was of Arab extraction.

"We'll see to it that it gets to the right people." Claimed Sam Eisen.

Martin Stein nodded happily.

From the corner of his eye, Jim noticed that Gabrielli was watching closely to see the reactions of the Israelis.

Mitchell then calmly and seriously, stated, "No, not your people. My people, the real Palestinians. The ones who are now living in cardboard boxes around the boundaries of the Beirut Airport. That's where the money is going!"

Gabrielli smiled broadly. Sam and Martin nodded in begrudging agreement.

Something was still bothering Jim, and he hastened to ask the question, "Those notes with Klein's signature where he crossed out. or erased, the letter 'M,' I was leaning toward the opinion that he was Mandil. What did you think?" He looked at the Chief.

"I thought so, too." Gabrielli responded. "But it turned out that he was tinkering with the idea of using the Italian name of Mandelli when he entered Italy. We learned that he used the name Mandelli when he was recuperating at Lago di

Garda. It seemed to work for him there and he continued using that alias all these years."

The boys from Israel nodded in agreement. They had kept that information from Mitchell so that it would not impede his personal investigations. It was just another case of "need to know". He had been kept 'out of the loop' to suit their needs!

As Mitchell turned away, Stein tossed me a bone by saying, "Comandante, you're uncanny recollection of the initials on the baton really cinched it for us. Hanging on to that stick that represented authority to him really did him in. That one thing from his past jogged your memory and put the nail in his coffin. Good work, I knew that we could count on you!" He mockingly saluted.

Il Comandante returned the salute and grinned wryly in response.

They all went home.

Jim and Dorothy Solomon